The War Brides of 24th Street

The War Brides of 24th Street

A Novel based on Actual Events

By

FRANCES MUNN ROBERTS

The War Brides of 24th Street

Published by Frances Munn Roberts
Bel Air, Maryland
United States of America

ISBN-10: 1723142832
ISBN-13: 978-1723142833

For information or additional copies, contact Amazon.com or visit my blog at francesmunnroberts.com

DEDICATION

To my beloved daughter Tammy who never quit believing and whose skill and labor made self-publishing possible for her computer challenged mother.

ACKNOWLEDGEMENTS

My heartfelt thanks go to my daughter Tammy for designing the book cover and for her steadfast encouragement and love.

I am indebted to my sisters Eleanor and Marian who were my caretakers at birth and my friends for life. Thanks for all the proofreading, the photos you generously donated, and your never-ending moral support.

Thanks to my niece Amy for convincing me that this was not an impossible dream and for providing the necessary sites.

With eternal gratitude to my grand-niece Ashlynn Yuhas for her inspired editing.

Thanks to my brother Roger and sister-in-law Monika who never fail to be there when I need them.

With loving thoughts to my grandchildren Mackenzie and Keith who are the hope of tomorrow.

And for the memories of an extraordinary period in history, I thank my mother and father.

Appreciation goes to Sarah and Nancy at Lovely Lane, and to Diane, for their consistent prayers and caring.

Gratitude goes to the English Literature Department of the University of South Carolina for my love of the classics.

Thanks to Colleen Webster for her writing classes at HCC.

Special thanks to the memory of Thomas Wolfe for writing "Look Homeward Angel," my eternal inspiration.

CONTENTS

The Real Danny

Prologue

I will be eighty-one years old this December, and I find my head swimming more and more with images of the wives, girlfriends, and mothers on 24th Street who waited and watched for their men to return during World War II.

My family lived in a row-house on 24th Street in Baltimore, MD. Without television or a phone to provide in-house drama, my sisters and I relied on the shifting romances of the neighborhood women and my father's sporadic encounters with alcohol and sobriety to give us something to talk about in the double bed we shared for ten years. It was a time when men wore fedoras and talked like Humphrey Bogart, while women wore housedresses and did the laundry by hand.

We were my father's second family, and our older half brother (Danny in the book) joined the Navy after the attack on Pearl Harbor, December 7, 1941. The goal was to free the Pacific Islands from Japanese invasion and to stamp out the tyranny of Nazism in Hitler's Germany. Danny would be lost on a raft for twenty-three days with eight sea-mates and no food or water after their ship was torpedoed. Only one would survive.

Today's world is changing so rapidly, I feel compelled to put down on paper the way it was then, when you loved fiercely for fear of loss and political correctness meant you sent family members away to battle with a brave face. It is an account of life in Baltimore when segregation held sway, a time when my sisters and I lugged ten cent bags of coal home from the grocery store because we couldn't afford the truck full needed to warm the house. It is a tale brightened by the colorful boarders who helped us pay the rent, a unique time in history that comforts me as I sit and watch the technical world spin by. Thank you for reading The War Brides of 24th Street.

The Dunn children and big brother

Chapter 1

Hollywood and World War II ran together in flickering shades of black and white. It was 1942, and the only battles we'd experienced firsthand were on the silver screen. In the dimness of the Centre Theater, my sisters and I sniffed our way through pockets of Kleenex, while Greer Garson and Ronald Coleman taught us to be brave and infinitely patient. Our duty, as we saw it, was to adapt valiantly to the absence of fathers, sons, husbands, and brothers. To this end, the women on our block dedicated themselves to the exasperating art of waiting.

Our widowed boarder, Lucille, waited for a better paying job so she could rescue her children from the financial security of their Grandmother's cheerless household. And my mother waited for a crisis significant enough to jolt my father out of his Don Quixote fantasies and into acceptance of a better paying job as a bookkeeper. Since that meant giving up his post as a coastguard policeman, turning in the pistol that helped him forget his rejection by the Army, it seemed as unlikely as the surrender of the Japanese from whose warplanes we taped our window shades shut so we could read during blackouts.

But the women who electrified my romantic imagination and fed nosy neighbors a feast of fabricated tales were the wives and girlfriends who littered the white marble steps of 24th Street. Perched like exotic birds, in breezy rayon dresses and boxy, open-toed high heels, they waited patiently for the return of their warriors. Thousands of our boys were stationed in London and New Zealand, while others stormed wide sandy beaches in the South Pacific, or lurked on iron-gray destroyers poised to strike Nazi submarines rising from the murky deep. When they returned - if they returned - the women would give up their front step musing and begin happily ever after in earnest.

To my mother, viewing their fresh faces from the house on the corner, these women offered an endless pool of inexperience, hungry for comfort and advice, ripe to fall under the spell of her lyrical southern drawl and relentless hospitality.

Fearing it might be in poor taste to approach newcomers from the front steps, Mama relied on the one person who spoke daily with everybody in the neighborhood. Bernie ran a combination grocery store and butcher shop on the first floor of the house next to the alley. He smelled of rump roast and sawdust sprinkled on the floor to soak up grease spills in the back, where he cut meat with long slender knives and wiped his hands on the bib of his apron, more blood-stained than white before the day was half done.

Rotund and good-natured, Bernie was also Jewish, yet he never burdened others with the plight of relatives trapped in Hitler's Germany. Instead, he concentrated on easing the lives of his customers, adding an extra slice of cheese when weighing it for a widow whose husband was killed in combat. Of late, he'd taken a special interest in Hazel Burnett, a willowy, freckle-faced blonde from Kansas who'd ridden a Greyhound bus all the way to Baltimore, hoping to find employment as a stenographer. From the bus station, she hailed a taxi to the YWCA to rent a room. One week later, in total violation of her contemplative, mid-western upbringing, she married the cab driver, Stanley Polanski, and set up housekeeping down the street from us.

"Are you sure you want to spend all your stamps on sugar?" Bernie asked, after Hazel handed him her ration book.

"I'm baking Stanley a birthday cake. Wish I could afford vanilla," she sighed, turning to gaze at a nearby rack of McCormick condiments.

Taking advantage of the distraction, Bernie made his way to the far end of the store, where my mother waited patiently for chicken stew parts while I gazed at the flat, black fish eyes scrutinizing me from their icy crypt. "That cake 'ull be little more than moldy crumbs by the time it reaches Stanley," Bernie mumbled, slipping an extra wing into the tiny pile of poultry before wrapping and handing it to my mother. "He's a machinist's mate on a freighter somewhere off the coast of Hawaii."

Mama smiled, knowingly, and ambled back to where Hazel stood admiring a stack of miniature brown bottles. "I'm Claudia Dunn. I couldn't help overhearing. I have half a bottle of vanilla and you're welcome to a teaspoon for your cake."

"Oh, I couldn't possibly…" Hazel stammered.

"You mustn't let formality stand in the way of neighborliness – not with a war going on."

"Well…if you're sure you don't mind…"

As we followed Mama past the narrow row of red brick houses, Hazel casually mentioned that she lived over Bernie's store in the second floor front.

"Then you must know the tenant in 2-B," Mama commented, a marked quickening in her voice. Even Bernie was at a loss to provide specifics about the reclusive girl upstairs. The most he knew was that her features were decidedly Asian and she'd been seen on more than one occasion getting out of a taxi in the fading light of a corner lamppost. Not many women on 24th Street could afford a taxi, and fewer still, to Mama's way of thinking, had any business being out after dark. Even more suspicious, the postman had been spotted delivering a large white envelope with a foreign return address to her door. What if she were a spy, an American Tokyo Rose, primed to sabotage the war effort with Japanese propaganda?"

"Here we are," she said cheerfully, leading Hazel down the hall, stepping over my sisters playing jackstones on the cool linoleum floor. They jumped up and followed us into the dining room, eager to meet the newest of the young ladies my father sarcastically referred to "Mama's gossiping chicks."

"Don't pester Hazel," she cautioned, courtesy being at the top of her list of godly virtues. "Do you have children?"

"No ma'am. Stanley joined the Navy a few days before we met and shipped out right after the ceremony. But we plan to start a family as soon as he gets back."

"Four is the most practical number," Mama stated flatly, astonishing my sisters and me, since she constantly complained that having four children made her old before her time. "Did I hear you correctly? Did you say you'd only known your husband a few days before you married him? Wasn't that a bit impulsive?"

"Most people would probably say so, but there's something about Stanley – a kind of take charge, man about town that's irresistible. It was my first time in a city of any size, and I was scared to death. He picked up on my apprehension and drove me free of charge to see everything from the nearest Lutheran church to the Baltimore Savings and Loan so I could deposit the eight hundred dollars I spent four years saving. If it hadn't been for Stanley, I'd still be holed up at the YWCA, trying to get up the nerve to introduce myself to the other girls."

"But what do you know about his character, his family background, political orientation? He could have an ex-wife and six children he's struggling to support on a cabdriver's salary."

Hazel accepted the cup of steaming black coffee Mama placed in front of her. "I know he goes out of his way to be helpful and his taxicab is spotless. I know his parents migrated from Poland and he was born and raised in Dundalk, where he attended Catholic school and drove the nuns crazy with his constant chatter. Actually, I find that kind of endearing. And I know he smells of Old Spice and shaves every day. My mother always told me a clean shaven man has nothing to hide."

"I can't believe she turned you loose in a city full of sailors with only that to go on. Don't you think it's an odd coincidence - his signing up and leaving for combat immediately after talking you into marrying him?"

"That just proves he's more patriotic than practical. There is one thing that bothers me, though. I've asked several times, but he hasn't told me exactly where his ship is anchored. I have a million things I want to write and tell him – not to mention all the questions burning a hole in my head. And I need an address to mail his birthday cake. He was pretty sure they were headed for the Hawaiian Islands, but every time he tries to pinpoint his location in a letter, the military censors black out the words."

"Surely they don't suspect a nice girl from Kansas of consorting with the enemy…unless they found out you live down the hall from that Asian woman in 2-B. I'd send a letter to President Roosevelt. He always takes the side of the people. He'll help you find Stanley. Getting back to that birthday cake…" Our ears perked up.

"What are the chances it'll make it all the way to Hawaii in one piece?"

"Not very good," Hazel admitted.

"Lord knows I'd be the last person to offer unsolicited

advice, but you might consider baking a cake and inviting several friends to sign a card for Stanley. A handful of friendly greetings would be far more welcome than a box of stale crumbs."

"You're probably right, only…I haven't had time to make any friends."

"What on earth are you waiting for? Oh, well; nothing's so wrong it can't be rectified. Just leave everything to me."

"I really wish you wouldn't…"

"It's no trouble," Mama said, determined to be accommodating.

Not wishing to seem ungrateful, Hazel murmured "Thank you," and stirred a spoonful of sugar into her coffee, passing the bag to my mother.

"Never look a gift horse in the mouth," Mama grinned, letting the fine white granules trickle slowly into her coffee. "To Stanley," she said, lifting her cup.

"To my Stanley," Hazel echoed, in a voice less certain since following Mama home from the store.

**

Lila was the most exotic of the cloistered ladies who hovered around our dining room table during those lonely, drawn-out years. Her blazing red curls were swept back by vibrant silk scarves, accenting her Pacific blue eyes and changing her complexion from warm rosy to ethereal ivory, depending on the color she wore. Lila dabbled in the paranormal and claimed to have contacted Harry Houdini in a séance on the tenth anniversary of his unintended death.

According to Mama, Lila's otherworldly ways were caused by growing up in Hoboken, New Jersey, a Catholic Italian stronghold where she was convinced mobsters bartered their way into heaven by chanting hail Marys and counting a string of beads in the correct order.

A Bing Crosby fan since 1931, when he sang White Christmas on the radio for the first time, Mama's protestant Celtic upbringing fed her suspicion that the Catholic Church had cast a spell and made an Italian crooner named Frank Sinatra an overnight sensation, rivaling the Irish-rooted Crosby for record sales and stardom. Nobody had the heart to tell her Bing Crosby was also Catholic, and if they had, she'd have insisted Irish Catholics were less Catholic than Italians, the Pope living right there in Italy and all. She never forgave Frank Sinatra or the Catholic Church for competing with her beloved Bing, although she stopped short of turning off the radio when they played "All or Nothing at All," her favorite Sinatra song.

Having fulfilled her maternal duty - cautioning us about the dangers of Italian Catholic crooners - Mama was able to embrace Lila's friendship with complete abandon, even opening the Baptist boundaries of her southern upbringing to the black art of astrology.

"What can you expect from a passionate Leo with Scorpio rising?" Lila reminded Mama, every time she complained about Daddy's drunken tirades. "Fire signs are proud, and water signs are insecure. You're lucky he doesn't blow up more than he does."

Mama found this extremely comforting; it relieved her of the nagging suspicion that she might have been the cause. Lila's pursuit of metaphysical enlightenment also benefitted my sisters and me, validating our daily experiences, making real what we were generally expected to expunge from memory in the name of peace and Mama's migraine headaches.

Still, my oldest sister Marjorie thought Lila's justification of Daddy's moodiness was total bunk. Thirteen years old, she remembered him before the drinking years and was convinced he had the power to put things back the way they were - but didn't love her enough to bother. This deep sense of betrayal led to endless hours curled up on the sofa, devouring the library books that transported her from the troll bridge to a pink and white Alcott world. Never having known my father sober, I thought his basic nature ranged from drunk to not quite as drunk, so my expectations of improvement were less lofty.

Lila was the only one of Mama's devotee's still single. She and Garret Cummings had been in love since the eighth grade, but Lila, for all her pull with esoteric forces, had been unable to talk him into marriage. "He's been obsessed with the fear of losing a limb since the day he joined the Marines and I made a casual comment about his vulnerable Capricorn knees. Doesn't he know I'd love him all the more if he came back wounded?" In the end, Lila succumbed to the blind faith of one whose reasoning resided in the cosmic clouds, where the alignment of planets was more likely to get her down the aisle than the most logical argument. After all, she was born in the sign of Libra, where marriage is a virtual certainty.

My next to the oldest sister, Betsy, singled out by Mama as "the only green-eyed child I have," found Lila's wishful thinking too vague for comfort and chose to bask in the shadow of the most glamorous and persnickety of Mama's drop-by friends, Brynn Vanderburger. A pale stick of a woman, Brynn defied tradition by cutting her raven tresses up to her ears at a time when shoulder length was the *do* of the day. She was regal in bearing and prone to critiquing family and friends with chilly disdain. Although Betsy had few illusions about Brynn's self-centeredness, her flawless sense of fashion made it worth the aggravation.

Brynn's mother was convinced her daughter would bloom best in an elitist environment, so she enrolled her in Goucher College - a prestigious school for young ladies of promise and presumed character. But Brynn was not willing to wait four years for her own spending money. Relying on the unearned luck that had graced her from birth, she camped out in front of her parents' living room window, directly opposite Military Police Headquarters from which dozens of soldiers in military garb emerged each day at five, on their way back to Ft. Meade.

Six weeks later, she eloped with a dress-uniform emblazoned in gold stripes and brass buttons named Hugh Pillstick. Together, they took over the third floor of her parents' house and soon after, Brynn went to work as a salesclerk in the millinery department of the May Company in downtown Baltimore, where she invested every dime of hers and her young Lieutenant's money in hats, handbags, and leather pumps.

Thanks to Brynn, my middle sister Betsy was designing and making her own clothes on Mama's pedal Singer by the time she was fourteen. Unfortunately, my parents were too preoccupied with mundane survival to encourage their second daughter's special talent, particularly one as unrealistic as clothing design in a hand-me-down household. Daddy had long ago decreed that we'd grow up to be secretaries with an eye toward marrying the boss, since he could not afford to send us to college. Betsy ultimately devoted her talented fingers to typing reports for the local gas and electric company, looking every inch the professional in her handmade linen suits and fuchsia silk blouses.

Unlike Betsy, I was far too sensitive for Brynn's verbal zingers and trailed, instead, after the oldest of Mama's best friends, Lucille. Although she was not officially a war bride, Lucille's son Andy had joined the Army, and that made her an honorary member of the group. Betsy did not care much for Lucille, and I must say, not without reason, although the fault lay squarely with me.

Lucille showed up on our doorstep one crisp Halloween afternoon, five weeks before the Japanese sank our naval fleet at Pearl Harbor. Mama was drawing hobo whiskers on my chin with a scorched wine cork when we heard the doorbell ring. My sisters and I raced headlong down the hall, pulling up short when Marjorie opened the door.

Standing in the vestibule was a short, stocky woman, at least fifty, with frizzy gray hair, deep set eyes, and a far-away look - like the disremembered faces in the oil paintings at the Museum of Art where my sisters and I took finger painting lessons in the summer. Mama enrolled us in everything Baltimore provided free to children of the displaced poor, those out of work blue collars and dust-bowl agrarians from the Midwest and South who swarmed to the big city in search of factory work.

"Oh my!" the woman exclaimed, in mock horror. "Who are these scruffy bums?"

"We're unemployed vagrants from the Great Depression," Marjorie announced proudly. From the time we were old enough to hold a spoon, Mama drummed into our heads tales of my grandfather's rise from poor farm boy to owner of a General Motors dealership. Investing his hard-earned cash in the down of his mattress instead of the local bank allowed him to escape the paralyzing losses of the Wall Street crash of '29. To us, T. W. Silby was a fiscal icon as wise as Uncle Wiggly, and we were proud to emulate his early struggles in costume. The fact that we never benefitted from his wealth would remain a mystery long after it might have made a difference in our lives. "We're going trick or treating" Marjorie explained. "Come on in."

Mama jumped up at the sight of company and wiped the

charcoal from her fingers on the wad of Kleenex she kept tucked in her apron pocket. "I hope they didn't scare you to death. I'm Claudia Dunn. You must be Lucille."

"Yes. Lucille Harrington. Bernie told me you have a room for rent."

"Sure do, on the third floor front. Pull up a chair," Mama said, lighting an unfiltered Camel.

Lucille smiled with relief and removed a pack of Kools from her pocketbook. We quickly discovered she only wore her bottom dentures on special occasions. Each time she inhaled a puff of smoke, her lower lip caved in and her boney chin jutted out, creating the jagged profile of a witch - an image quickly softened by the laugh lines framing her warm brown eyes.

"Marjorie, you'll have to finish charcoaling Silby's whiskers."

"Unusual name; I don't believe I've heard it before."

"Silby is my maiden name. Daddy was one of the Spartanburg Silbys of upper Piedmont South Carolina. His great-grandfather distinguished himself in the Battle of Cowpens, defeating the British in the Revolutionary War. How about a cup of coffee?"

"I'd love one," Lucille said, lighting a second cigarette, cozying down for a friendly chat.

"Room and board includes breakfast, supper, and Sunday dinner," Mama explained, shaking a handful of vanilla wafers onto a saucer, apologizing for the lack of homemade cookies. "It's impossible to keep enough sugar on hand with four kids and a husband with a sweet tooth. Speaking of husbands, I fix eggs and grits for Thurston every morning, but you don't have to eat the grits. Most Yankees don't care for them."

"I'm a Louisiana girl, born and bred. I moved to Baltimore when I married Mr. Harrington, but I still love grits," she laughed, a low, throaty sound, like muffled thunder in a distant quarry, interrupted by a wheezy cough at the end. "And you're welcome to my sugar rations. I have a touch of diabetes, so you'd be doing me a favor."

"That's mighty nice of you. Do you have children?"

"Yes, but the girls are staying with my mother-in-law in

Delaware until I find a job that pays enough to get them back. Both of my parents were killed in the flu epidemic of 1918, so they can't help us." Lowering her voice, she confided, "Mr. Harrington got hit by a streetcar on his way home from a St. Patrick's Day celebration at Finnegan's Pub, and he had no life insurance. My son Andy sends what he can, but he's in the infantry stationed in the Philippines, and he can barely afford toothpaste. I worry about something happening to him every minute of every day."

"Have you considered remarrying, if only for financial security…so you can bring your girls to live with you?"

"I can't. I'd lose my widow's pension – not that it's all that much. But if I add it to a modest income from a job, I can bring the girls to live with me without being beholden to a man. It's the rare stepfather who's willing to support another man's children without getting resentful and mistreating them."

"We'll have to find you a rich widower with a better pension plan and children of his own. That way, he'll have a stake in being nice to yours," Mama laughed. "Getting back to meals, Thurston's a creature of habit, so we eat supper promptly at six. Room and board is $3.00 a month and for a quarter more, I'll wash your clothes along with ours."

"That sounds fair. Is this weekend too soon…?" Footsteps in the hall caused Lucille to turn halfway round. A slightly built man with leathery skin and a deep crease between his heavy brows entered first, his glacier blue eyes darting sharply toward his offspring. "What are they doing?" he grumbled, irritated by the lack of giggling to complain about.

"Marjorie's fixing their faces for trick or treating. This is my husband, Thurston Dunn, and the man behind him is Mick Mosely. Lucille will be moving across the hall from you this weekend, Mick."

"Well now," the older man said, in his upbeat Irish brogue, "this must be m' lucky day."

"Where's the boy?" Daddy grunted."

"Brother Boy's out back. He doesn't get enough sunshine," Mama complained, in the slightly defensive voice she used when justifying her actions to my father. My sisters long ago concluded that her marriage had been an atonement of some sort; we just hadn't identified the nature of her offense. She'd been the more affluent and some would say the more attractive of the two, with her proud chin, marble smooth skin, and composed gray eyes. Yet she always fell short of pleasing him. "Thurston hates it when I call him Brother Boy," Mama explained to Lucille, sending a black scowl across my father's somber Scottish features.

"I'd better go," Lucille said, rising quickly from her chair.

"No!" cried Mama. "We want you to stay for dinner, don't we Thurston?"

"I don't want to impose..."

"You wouldn't be imposing," Mick said, surprising Mama, since he generally shied away from contact with her female friends.

By six o'clock, we were seated in our assigned chairs at the table, with me on the far side between Lucille and my sister Betsy. Lucille had mashed the potatoes and added extra pepper to make up for the shortage of rationed butter, and I could feel a telltale tickle in the back of my nose.

Sneezing on Lucille was inconceivable, sneezing into my plate, almost as unthinkable. I turned my head and sneezed a mouthful of mashed potatoes onto my middle sister, who began wailing at the top of her lungs. Mama passed her a napkin to wipe off her arm, but it seemed like an eternity before Betsy quit shrieking: "You sneezed on me! Mama, she sneezed on me!"

As I shriveled in my chair, mortified and guilt stricken, Lucille leaned down and softly said, "Darlin,' next time just sneeze on me."

Chapter 2

Mama soon discovered she and our new boarder had more in common than southern roots. Lucille's son Andy escaped the Philippines just before the Bataan death march of 1942 that killed thousands of Filipino and hundreds of American prisoners of war, and my half-brother Danny survived near death from pneumonia while running desperately needed supplies from America to a freezing seaport in Murmansk, Russia – thanks to the uneasy alliance we'd formed in an effort to stop Hitler.

Danny was on his second day of medical leave when Hazel burst into the dining room, her yellow hair bouncing lightly across her shoulders, a single strand of white pearls around her neck. His amber eyes locked instantly onto her lemon cashmere sweater, and a jolt of adrenaline shot through his bulging, twenty-one year old veins. He stood up and offered her his chair.

"This one's fine," she said, squeezing in between Betsy and me.

"Well, Hazel!" Mama exclaimed, sliding a stack of pancakes and scrapple in front of Danny. "What brings you by this early in the morning?"

"It's Stanley. His ship is docking in San Diego for repairs, and he's apparently being assigned to a new one. I wouldn't have known if Bernie hadn't spotted it in the Baltimore Sun. I still don't have his mailing address, and knowing the name of his ship hasn't helped, since the Navy insists I'm not listed as his wife."

Mama was on the verge of saying "I told you so," when Danny grinned and said, "It just so happens I'm being deployed to the SS Flashpoint, which is also docked in San Diego."

"Wouldn't it be nice if you and Stanley ended up on the same ship?" Mama sighed, never one to let unlikelihood stand in the way of a good idea.

"Is Stanley your husband?" Danny asked, noticing a cheap gold band on Hazel's finger.

"Just barely," Mama chimed in. "He shipped out the day they got married."

"That doesn't make us any less married," Hazel replied, stiffly.

Seasoned in the art of peacemaking by my father and his mother's haggling divorce, Danny assured Hazel that Mama didn't mean it the way it sounded. "I'm leaving for the naval base in Charleston, South Carolina on Friday, and from there, I fly to San Diego. If you want, I could look Stanley up and try to get his address for you."

"Why don't you ride along when Mick takes us to the station to see Danny off," Mama urged, trying to make up for trivializing Hazel's wedding vows.

"Oh, I couldn't intrude on your goodbye. Mr. Dunn might not like it."

"You wouldn't be intruding," Danny insisted. "I haven't had a pretty girl see me off since I enlisted, so I'd consider it a personal favor. And I promise to square it with my Dad."

Betsy and I crossed our fingers and prayed she'd say yes. Stanley had been cast in the shadow of Mama's critical yardstick, but we adored our half-brother Danny, with his Indian autumn eyes and boyish brown hair parted neatly on the side. "I guess I could," Hazel whispered, clearly not comfortable with the idea.

Danny strolled across the room and turned up the volume on the radio. The mellow syncopation of Glen Miller's *In the Mood* pulsated off the walls. "Dance with me," he coaxed, taking Hazel's hand in his.

"Oh, I can't dance."

"Sure you can." Drawing Hazel to her feet, he spun her in circles, his warm palms lightly grazing her waist. My sisters and I joined in, dancing along behind.

Hazel wiggled free and sat down before the song ended, so Danny finished it with Betsy, unaware he was creating her most cherished childhood memory. When Mama asked Hazel why she stopped dancing, she said she was having more fun than girls from Kansas were supposed to have. I wondered how much was too much for girls from Baltimore but was afraid they'd think me stupid if I asked.

Later that night, Danny insisted on walking Hazel up the street to her door. As they started down the front steps, I noticed Lucille glower when he slid his arm across her shoulder. "Is Hazel having too much fun?" I asked.

"No, Honey. Danny is."

**

On Danny's last night at home, we were allowed to stay outside longer than usual, so they could say their grownup goodbyes without interruption. As darkness settled like a cloudless canopy over one row house after another, we decided to play hide-and-go-seek in the alley. The unfenced backyards were cluttered with shadowy objects to hide behind: bushel baskets of sooty coal furnace ash, dented tin trashcans, overstuffed chairs waiting for someone worse off than we to give them a secondhand home.

My favorite hideout was the backyard of a woman the mothers on our street called Jezebel, although her real name turned out to be Virginia. She kept a tiny red lantern in her kitchen window, a beacon for stray mutts seeking shelter. In a surprising display of neighborliness, my father built her a dog house, and on mild winter nights, when the sky would soon be seared by a billion stars, it stood empty. So I crawled inside and became invisible.

Before long, a young sailor approached, lit a cigarette, thought better of it, and tossed it away. Then - surrendering to whatever lures homesick sailors to a woman's door – he knocked. She opened immediately, and I caught my first close-up glimpse of her. She looked surprisingly ordinary, except for garishly rouged cheeks and weary emerald eyes. I knew her best as the butt of tasteless jokes around Mama's dining room table, but I couldn't help feeling they were underestimating the redeeming qualities of a woman who would offer refuge to lost, lonely dogs.

Suddenly, a group of noisy drunks came staggering down the alley, and I panicked and scurried home, crouching in the corner beside my front steps, unwilling to reveal myself before the game ended. Daddy and Danny unexpectedly appeared in the doorway, a bottle of beer in one hand and a cigarette in the other. They sat down on the front steps for a final conversation before Danny left for his new assignment.

"Now, Son," Daddy began. "Don't volunteer for any duty you don't have to. Arlington National Cemetery is lined with the crosses of boys who tried to be heroes during World War I. You just do what you're told as inconspicuously as possible and avoid taking risks."

"Don't worry, Dad. Nothing's gonna happen to me; I have too much to live for. Did I tell you the bank manager offered me a job as a teller when I get back? He probably offers the same job to all us returnees. It's a safe risk, since only a handful will show up for the position once the War's over…"

"Don't say that, Danny. I missed six years of your childhood thanks to Claudia, and I don't plan to miss any more of your adult years than I have to. You should think about settling down in Baltimore when you get out. There are piss-poor job opportunities in Lee County, South Carolina. If Roosevelt gets the GI Bill passed in Congress, you can go to college and become a lawyer or a stock broker – although a man who's good with his hands doesn't really need more education. Mick could probably find you something in carpentry, if you're interested."

"Actually, Dad, I've been thinking about a degree in education and teaching English literature. I've always wanted to write, and teaching would give me summers off…"

"I can tell you right now, there's no future in writing. Only a handful of teachers ever get published. And even if they do, there's no real money in it. How about a career in the Navy? Hell, Boy! You could be an Admiral if you got in at the Naval Academy. All it takes is a reference from a U.S. Senator. Claudia's father knows "Cotton Ed" Smith personally. She could get him to recommend you. Only promise you'll wait until the War's over before making up your mind…"

Early the next morning, the sky still rosy with dawn, Mick Mosley pulled up in front of Pennsylvania Station, between Charles and St. Paul Streets, where we spilled out of his '39 Ford and into ancient Rome. The entrance was lined with graceful, curved archways. Above the center arch was an enormous clock with gilded Roman numerals and over that, a majestic eagle flew, its stone-carved wings spread protectively over all who traversed beneath its watchful eye.

We walked through the center door and entered a cavernous waiting area, four stories high with three glass ceiling domes, the sunlight from each drenching the pink and white marble below.

Six months later, when we picked up Hazel's husband Stanley from the same station, the glass domes would be painted black, for air-raid protection, muting the marble and taking away the magic. But on that Friday, the only gray lay in Danny's going away.

As we descended the stairway to the tracks below, the openings to the north and south tunnels were dark as midnight, creating the illusion that departing voyagers disappeared into a mysterious mosque, while those arriving were unexpectedly thrust into the glare of oncoming relatives.

We heard a shrill whistle in the distance and felt the pounding pistons, the slackening of the chugging engine, the squeal of iron against iron as the brakeman brought Danny's train to a steamy standstill. Redcaps raced to the openings between cars, placing rubber stools under the feet of middleclass traveling ladies dressed in cheap fur coats, wide-brimmed hats, and black kid gloves. The word *boooard* echoed up and down the tracks, and I started to cry, for it sounded like goodbye.

Danny hugged Mama and Lucille, and shook hands with Daddy and Mick, slapping them affectionately on the shoulder, the way men do. He tousled the tops of our heads, then turned to Hazel and asked if he could kiss her goodbye, but she blushed and looked away.

"It's just that I don't have a girl of my own and where I'm going, I may never get the chance…"

Hazel lifted her head and pressed her lips against his. He kissed her long and hard, then grinned, threw his white Navy cap into the air, grabbed his duffle bag, and jumped on board, waving out the window until his train vanished into the black belly of the southbound tunnel.

Chapter 3

"Dearest Lila:

"I'm sorry there was no way to get a letter to you. We shipped out of Wellington Bay, New Zealand over a month ago, headed for Guadalcanal to relieve troops pinned down for weeks on that god forsaken island. Our landing was a disaster. The Navy packed us into amphibious tanks and dumped us on the shore, while Japs shot at us from higher ground, picking us off like ducks in a barrel. We had to crawl over the bodies of our own wounded to keep moving, shooting into the air, having no idea where the enemy was. I got nicked by a piece of shrapnel. Don't panic; a couple of stitches fixed me up like new. But it's a hell of a war when you can't even see the guy you're aiming at. On the other hand, maybe it's better that way.

I miss you like crazy and can't wait to make it stateside. Think I'll try for a more serious injury; it's an automatic two week leave - almost worth it to see you. I should have listened when you told me to join the Air Force, where the enemy can't reach me. Truth is, the guys giving us air cover are getting shot down faster than buzzards in a road-kill relay. Besides, I really am proud to be a Marine and hope we can wrap this thing up soon, so I can come home to you. Pray for me and the guys, and stay your sweet self until I see you again.

Almost forgot. Remember Billy Brooks, the kid who glued the latrine seats closed in boot camp? Well, he didn't make it. I'm sending his address so you can write and tell his mother how sorry we are. And say hello to that odd little woman down the street, the one with all the friends."

Love always, Garret

"That's all he had to say," Lila sighed, folding Garret's letter, slipping it inside her blouse next to her heart.

"How can you do that, read his letter out loud without

crying?"

I was relieved that Hazel asked the question. The last thing my sisters and I did at night was cry our way through prayers for the safe return of our boys – and General MacArthur, without whom, Daddy assured us, we could not hope to win the war. I was finding it increasingly difficult not to tear up at the very mention of Danny or Garret.

"I cried myself dry before I got here; that's how," Lila said, her hand moving perilously close to a box of Kleenex sitting on the dining room table.

"Did that last line refer to me?" Mama asked. "What did you say that made Garret think I'm odd?"

"Don't worry, Claudia, he thinks I'm odd, too."

"You *are* odd," Brynn snickered, "thinking the planets can predict the future. What rubbish. I wish they'd send Hugh overseas. Having him underfoot all the time is a pain in the neck. I'm beginning to hate the smell of his aftershave," she hissed, like a serpent caught in a thorny rosebush.

"You can't mean that!" cried Hazel. "I would thank God everyday if Stanley had a cushy desk job instead of rattling around in a tin can on the ocean - being bombed from above, torpedoed from below, and shot at by ships along the horizon."

"You'll see what I mean when Stanley gets back and expects you to be in the mood for *you know what* every night. You have no idea how boring sex is when you've been married a couple of months."

"You kids go find something to amuse yourselves," Mama said, as she always did when the "s" word came up. "You think that's bad," she continued, "wait till he smells like a brewery and hasn't shaved for two days. You and Lila are still in the honeymoon stage, Hazel. Wait till Stanley's been home six months. You'll be looking for excuses to stay up until he falls asleep."

"Never!" she exclaimed. "Lucille, you were married a long time. Did you get tired of the physical side of marriage after a few years?"

"No, I can't say that I did…"

"That's because you're a hopeless people pleaser," Brynn interrupted. "You'd gnaw your lips off before complaining, no matter how much you hated it."

Ignoring her accusation, Lucille remarked dryly, "It sounds to me like you're waiting for Hugh to make it better. Does he have any idea how you feel?"

"Are you crazy? I can't talk to a man about a thing like that."

"You don't have to tell him directly," Lucille assured her. "In fact, talking to a man about a personal need is the quickest way to ensure he'll resist satisfying it. No man wants to face up to the possibility that he's not performing adequately. You have to show them what needs changing, the way you potty-train a toddler. Once he sees that something pleases you, I guarantee he'll repeat it."

"How am I supposed to show him?"

"You can move, can't you? Shift your body until he's in the right place."

"I try not to move at all," Hazel said, gloomily, her cheeks aflame with embarrassment.

"Good grief! You girls are as prudish as Presbyterians. You need to think beyond yourselves and look at it from their point of view. Those boys don't have much more experience than you…at least they didn't before they went overseas. They'll be grateful for any direction you give them, as long as they don't have to talk about it."

"I think it boils down to a question of duty," Mama said, in the resigned voice of one accepting a prison sentence. "Sex is one of those things you simply have to do, and it's unrealistic to expect to enjoy it - or get away with not doing it. I still remember how disappointing my first time was."

"Oh, Claudia," Lila sighed heavily. "That's so sad. There must have been a time when you didn't feel that way, when you looked forward to Thurston touching you. You have an Aries moon, for Pete's sake. There has to be a streak of passion behind that polite southern facade. I love the hardness of Garret's body, the hammering of his heart when I rest my head on his chest. That's all I need to get my juices flowing."

There was a muffled giggle under the table, and Hazel cried, "Oh, my lord. Those kids have been listening to every word we said."

Mama flung back the edge of the tablecloth and Marjorie, Betsy and I crawled out, hands over our mouths, trying not to laugh.

"I thought I told you to leave the room," Mama snapped.

As we scrambled out the door, I remember thinking I'd learned something important about men and women, but by bedtime, I was too busy praying to remember what it was.

Mama

Chapter 4

On Thursday afternoon, Mama wrote the secret word on a piece of paper and folded it to fit in the pocket of my dress. I was supposed to give it to Bernie in exchange for a box of mediums, wrapped in plain brown paper. Marjorie and Betsy had performed the monthly ritual before me, and I wondered who would carry it out once I got too old. It seemed unlikely that Mama would send Brother Boy, since his gender excused him from all household chores except taking out the trash and handing tools to Daddy. Still, Bernie had to give the box to somebody.

We had no way of knowing in a few short years postwar prosperity would lead food chains to swallow up neighborhood grocers whose congenial credit was no longer needed. Acme and the A & P would render shoppers and salesclerks anonymous by sheer volume, and nobody would bother to wrap sensitive items in plain brown paper. But on that Thursday, when Mama slipped the note into my dress pocket, the world was still deceptively personal, and propriety ruled when it came to feminine products.

As I passed the doorway leading to the apartment upstairs from Bernie's store, I heard a soft voice call, "Ritta gura. Coma here, ritta gura." My heart leapt in my chest, for I recognized her Asian accent from the war movies my sisters took me to see every Sunday after dinner.

The woman calling me poked her head a little farther out the door, and I could see she was either Japanese or Chinese. We were not yet acquainted with Taiwanese, Vietnamese, or Cambodians, and it would be another eight years before we engaged in combat with North Korea.

"Rita gura," she repeated, an edge of impatience raising her voice an octave as she gestured for me to come closer. I weighed my mother's emphasis on politeness against my nervous stomach and hesitantly approached the door.

"You rika earn ten cents?" she asked, her round face only

inches from mine.

My voice stuck in my throat, and I gave a feeble nod.

"You scruba my froors, I pay you ten cents."

"Yes ma'am," I whispered, backing away from the door. "I have to go, now. My mother is waiting for her box."

She smiled and nodded, bowing her way back inside, her shiny black eyes following me all the way to Bernie's door.

My hand trembled when I passed him the note, and I was grateful he didn't notice. He slid Mama's parcel toward me. I picked it up and headed for the door, stopping short, wondering whether the woman with the slanted eyes would be waiting for me.

"Did you want something else?" Bernie asked.

"No sir," I answered, easing the door open, tentatively stepping outside. I decided to cut through the alley that ran alongside the store to avoid passing her door again. It led to what we called the "colored playground," to distinguish it from the recess yard at Public School #53, since legalized segregation prohibited black children from attending white public schools.

Separation by race and income was further evident in what lay at opposite ends of 24th Street. To the east, were the lavish row houses of Maryland Avenue, with their floor to ceiling windows and brass hand rails leading up glistening marble steps to distinctive oak front doors. Our school was located on that side of the block.

Howard Street, nearer our end, had a saloon or shoe repair shop on every corner, with a handful of poverty-infested houses in between. Lumbering up and down its asphalt highway were trackless trolleys with poles attached to overhead wires taking those lucky enough to be employed to downtown factories and waterfront warehouses, where my father once patrolled the harbor with a loaded gun. The Coastguard fired him for beating up a co-worker during an argument over whether or not labor unions were part of a communist plot to bankrupt big business. The alley that ran along the playground was nearer Howard Street, where mostly black people lived. 24th Street was the culturally integrated cord connecting uneasy poverty to restrained affluence.

Sitting on a squeaky swing inside a six-foot chain link fence was a dark skinned girl about my age, her bristly black hair twisted into five or six short braids, wearing a white dress with bright green leaves on it and brown tie oxfords with holes in the soles. I stood at the open gate while we studied each other. As different as we were on the outside, we had two traits in common: curiosity and an open-hearted readiness to like anybody who liked us back.

"What's your name?" she asked.

"Silby."

"That's pretty. Mine's Cricket."

"Cricket! Is that really your name?"

"That's what my grandma calls me 'cause I bounce from one thing to the other and never finish anything I start. My real name is Leona Love Johnson. My mother's a cook at a fancy hotel downtown, but my stepfather doesn't like kids, so I live with my grandma on Howard Street. But they're gonna come for me one day and take me to live in a fancy house on North Avenue. You live around here?"

"On 24th Street. I have a grandmother, too. She came all the way from South Carolina on a train to visit us once, but I was too little to remember. Mama said she had asthma and used to sit and rock me while we wheezed together. I wish I could remember. My grandfather won't let us visit them because he hates my father."

"What did your father do?"

"I don't know, but it must have been pretty bad cause my mother won't talk about it - and she talks about everything."

"You wanna play hopscotch?"

"Sure. You got a piece of chalk?"

"Don't need one," she laughed, leading me to the other side of a green shed, where a rough hopscotch was painted on a slab of crumbling cement.

"Wow! Wait till I tell my sister. Betsy's the hopscotch champion of the whole block."

Cricket took a worn rubber shoe-heel from her pocket and held it out to me. "You can go first."

"I don't mind going last," I assured her.

"Neither do I," she grinned. She had the whitest teeth I'd ever seen, and we played for hours, until I heard Daddy whistle for me to come home to supper. Only then, did I remember I'd forgotten to take Mama her brown paper box. Three days later, I got the worst spanking of my life for inviting a group of Cricket's friends to use the bathroom when my parents weren't there. Daddy said it was Mama's fault for not teaching me that Negroes aren't allowed to use the same bathrooms as white people. I asked why, but his only response was an angry warning to stay away from the playground.

Banned from our usual hangout, Cricket and I branched out to the snow cone stand three blocks away, inadvertently altering the course of my spiritual future forever.

**

Vera Washington was an anomaly in 1942: a black woman who owned her own business - initially selling snow cones – then graduating to a successful ice cream parlor, operated from the first floor of her row house on Lorraine Avenue. She had not set out to become a self-sufficient woman, although she'd always had a fiery spirit, refusing to be dominated by a male, even for financial security. She had her mother to thank for that, for reminding her every day that she was smart, well-loved, and fully capable of surviving whatever decisions she made. This latter belief allowed Vera to trust her instincts entirely and proceed as though everything would turn out well.

She and Mama got acquainted when I pestered her into taking us for snow cones one day when Cricket couldn't come out to play. Vera had written "2 cents" on a piece of cardboard, and was sitting on the front steps shaving ice into handmade paper cones and flavoring them with Nehi grape soda. Lucille had gone along, as she did whenever we undertook a new adventure.

"Mighty pretty little girls; I can see they resemble you." Vera smiled, scraping the shaver smoothly along the clear cold ice.

"Oh, I don't know if I'd describe them as pretty, but they *are* all mine." Mama confessed.

"Do I hear a southern accent?" Vera inquired, grinning broadly.

"Yes ma'am," Mama answered - gasping when she realized she'd said "yes ma'am" to a black woman. Returning the conversation to her view of a more appropriate exchange, she added, "I'm Claudia Silby Dunn. My father is one of the Silbys of

Spartanburg, South Carolina, and this is my friend Lucille."

"Nice to meet you. I'm Vera Washington, and my mother was born and raised in Kershaw County, so I know South Carolina well."

"You don't say," Mama commented, softening in spite of herself. "Daddy had a brother who lived in Kershaw County. He worked for the Post Office until he fell off the back end of a train and killed himself. He had a tendency to drink a little too much," she added, lowering her voice.

"I know what you mean. My daddy got run over by a garbage truck on his way home from a three day binge when I was twelve."

"You poor thing; how sad to lose your father so young."

"Oh, he's not dead. I don't remember much about it, except that my mother had to take in washing, and they squabbled a lot more. But having to support my sisters and me made her stronger, in the end."

Mama appeared puzzled by her last remark but on the whole, liked Vera very much, as did Lucille. By the time Vera expanded her business to include refrigeration and readymade ice cream cones, Lucille and Mama had established a routine of dropping by her shop for a cup of coffee on Wednesday afternoons, when Vera closed the doors to the public for her deliveries. It was a habit Mama considered harmless…until the day the preacher came to call.

Chapter 5

Neither of my parents was noticeably religious, although both had been raised in fundamental, southern churches and went out of their way to have us christened, just in case. When Marjorie was ten years old, Mama decided she should take Betsy and me to Sunday school. The nearest Methodist church was six blocks away, forcing us to cross three lanes of traffic on Maryland Avenue and Charles Street, fast-tracks for streetcars, trucks, and taxi cabs. It was a daunting task, even for one as responsible as Marjorie.

There we stood, three blind mice, in front of the mother church of American Methodism, matching paper-dolls, joined at the hands. Until that Sunday, the most exotic sights we'd seen were the frozen fish eyes at Bernie's market and the shiny chrome on Mick's new Ford coupe. Now, we were surrounded by such splendor, Marjorie had to remind us to close our mouths and breathe.

The domed ceiling was painted pale blue, with a huge swath of white stars making up the Milky Way. Snow white candles in brass holders flickered on either side of a bronze altar cross, sending smoke signals to the nameless Creator of the universe. And up and down the aisles of maroon theater seats stood huge mahogany pillars, providing an enduring foundation for the balcony and choir loft overhead.

Discovering such magnificence only six blocks from our blue-collar neighborhood would inspire Marjorie to rise like a phoenix out of the ashes of poverty and into a life of greater opportunity, but not before she herded us home to dinner and hung our Sunday dresses on the nails Daddy had hammered in the thirty inch closet of our shared bedroom.

The decision by my mother to send us to Sunday school would have fateful consequences four years later, when the Reverend Dr. Blossom discovered, while leafing through attendance records, that the three Dunn children were missing a set of parents. It might have gone unnoticed in today's listings, lost in a profusion of stepparent names, but back then, people could not afford to divorce themselves from the perceived perpetrators of their acute unhappiness. Dr. Blossom immediately decided he must make a home visit to correct the irregularity in his records.

Mama was wearing a flowered housedress, socially presentable, except for the chicken white skin and pale blue rivulets of varicose veins running from her bare knees to her dingy, terry-cloth scuffs – casualties of washing, ironing, cooking, and cleaning for a family of six, plus two boarders. Her hair was meticulously tucked around a brown padded donut, pulling it away from her face in a smooth, soft circle. Mama had exquisite cheekbones, by far her finest feature, which she rouged in pastel pink. Her lips were thin and unforgiving, her chin strong and resolute, her waistline lean as any girl's. When you added the stormy gray eyes, she was not unattractive, even to Dr. Blossom on a weekday afternoon.

"How do you do, Mrs. Dunn? I'm Dr. Blossom, from the First Methodist Church, and I wondered if I might chat with you a few minutes about your children."

"If they've done anything wrong, I can assure you it won't happen again," Mama said, her chin shifting forward on its hinges, eyes glaring at me suspiciously.

"Oh my, no. Mrs. Mitchell says they are lovely children, sweet and curious to learn more about our Savior. No. I'm here to invite you and Mr. Dunn to join our congregation."

"Oh," Mama sighed, disappointed. She was more at home disciplining children than discussing the state of her soul with the preacher - much less Daddy's somewhat ambivalent relationship with his maker.

"Do you and Mr. Dunn have a home church, perhaps the congregation where the children were baptized?"

"Well, I grew up in the Baptist church, and Mr. Dunn's family was, for the most part, Methodist. The few who were Presbyterian settled in Pennsylvania, after migrating from Scotland. That's why we sent the girls to your church – to get a foundation in…in matters related to attending church."

"And it's good that you did. But I'm sure you'll agree it's important to set a good example by attending church with them…" At that moment, he was interrupted by a chipper voice down the hall.

"Claudia! What happened? You missed your coffee this morning? Oh! I'm sorry. I didn't know you had company..."

Mama's eyes froze in their sockets as Vera stepped through the dining room door. Making a hasty recovery, she mumbled..."Umm...this is Vera Washington. She runs the ice cream parlor on Lorraine Avenue. Vera, this is Dr. Blossom, pastor of the First Methodist Church."

"Nice to meet you, Vera," Dr. Blossom responded in a smooth, unruffled voice.

Sensing Mama's discomfort, Vera apologized for the interruption and hurried down the hall and out the door. Mama set about proving to the minister that she was not in the habit of inviting Negroes to her home for coffee.

"Lucille and I occasionally take the children to Vera's for ice-cream, and she apparently thought it was an open invitation to drop in on us."

My heart sank, for I recognized the deceptive voice of betrayal when I heard it. And I couldn't help believing my mother heard it too, and cringed a little inside, for it was not her nature to be unfair - misguided, even ridiculous on occasion, but never intentionally unkind.

"I understand completely." Dr. Blossom said. Then, banking on her momentary discomfort, he added, "So we can expect to see you and Mr. Dunn at this Sunday's service?"

"I'll be there if I can, but with four children, plans change at a moment's notice..."

"Well, give my best to Mr. Dunn," said Dr. Blossom, adjusting his clerical collar, sauntering down the hall with the confidence of one who had righted an irregularity in church records and increased his congregation at the same time.

"Do drop in again," Mama said, rolling her eyes at Lucille as he started down the front steps.

"Oh my god! What must he think of me?" Mama groaned, once the coast was clear.

"He doesn't think anything," Lucille assured her. "He's a man of the cloth. He's not allowed to be judgmental."

"You can't be serious," Mama said, relating a faith-shattering experience from her teen years, when the preacher's wife lied to my grandfather about hitting his car while she, Mama, was driving. Granddaddy believed the preacher's wife, who claimed Mama bumped into her, rather than the other way around. Mama never forgave God for letting her get away with it and except for christenings and weddings she refused to darken the inside of a church again. Still, she did her best not to allow her personal grudge to affect our relationship with the Almighty.

"Why isn't Vera allowed to visit us?" I asked, wanting to get rid of the queasy feeling in my stomach.

"You'll understand when you're older," was all she said. And she was right. A few years later, after our block was integrated, Daddy sat on the front steps night after night, talking with an elderly black man about the collapse of the railroads, for which they blamed Union wages; and the bombing of Hiroshima, for which they praised Truman. Despite their congenial conversations, the man always stood and never sat down next to my father. Nor would it have occurred to Daddy to invite him inside. Such were the unspoken rules, as conditioning bound the heart to behaviors that compromised conscience.

In discussions with white men at work, Daddy recited the classic southern bigotry he grew up on. In his personal interactions, with the exception of Stanley Polanski and a few die-hard Union supporters, he never met a man whose opinion he did not respect on some level. That contradiction – along with others - made my father an emotional conundrum to those of us who felt compelled by birth to love him.

Chapter 6

"Why are we using the good tablecloth on a Tuesday?" Betsy asked, as Mama snapped the crisp white linen into the air, letting it float onto the table, centering all four corners with military precision, a ritual usually reserved for Sunday company and Thanksgiving dinner.

"Lila's coming to read my horoscope."

"What's a horoscope?" I asked, mesmerized by the word. It made me think of pirates squinting through spyglasses for hidden treasure on some exotic island.

"If you must know, there's a job opening at Julius T. Gutman's in the pots and pans department, and I'm thinking about taking it, at least until your Daddy finds something."

"You mean...you're going to work? Who's gonna take care of us?" I cried, waves of panic clamming the walls of my stomach.

"Don't make a mountain out of a molehill. Lucille and Marjorie will be here; it will be just like it's always been."

I didn't find much comfort in that, but I liked Lila and trusted her to use her mystical powers to keep Mama from deserting us. Besides, I wanted to tell Lila about a dream I'd had the night before. She was always telling Hazel and Brynn what their dreams meant. Maybe she could take some of the scary out of mine. All I knew was that it paralyzed me with dread and held me captive in a dark hallway, staring at a corpse in an overflowing bathtub. The body was dressed in navy blue, bellbottom trousers and appeared to be a young sailor, with frozen amber eyes and hair parted neatly on the side. I screamed as loud as I could, hoping Marjorie would rescue me, but all that came out was a thin whimper. I finally wheezed myself into consciousness with an asthma attack.

As if she read my thoughts, Lila poked her head into the dining room, her wild auburn hair tamed by a midnight blue scarf sprinkled with silver stars, her uniform for reading the cosmic future.

"Bring us a cup of coffee," Mama called to Marjorie, who

was already in the kitchen filling their cups. Lila sat down next to Mama and began spreading out pages of glyphs, with blue and red lines connecting them. She explained that the blue lines were positive, representing harmonious periods and good fortune, while the red were stressful, indicating a negative occurrence from outside oneself, or an internal position held so stubbornly, it caused the individual to self destruct in the face of positive opportunities.

"There is an opening at Gutman's department store," Mama began. "Can you tell from my horoscope whether or not I'll get it if I apply?"

"Well," Lila began, "the Sun is transiting your 10th house of career, so I would say you will not only get it, you'll receive the recognition you deserve from your supervisor, most likely a man whose authority you respect."

My heart sank.

"However, I'm more interested in the square from Uranus to Saturn."

"What does that mean?" Mama asked, in an uneasy voice.

"Maybe nothing; maybe everything," Lila murmured, cryptically. "Uranus is associated with unexpected change, often of the least desirable kind. Saturn is famous for forcing lessons on us we'd rather not learn. When I see activity between these two, I generally warn the individual to be prepared for the last thing she wants to see happen. My guess is that it refers to Mr. Dunn losing his job, particularly since Uranus is in the 8th house of joint assets, presumably yours and his.

"It could also reflect something as subtle as the demise of your role as mother and rebirth as a working woman. But if that were the case, I'd expect to see activity involving the Moon in your 4th house of family. That's what makes me wonder whether something more upsetting is on the horizon, particularly with Saturn in Thurston's 5th house of children."

We heard a raspy intake of air from Mama.

Shielding her from an unpleasant prediction, Hazel sidetracked Lila. "Is it true that Hitler has his own Astrologer?"

"I've read that he has. But astrology won't help him win the war, at least not the way he's hoping. Astrology is simply a way of understanding God's handiwork through behavior and history. By studying the positions of planets and stars when significant events take place, we can guess the probable outcome of similar occurrences in the future."

"Does the position of the stars during World War I give us any reason to hope we'll win the current War?" Hazel asked.

"Well, the most fascinating difference between then and now is the discovery of the planet Pluto, thought to rule violence and destruction - ushering in the War as it did. But Pluto also brought the science of Psychiatry, second only to Christianity in its power to inspire men to lead better lives. In opening our minds to the horrors of the subconscious and unmasking its destructive impulses, we may be able to prevent the rise of another Hitler and avoid ever going to war again."

"Maybe psychiatry can eliminate not only war but alcoholism and infidelity," Hazel said, warming to the possibilities.

"That's asking a lot from a planet that takes two hundred and fifty years just to orbit the Sun," Lila grinned.

"Only God and an honesty bordering on the divine could keep husbands from cheating," Lucille chucked, just before the doorbell rang.

My sisters and I raced down the hall, always happy to welcome strangers, since my parents were less likely to argue in front of them.

"Telegram for Thurston Dunn," said a diminutive man, wearing a black uniform with yellow stripes down his pants-legs and a duckbill cap on his head. No one at our house had ever received a telegram, and my mind flashed instantly to my dream.

Mama's fingers seemed to work in slow motion as she tore away the flap and meticulously removed the yellow sheet from its envelope.

"Unexpected leave Stop Arrive 2 pm Saturday Stop Love Danny"

Chapter 7

It was the sweltering summer of my tenth year. Mosquitoes melted through the window screens and buzzed around our sheet protected heads. Next day would be the 4th of July, and we'd seek relief sipping lemonade at the outdoor band concert in Druid Hill Park. A fear of air-raids forced the canceling of fireworks, but there would still be music and dancing.

After a full day's coaxing, Hazel agreed to join us, along with Danny, Mick, and Lucille. Hundreds of people spread their blankets on the ground, many planning to escape their un-air-conditioned bedrooms by sleeping under the stars.

The band, mostly brass and percussion, opened with "God Bless America," bringing the crowd to its feet. They moved on to "The Boogie Woogie Bugle Boy of Company B.," as couples put on a show for the crowd. A group of sailors from Bainbridge Naval Base hurled their dance partners into the air then slid them between their legs, dragging them back to their feet again. Mama expressed relief when they settled into a medley of love songs, beginning with "To Each His Own." Danny's persistence finally paid off, and Hazel consented to dance with him. We watched as he twirled her gracefully to the far edge of the crowd, sitting down on a bench beneath a slice of moon at the crest of a hill.

From our blankets in front of the bandstand, we could make out their silhouettes as they talked – or rather Danny did. She sat still as porcelain, gazing into his eyes. By the time he leaned forward and kissed her, my sisters and I had them wooed and wed in our imaginations. Our bubble burst when she pushed him away and ran down the hill to where we sat.

"Are you all right?" Mama and Lucille asked.

"Good grief! Was everybody watching?" Hazel cried, turning on her heel, disappearing into the darkness. By the end of the concert, Danny had talked her into coming back, but neither said a word on the long ride home.

Three days after the concert, Danny returned to his ship, and Hazel donned a mantel of guilt so profound, it led the entire neighborhood to weigh in on the merits of confession.

"I have to tell Stanley," Hazel sighed. "I owe it to him."

"One kiss on a park bench is not a confessional crime," Brynn insisted.

"Of course it's not," Mama agreed.

Lila took a surprisingly analytical approach, citing the importance of honesty in relationships. "Do you think Stanley's not going to notice on his next leave if she mopes around the house feeling guilty?"

"I don't mope," Hazel assured her.

"Maybe not, but if you believe you're harboring a guilty secret, you'll think you deserve it when he treats you like you've done something wrong. Confidence generates respect, and if you lose that, you'll end up letting yourself be bullied."

"I wouldn't go that far," said Lucille. "But I do think you need to measure the cost of hurting Stanley against the value of reducing your guilt. You might feel better, but Stanley would be haunted forever by an image of you kissing Danny in the moonlight. And what happens when the War is over and Stanley and Danny both come home. There is no way we could have a get-together without the past casting an awkward shadow."

"I hadn't thought about that," Hazel said. "I don't think I could handle being in the room with both of them - especially if Stanley knew."

Marjorie, with the rarified wisdom of a fourteen year old, stated emphatically that Hazel should tell Stanley. "If he really loves her, he'll understand. And even if he doesn't, she'll have the satisfaction of knowing she did the right thing."

"She'd be crazy to tell him," pragmatic Betsy argued. "Why make Stanley mad if she doesn't have to?"

I took my usual stance – mired in the face of conflicting points of view.

Mick told Hazel he didn't think it made that much difference but whatever she decided, she must not tell him while he's overseas. "He might go AWOL, or do something equally destructive."

Daddy complained that we were turning a momentary

impulse into the crime of the century and suggested, in no uncertain terms, that we drop the subject. His timing could not have been more perfect, for two weeks after the kiss in the park, Stanley Polanski had an unfortunate stroke of luck. A bullet nicked his elbow, sending him home for an injury earned leave. I wheedled mercilessly until Mama said I could ride in the rumble seat of Mick's Coupe when he and Hazel drove to Pennsylvania Station to pick Stanley up. In a world unaccustomed to privately owned automobiles, it seemed a magical car, the color of dark ripe plums, with whitewall tires and glinty chrome accessories. Mick liked to brag that he could afford a wife or a car and had chosen the latter, parking it two houses up to protect it from us.

The rumble seat was separate from the interior of the car, opening out from what would now be the trunk, exposing the rider to the elements but providing a warm leather cushion when the sun's rays reached the highway. Having slept all my life between Marjorie and Betsy, bathing in their leftover tub to conserve hot water, seldom completing an uninterrupted sentence, the rumble seat provided the first real privacy I'd ever known. I reveled in the freedom that comes with absolute aloneness, nestled in a snug corner as rows of tall buildings zoomed by, lulling me into delicious daydreams of having hair as long as Rapunzel's and being rescued from my siblings' second floor bedroom by a prince with shiny ebony eyes.

Hazel rode in the front with Mick until we picked Stanley up. Then I moved to the front, where I could watch but not hear them through the back window, kissing and staring into one another's eyes, trying to resurrect the stranger each had married after a brief courtship a year earlier. I knew Hazel was nervous. I'd heard her running catastrophic scenarios by Mama and Lucille every day since receiving his letter.

"What if he doesn't love me anymore? We only had two official dates before he proposed. What if he's been fantasizing about somebody who doesn't exist? He might hate me after he gets to know me?"

Lucille chuckled softly. "Nobody could hate you, Hazel. All young folks are on their best behavior before they get married; otherwise, nobody would do it. Marriage is all about uncovering the true nature of your partner and loving them anyway. It's the same for all newlyweds. But you'll survive and develop a more durable bond, especially after the babies start coming."

"Don't set her up in false hope," Mama cautioned. "It could turn out they really *don't* have anything in common. Here's the thing, Hazel. Divorce is not the pariah it once was. Thurston's divorced, and it hasn't hurt him any. It created complications between my father and me, but that had more to do with my being eighteen than anything Thurston did. Keep in mind you're not required to work it out if you don't want to. Nobody's gonna hold a hasty husband against you during a war. And you wouldn't be alone for long. Look how quick Danny took a liking to you."

"Good grief, Claudia. The last thing I want is to settle for my marriage not working out."

"I know. I'm just saying there's no need to put the cart before the horse."

Overhearing that conversation nudged me closer to a growing suspicion that much of what my mother said was profoundly irrelevant, a vacant voice generated by years of codependent denial and reliance on hackneyed clichés, skimming the razor's edge of reality without getting nicked. Yet, she spoke with such conviction, I spent the majority of my childhood thinking she was gifted with an insight into human affairs I would never be able to master.

The day we picked Stanley up from the train station, Mama and Lucille threw him a welcome home party, with pound cake covered in my grandmother's homemade custard - a substitute for ice cream, since our tiny ice-box had no freezer. I'd forgotten how piercing Stanley's green eyes were. His hair was the color of burlap - kinky and course – his skin, slightly pock-marked along bony cheekbones.

Stanley and Mama hit it off surprisingly well, thanks to her mistaking his disarming charm for genuine interest. He talked Hazel into dropping by our house every Friday on Mama's day off so he could dazzle her with tales of close encounters with Japanese submarines on the open sea. It was during one of those visits that Daddy happened to lose his job.

Stanley was seated in Brother Boy's place at the table, cattycornered from Mama, drinking a beer, straining his neck toward her, sharing an off-color joke to which she responded with unladylike cackling guaranteed to rub Daddy the wrong way. Hazel and Marjorie sat across from Stanley, with Betsy and me hovering nearby, mindlessly debating whether Doris Day could sing better than Rita Hayworth.

Daddy suddenly appeared in the doorway, glaring at Stanley, his sweat glands reeking of sour whiskey, a telltale sign he'd stopped by Sammy's Side Street Saloon and drunk himself into a nasty mood.

I've always believed my father's drinking was a side effect of misguided idealism. Convinced that the bravest were the first to die in battle, he ran away from home at seventeen to enlist in World War I and prove his gallantry. But my grandmother tracked him to the recruiting office in Charleston, South Carolina, and dragged him back to their whistle-stop, parched wood house in Leesville, next to the railroad yard. Two weeks later, she shipped him off to business school in Poughkeepsie, New York, where he learned accounting, a job he was good at but too ashamed to settle for. Once he discovered that hammering nails gave him more satisfaction than scratching figures into columns with a fountain pen, he switched to cabinet making and devoted the next twenty years to constructing finely grained tables and chairs, while drinking away his unfathomable shame at turning out to be ordinary.

By the time World War II broke out, his oldest son Danny had joined the Navy, making Daddy more determined than ever to distinguish himself as one of the valiant few on the front lines. To his incontrovertible regret, he was turned down because of an enlarged heart. He tried joining the Coast Guard but only succeeded in being hired as a watchman.

When Daddy walked into the dining room and saw Stanley in his crisply pressed Navy blues, youthful and full of promise, hypnotizing my mother with his clever banter, a mixture of self-loathing and jealousy washed over him. In a voice sarcastic enough to splinter stone, Daddy demanded to know what Stanley was doing flirting with his wife. Then he lunged past Stanley and pulled Mama to her feet, slamming his fist into her face. She collapsed onto the floor like a puppet with severed strings.

Betsy grabbed Brother Boy and dragged him under the table. Marjorie stood frozen, her stricken eyes unable to accept what they were witnessing. Then, she turned and raced out the door to Bernie's, to call the police. I tried to pull Stanley to his feet, screaming at him to stop Daddy before he killed her. But his response sounded strangely hollow, like a preacher advising his congregation in slow motion from a pulpit too high to reach. "You never interfere in a marriage," he said, not budging from his chair.

All at once, Lucille appeared from nowhere, wedging her body between Mama's and Daddy's, sliding her arm through his, saying as calmly and repetitively as rain on the roof, "Come on, Thurston, you've done enough damage." Daddy snorted like a grizzly bear but let himself be led upstairs, mumbling, "How'd he make it into the Navy, anyway?"

Hazel pressed a cold rag against Mama's nose to stop the bleeding, and the police arrived a few minutes later. But they refused to get involved because Daddy had fallen asleep and Mama would not press charges. We never spoke of the incident to each other, not even my sisters and me, but being the emotional child, it took Lucille over an hour to quell my pleas for God to damn Daddy to everlasting hell.

Most disappointing in the week that followed was Hazel's continued devotion to Stanley. I guess it was easier for me to focus on Stanley's cowardice than my father's, on Hazel's blind devotion than my mother's abject dependency on Daddy. Adding to my confusion was the awareness that my grandparents were not only affluent, but willing to take us in. All Mama had to do was write a letter and board the same train that took Danny away. In later years, when pressed for an explanation, Mama claimed she could not go home because her sister Belle had left her abusive husband and returned with two children for my grandparents to raise. She was determined not to do the same thing. Mama was nothing if not proud, except where Daddy was concerned.

The following week, Stanley returned to his ship, and we settled into the business of not noticing how unhappy things were becoming at our house.

Chapter 8

Lila had reached the limit of her ability to self comfort when she brought her troubles to our dining room table. "It's been almost three months since I heard from Garret. He's never gone this long without writing, and Saturn is transiting his 6th house of health. I just know he's lying wounded in a muddy trench or clinging to life in a prisoner of war camp. I've called the War Department over and over, but all they'll tell me is I'm neither wife nor relative. What about the thousands of girlfriends left behind? What are we supposed to do?"

"Doesn't Brynn's husband work at Military Police Headquarters? If I were you, I'd walk over there and see if he can help."

"He'll probably tell me the same thing everybody else has. Still, I can't just sit here and do nothing."

"The Military Police helped our dog Fleabite when he got run over by a car," I chimed in, trying to make her feel better. "They hit him in the head with a Billy-stick so he wouldn't suffer anymore. I'm sure they'd be glad to help you, too."

Lila burst into wrenching sobs.

"Good grief, Silby," Mama sputtered, patting Lila on the hand, assuring her Garret was more likely a victim of red tape than the Japanese army.

Lila wiped her nose on the mound of Kleenex Mama offered from her apron pocket. "Maybe it's not such a bad idea."

"That's the spirit. Take Marjorie along for moral support."

"Come on, kid," Lila sighed. "Let's go see what we can find out." Betsy and I followed at a discreet distance, determined to be helpful whether they wanted us to or not.

Military Police Headquarters was as foreboding as the haunted house on Calvert Street, where we peeked in the window on Halloween to watch old lady Wortley cast spells over her twenty-nine cats. Known as the MP building to those who lived nearby, its red brick exterior took up the entire corner. In the back, there grazed a fenced in flock of fat, gray sheep, rumored to have been used as Guinea pigs for germ warfare. But most of all, it was known for housing a handful of German prisoners of war who cooked and served meals to the solders on duty. Betsy swore she'd seen them clad in black and white stripes, dipping mashed potatoes in the cafeteria. We inched closer to Lila and Marjorie, lest we end up dipping mashed potatoes too.

Meeting Hugh Pillstick in such a structured setting did little to convince Lila he'd be helpful. He was a slight man, with reddish hair, a weak chin, and a polite but impersonal manner - and he had married the only woman on 24th Street with little interest in doing favors. He cleared his throat, nervously, and led us to a small, second floor office.

"What can I do for you?"

"I haven't heard from my fiancé in close to three months, and I was wondering whether you could check to see if he's been transferred to another location."

"I'm sorry, but our unit only has jurisdiction over Bainbridge Naval Base and Baltimore City, wherever servicemen are working or socializing. We have no authority overseas and don't receive information about anyone who may or may not be missing in action."

"But you can access military records can't you? You could look up his battalion and find out whether they are on their way home or have been sent to a different country. You could do that, couldn't you?"

"No, ma'am."

"Please Hugh. I haven't slept in weeks. I'm beside myself with worry. Couldn't you go out of your way for a friend of Brynn's?"

Lieutenant Pillstick was more comfortable following orders than he was saying "no," which, along with his stripes and brass, is what led Brynn to choose him in the first place. "I guess I could check on his last mission, but I want your word you won't send your friends to pester me about the whereabouts of boyfriends behind in their letter writing."

"I swear on the planet Jupiter."

He excused himself and Lila decided to read our palms to make the time pass more quickly. Marjorie and Betsy, she concluded, were gifted with practical palms, while I was destined for a troubled future. But I thought it small price to pay if it helped us find Garret.

Hugh returned almost an hour later with a handful of carbon smudged pages. "Are you sure you want to hear this? The news isn't all that encouraging."

"I don't care!. I have to know."

"Should they be in the room?" he asked, nodding in our direction.

"Absolutely. They're my best friends."

"Have it your way," he muttered, picking up the first sheet. "After their victory at Guadalcanal, the 2nd Marine Division, to which Garrett had been assigned, was sent back to New Zealand for rest and recuperation. In October of this year, '43, they were deployed to a group of battleships led by the escort carrier USS Liscome Bay, to take part in an attack on the Island of Betio, southwest of Hawaii. Betio itself is only three miles long and half a mile wide. Even so, it was occupied by four thousand Japanese troops, and they'd had a year to fortify themselves with planes and submarines to attack American aircraft carriers on their way to Hawaii and the Philippines.

"Thanks to naval gunfire and the 27th Infantry, the Marines were finally able to take the Island. The following day, November 23rd, our escort ship USS Liscome Bay was torpedoed by a Japanese submarine. It was carrying 8,000 lbs of bombs and instantly exploded in a firestorm of burning metal, killing over five hundred American officers and enlisted men.

"Altogether, 2,000 lost their lives taking that island, and many more were wounded. The good news is that Garrett's name does not appear among the dead. The bad news is I don't have a list of the wounded."

Lila's face was ashen and tears streamed down her cheeks. "Why?" she whispered, her voice deadened by the horrific cost of taking a three mile stretch of worthless sand in the middle of the ocean.

"To place us in a more strategic position for retaking the

Philippines. It was critical to the war effort…"

"That's not a good enough reason," she sobbed, burying her face in Mama's Kleenex.

"I…I'm…truly sorry," Lieutenant Pillstick stammered, as if he were personally responsible.

Lila wiped the tears from her cheeks and fixed her eyes on his. "I believe you are," she said, reaching out but drawing her hand back without touching him. Then, she rose, thanked him for his help, and walked slowly home, with us on either side, longing to comfort her but too afraid of making it worse to say anything.

Chapter 9

As happy as she was when Lila told her Garret might still be alive, Hazel could not shake off the need for confirmation of Stanley's enlistment in the Navy. She agonized for weeks over whether or not to approach Hugh Pillstick – particularly after Lila said she'd promised not to pester him with friends seeking information about their partners.

On the positive side, Stanley always received the letters she mailed to the San Diego post office box he insisted all military mail must be sent for distribution overseas. Making it even more plausible was the lengthy delay between Hazel mailing her letters and Stanley responding to them - consistent with such a circuitous route. He'd also left home in full uniform, with a duffle bag of clean underwear. When Hazel added this to the list of reasons to believe he'd enlisted, Mama argued that you don't get a military uniform until you complete six weeks of basic training which, as far as Hazel knew, he had not done.

Then, too, there were the insurance documents Stanley had her sign as his beneficiary in case he was killed in battle. Every time she asked about them, he assured her she'd be receiving a copy of the policy any day. She'd also stumbled onto a suspicious cardboard box taped on every side, with the word "personal" printed in bold black ink on the top. It showed up in the back of the closet just before Stanley shipped out the last time. Brynn told her she was crazy not to open it, but Hazel feared Stanley would never trust her again if he found out.

One breezy Saturday afternoon, she spotted my father sitting on the front steps, tightening my roller skates with the key. She hurried over and asked the question to which she was certain all married males knew the answer. "How can you tell when a man is cheating on his wife?"

"Simple," Daddy answered. "You ask his wife. Women have a sixth sense when it comes to infidelity, even if they talk themselves out of acknowledging it – like you're doing now. A wife who is mistaken when she suspects her husband of cheating is as rare as a blind birdwatcher. And the more miserable she is, the less likely she will be to admit he can't be trusted. She'll claim it's not knowing that's making her batty, but in her gut, she knows the truth. What she's searching for isn't honesty, it's evidence of fairy tales."

"It's not so much that I believe there's another woman," Hazel explained. "it's just...we did rush into marriage. Maybe the cuffs of commitment are tighter than he expected, and he wants to leave a way out if he needs one."

"It might work that way in Kansas, but in Baltimore, there's only one reason a man would go to all that trouble. There's another woman making demands on his time or money and he needs a legitimate cover for not getting caught."

"All he has to do is tell me there's somebody else, and he'll be free as a bird instantly."

"Like hell he will! The minute a man confesses he no longer wants a woman, she begins tallying up all the ways he did her wrong. Before you know it her friends are recommending the lawyer that got a hefty settlement for Aunt Sue. Then boom! He's broke for the rest of his life."

"Is that what happened to you?" Hazel couldn't resist asking.

"My first wife was a coldhearted, money grubbing...Oh, no you don't! We're talking about you, not me."

Shortly after that conversation, an older, dowdy woman came into Bernie's store asking if anyone knew which house belonged to Stanley Polanski. Bernie, who'd always had a weak spot for Hazel, sent the woman to our house so my mother could field any uncomfortable questions that might upset his gentle friend.

Mama tried her best to be cagey. "I think there used to be a neighborhood cab driver named Stanley. Last I heard, he had joined the Navy and was on board a ship headed for...I think it was Rumania. Are you a relative of his?"

"I'm more than a relative. I'm Blanch Polanski, his common-law wife. Have been for almost a year now. A friend of his told me he bought a house on 24th Street, near Howard. All I want is what's coming to me – not a penny more nor a penny less."

"You have to live together seven years to be considered a

common law couple," Mama retaliated.

"Depends on whose side the judge is on," Blanch giggled, clearly experienced in marital litigation.

"I can pretty much guarantee nobody by that name owns a house on this street. Why don't you give me your address, and I'll let you know if any of the neighbors run across a forwarding address. How'd you come to meet Mr. Polanski?"

"I moved here from West Virginia to look for a job waitressing and he happened to pick me up at the bus station and drive me to the YWCA to rent a room. When he heard I didn't know anybody in Baltimore, he took pity and drove me all over town, showing me the sites. It wasn't two weeks before we rented a room together in Hampden. Then, a couple of months ago, he suddenly vanished, along with his clothes. I'm relieved to know he joined the Navy. I was afraid he left me for another woman."

My sisters and I were mesmerized by Mama's coolness under pressure. "I'm sure you'll hear from him as soon as he gets leave."

The woman wrote down her address and thanked Mama for her help. We followed her to the front door and watched from the top step until she got on the streetcar that would take her home to Hampden. Then Mama sent Marjorie scurrying to find Hazel. "And don't dally along the way."

Hazel rushed in a few minutes later, breathless and frightened. "Has something happened to Stanley?"

"Well," Mama said coyly, "in a manner of speaking, it has. His common-law wife of the last year hasn't seen him since he left home – apparently around the time he met you."

The color drained from Hazel's cheeks, and she gasped, "Oh my Lord! Thurston was right. He just had the wrong victim. Stanley's not cheating on me, he's cheating on her. At least they're not legally married. That makes it less like adultery."

"He didn't tell you about her. That's as close to infidelity as he needs to get," Mama stammered.

"Whatever existed between them was before he met me. And it sounds like he hasn't seen her since. My doubts about his being in the Navy are based solely on my own insecurities, not anything he did."

"If you really believe that, you'll have no problem asking

Hugh Pillstick to confirm it."

"There's no reason to, now," she smiled, contentedly.

After Hazel left, Mama contacted Brynn, who agreed to talk Hugh into checking on Stanley's military background. Less than a week later, Brynn told us he had indeed enlisted in the Navy, but he'd named one Agnes Bolton as his spouse and the beneficiary on his life insurance policy.

"There are two of them," Mama cried, when Lucille got home from her daily job search. "I think it's time we told Hazel to quit waiting for the life insurance policy."

But Lucille insisted that would be unnecessarily hurtful.

"It will hurt a damned sight more if Stanley gets killed and a stranger named Agnes Bolton turns up to claim her inheritance. As his legal wife, Hazel will still have to pay for the funeral. I think it's safe to assume Agnes and Blanch won't be waiting at the cemetery to do it."

"What matters most is Hazel's name being on the 24th Street mortgage so she doesn't lose the house," Mick stated firmly, never far behind once Lucille entered a room. "The Navy will pay for his burial if she can't afford to."

"Not if she isn't listed on military records as his wife," Mama argued. Then, she suddenly reversed her stance and pretended to buy Hazel's belief that Stanley was a loyal man who loved her with all his heart. When my sisters and I questioned the virtue of such a sham, Mama told us when it comes to friendship, being sparing with the truth is sometimes the better part of kindness. "And, it never hurts to bide your time…"

Chapter 10

A package arrived from my grandmother two weeks before Christmas. Although she was asthmatic and had to cover her nose with a damp cloth to avoid inhaling the flour, she mixed and baked a fruitcake filled with plump pecans, candied cherries, and juicy pineapple – nothing like the dry blocks of bitter citron sold nowadays. She also included homemade butter mints, pulled with her own arthritic hands until they were the perfect, melt in your mouth consistency. My grandfather added twenty-five dollars, five for each of us, except my father. Mama was so excited by what she considered a partial sign of redemption, she decided to invite Hazel, Lila, Brynn, and Hugh to a Christmas Eve party to celebrate.

But it was not just the gift from home that put Mama in a festive mood. While gluing red sequins on her handwritten invitations, she learned there was going to be a surprise guest at the party. She adamantly refused to tell anybody who it was, although Marjorie probably knew, since she shared Mama's gift for keeping secrets. But the rest of us were doomed to a week of front step speculation.

I prayed constantly that Danny would be the one coming home but was careful not to say anything for fear of setting Daddy up in false hope. It never occurred to me that whatever Mama knew, Daddy also knew. My parents lived in separate quarters, Mama in the kitchen and Daddy behind his newspaper in the living room. They met in the dining room for meals, where she kept him informed about our ailments and misdemeanors while he grunted and complained to Mick about the incompetence of the men at work. I had no idea they talked about personal things once they went to bed – unless, of course, they were arguing. Then the whole house knew.

The week of wondering was finally coming to an end, and Santa Claus was scheduled to arrive two days later, two days after my eleventh birthday. But the man in the red suit paled in comparison to the first Christmas party ever held at our house -

certainly the first one with a mystery guest. I should have known anything my parents planned together would end in squabbling. Lucille said it was because my mother didn't know a losing cause when she saw one, but Mama rejected that as nonsense and set about trying to change the way Daddy had celebrated Christmas for over fifty years.

"You have to get the tree today so we can decorate it in time for the party."

"No such thing as putting the tree up before Christmas Eve."

"Lots of people do it."

"Lots of people are Fascists too, but that doesn't make it right."

"It's not a question of right or wrong. It's a question of convenience."

"Well, it suits my convenience to get the tree on Christmas Eve," Daddy bellowed, the spidery veins in his cheeks turning blue, as he stomped down the cellar steps to sip whiskey behind the furnace and hammer nails until suppertime. Mama agreed, grudgingly, to wait until the following day for the tree.

Tension at the dinner table combined with Christmas anticipation to give me a night of fitful sleep. I kept finding myself lost under the covers at the foot of the bed, entangled in my sisters' feet, until Marjorie dragged me back to the head. Finally, I gave up sleeping altogether and crawled between my sisters to the cold linoleum floor, tiptoeing down the stairs, where Lucille sat stirring her coffee at the dining room table. I raced across the room and into her arms.

"You know what your Mama's gonna do if she finds you out of bed?"

"I know, but I'm too excited to sleep." Lucille smiled and offered me a sip from her saccharin laced cup, snatching it away when she heard my mother's scuffs flip-flopping down the stairs.

"What are you doing up this early? I declare, Lucille, you spoil her rotten."

"She wants to watch us fix breakfast," she fibbed, redirecting Mama's attention from my wakefulness to cooking breakfast. I climbed onto a kitchen stool and watched as Lucille opened the creaky iron door of our tiny hot water heater. Blue flames shot from the match-head up the coiled heating element in synchronized poofs. Slamming the door shut, she began cracking eggs while Mama scraped a heaping spoon of day-old bacon fat into the frying pan. All sorts of lovely sounds filled the kitchen: grits gurgling in a double boiler, bacon sizzling in the pan, coffee drizzling in the dripilator. Lucille and Mama worked in perfect unison, reaching in front of each other to turn the bread in the two door toaster so each side could brown evenly. The concert stopped the minute Mama heard Daddy's footsteps on the stairs. She filled his plate, poured his coffee, and waited in the kitchen doorway, poised to serve.

Daddy entered the room smelling of sweaty undershirts and wood-shavings caught in the cuffs of his trousers. Having grown up with only a back-porch pump, he had an aversion to bathing after dark, when bats circled overhead and field mice tried to dart up his trouser legs. Consequently, he awoke each morning reeking of the day before, hair un-brushed and askew with cowlicks, bristly stubble casting dark shadows along the deep folds in his cheeks.

As I watched him sipping coffee, a reckless idea unaccountably took possession of my brain. I tried to replace it with more benign thoughts, but it held on with the tenacity of an addiction. It pestered me all day, as we trailed behind Daddy pulling my brother's Radio Flyer wagon to get the Christmas tree; it pestered me through an endless afternoon, as he meticulously arranged each light before allowing us to add the ornaments; and it pestered me as we hung the tinsel to the cadence of his booming voice: "Don't clump. Don't clump. Don't clump."

Suddenly, there he was, sitting at the dining room table reading the morning paper, killing time before bathing for the party. I walked over and stood next to his chair, anxiety rising in uneasy waves from my cold stomach to my thundering heart. My father's moods were unpredictable at best, and presenting him with an unexpected proposition was risky business. Yet, something about the magic of Christmas led me to believe a miracle might be possible. Throwing caution to the wind, I took a deep breath. "Daddy, can I watch you shave?"

He continued to read his paper as though he hadn't heard.

"Daddy, can I watch you shave?"

"Watch me shave? I guess so, if it's all right with your

mother."

I couldn't believe my good fortune. He started up the steps. I held my breath. "Come on," he said, almost as an afterthought.

I climbed onto the clothes hamper as he turned on the hot water and hooked his razor strop over a nail on the wall, honing the blade of his straight razor to a fine edge. Wetting the bristles of his shaving brush, he swooshed it in the soapy mug and lathered his face. Then it began – the part I loved best. It started as a distant rumble, bellows born from the floor of his lungs, full pitch at the vocal chords: "Oh...John Henry was a steel driving man..." The magic ended as abruptly as it had begun, with the ringing of the doorbell and Brynn's strident voice calling "Where is everybody?"

**

There are two types of people, excluding the withdrawn and morbidly depressed: those who take an edge, whose energy crackles like electricity, causing you to step back when they approach; and those so filled with goodwill they grant you generous space, creating a safe place you can lean into. Lucille was like that, but she was busy helping Mama, so I followed Lila around, thinking it would protect me from verbal blunders. I knew Lila wanted more than anything for the surprise guest to be Garret, and I was impressed by her ability to disguise desperate hope behind a cheerful smile. My sisters and I prayed it would be Garret if it couldn't be Danny. After directing us to fill our plates and glasses, Mama called to the kitchen pantry, "You can come out now." I held my breath.

A long lean soldier, wearing a cotton khaki shirt and tie from recent duty in the tropical Philippines, stepped into the doorway, his garrison cap cocked jauntily to one side of his curly black hair, eyes like his mother's, radiating warmth, a sheepish grin on his face, an easy 'uisiana accent when he said, "Hey, Mama."

"Andy!" cried Lucille, throwing her arms around him. He towered over her like a crane. Everybody except Daddy and Brynn got teary-eyed, although we masked our sentimentality behind mouthfuls of butter mints.

"Sit down, boy," Daddy cried enthusiastically, having reached the gregarious stage in his drinking, "and tell us about the fighting. Are we any closer to taking back Corregidor and Bataan? Shameful loss! A dark day for America..."

"No!" cried Mama. "No war talk tonight. It's Christmas Eve, and everybody has to be in a cheerful mood. Tell us something your mother would enjoy hearing, Andy."

"Yes, ma'am," he complied, grinning. "This should make you happy, Mama. They don't give us enough to eat, so I volunteered for KP duty and learned to peel potatoes and scramble eggs. We get to have what's left when the fellas are done." If he'd told her he had been promoted to General, she could not have been more pleased.

After doing her best to be cordial at the party, Lila slipped her coat around her shoulders and quietly disappeared to the front steps where she could watch the stars blinking in an inky sky – probably the one thing she was certain she and Garret might be sharing, assuming he was still alive. I noticed Andy following her with his eyes, and before long, he had joined her.

"Mind if I keep you company?"

Lila assured him she didn't and went back to star-gazing. I sat down Indian fashion on the cold vestibule tiles and settled into overhearing as much as I could. I knew Lucille would want to know. Neither spoke for the first fifteen minutes – until he offered her a cigarette.

"My mother wrote that you are worried about your fiancé. Still no word from him?"

"No," she said dejectedly.

"I wouldn't worry too much. It's a mess over there, with thousands of soldiers scattered half-in and half-out of enemy territory. Identifying the wounded can be a long, painstaking process. Not hearing doesn't necessarily mean he's not okay."

"Really," she cried, her voice trembling with fresh hope. "How long do you think it will take to find him? I have the additional complication of not being a wife or relative. I have to pry information out of them."

"I'd give it a good six months. Have you been engaged very long?"

"Seems like all my life," she sighed, relieved to be talking with someone who had shared Garret's overseas experience. "We met in the eighth grade during a drum and bugle parade at school. I twirled the baton and he attempted to play trumpet. To be completely honest, I first noticed him in the third grade, but he didn't know I was alive. I used to follow him home from school, ducking behind front steps every time he turned around."

"What attracted you to him?"

"His presence of mind. I'm kind of Neptunian in nature. You'd more likely find me reading a deck of Tarot cards than the Baltimore Sun. The minute I laid eyes on Garret, my instincts told me he was solid as a tree, with the perseverance of a mountain goat. I can't concentrate long enough to write a grocery list. He can store unbelievable amounts of data in his head. Garret grounds me. When my thoughts wander into lala land, he can pull me back just by whispering my name..."

She covered her face with her hands and began to cry. Andy put his arms around her and rocked back and forth assuring her it would be alright. It had been over a year since Garret held her in his arms, and she melted, now, into Andy's. "Just until we go inside," she whispered, half aloud. "Just another fifteen minutes..."

Chapter 11

The air was murky and smelled of rancid sesame oil and apricots. A naked light bulb dangled from a frayed cord in the center of the ceiling, causing jagged shadows to dance along dingy, onion yellowed walls. The only furniture was a paint-peeled table and chair placed just to the right of a sticky strip of fly paper, scotch-taped to the window sill. For all the rumors about her glamorous occupation as a spy, the diminutive Asian woman in apartment 2B did not seem to have reaped a great deal from her career. She handed me a bucket containing a scrub brush and a box of Duz soap powder and told me to get to work.

Relieved to find I was there to scrub floors and not the captive of a white slave trader, I dragged a chair to the sink and filled the bucket with hot water and Duz. Then I searched cabinets for an old newspaper to cushion my knees and came across several sheets of paper covered in curved tic-tac-toe shapes, drawn with a soft, black pencil. More afraid of asking permission than damaging her drawings, I placed the sheets under my knees and went to work.

After scrubbing my way out the kitchen door, I wandered into a combination living room and sleeping area. She stood beside a drawn window shade, peeking out at the alley below, chanting thin, nasal refrains, like a bird calling to its mate from an overhead branch. I debated for several minutes about the least intrusive way to interrupt and finally decided there was none. So I inched closer and closer, until she spotted me out of the corner of her eye and turned around.

"You finish?" she asked.

"Yes ma-am."

"Okay. Here your ten cents."

I took the dime and hurried down the stairs, not noticing her papers in my other hand until I reached my front door. After an initial flood of panic, I convinced myself it would be better to wait until the following week to return them. Secure in the armor of procrastination, I tossed them on the buffet and didn't give it another thought until Mick asked, at the dinner table, which of us spoke Chinese.

"Chinese?" Mama asked, glancing up from the bite-size bits of ham she was cutting for Brother Boy. "Why would any of us speak Chinese?"

"There's a letter written in Chinese on the buffet?"

"Where did it come from?" Mama asked, suspiciously.

"I accidently brought it home from the oriental lady's house when I scrubbed her floor."

"Why is she writing Chinese? I thought she was Japanese," Mama said, as though I had intentionally misled her.

"I'll get to the bottom of this," Daddy said, his chair scraping the planked floor as he left the table. He returned several minutes later brandishing the gun he'd used for patrolling the Chesapeake Bay, exhilarated by the prospect of a citizen's arrest. "I'll show those papers to Charlie Wong. He'll know what they say."

"I'll go with you," Mama and Mick replied, in complete accord.

"Can I go, too?" I asked, thrilled at the possibility of exposing a spy.

"No!" Daddy replied, sharply.

"Now, Thurston, she's been inside the woman's apartment. She might have something important to contribute."

Much to my relief, Mick supported Mama.

Daddy grunted and tucked the papers into his breast pocked, then led Mama, Mick, and me up Howard Street to the corner of 25th, where steamy white vapor smelling of starch and cotton hot irons poured from Charlie Wong's Laundry and Dry Cleaners.

Mrs. Wong looked up and smiled, her upper lip sliding effortlessly across slightly protruding teeth. "Can I herup you?"

"We'd like to see Mr. Wong," Daddy said, clearing his throat with authority.

She called to her husband in the back, "Mr. Dunn want to see Mr. Wong."

Mr. Wong entered on quiet feet, his narrow eyes locked in a position of polite receptivity, and asked how he could be of service.

Daddy slid the papers across the counter and asked if he could tell us what they said.

At first, Mr. Wong appeared anxious to help, but as he shuffled through the pages, his face grew troubled, then sad, and finally, angry. "Where you get this?" he asked, almost rudely.

"It doesn't matter where I got it. What matters is whether or not I need to turn it over to the War Department. What does it say?"

Mr. Wong licked his lips, nervously shifting his focus from Daddy to Mick, occasionally glancing at Mrs. Wong, as if her eyes held the solution to his dilemma. She said something to him in Chinese, and he heaved a sigh and said, "Not here. We go upstairs."

He led us to a modest room, where the furniture seemed sparse and the air, uncontaminated by cigarette smoke, a condition my asthma had taught me to value. He invited us to sit down, then unfolded the pages and began interpreting the words in a respectful, subdued voice.

"It retter to her mother in Shanghai. She say rife in America good and bad. Good in country not yet attacked by Germans or Japanese, bad in peopre mistake her for Japanese and treat her rike enemy. She change job at munitions factory to night shift so fewer workers to brame her when husbands wounded in war. She say a hundred thousand Japanese interred in prison camps in America. They ruse jobs and homes and terrified for future. She afraid this happen to her because of srant eyes and round eyes not knowing difference. She very afraid of this so she riv rike bat in cave. She fear every day rusing job and being sent away and never heard from again. She say it bad time to be Chinese, even though we not enemy of America."

Mr. Wong reached across the sofa and handed the letter back to my father, the two seeming to bond for a moment in common mourning for the peace and security they had taken for granted before Pearl Harbor. Then Daddy turned and led us home in silence. Even my mother had nothing to say.

Chapter 12

There seemed to be no policy more stringently enforced in 1944 than keeping the whereabouts of military personnel out of the hands of the girls they left behind. Lila was about to give up when she received a note in the mail from Lucille's son Andy. It was short and to the point: "Can't tell you how I know, but Garret is recovering at Walter Reed Hospital from wounds received in the battle to take Betio. Prepare yourself for the possibility of serious damage. Whatever you find, I pray the future will be a happy one. Best wishes, Andy."

"How did a cook in the Army get his hands on information Lieutenant Pillstick couldn't access?" Lila asked.

"I have no idea," Mama answered. "Maybe some high ranking officer likes his cooking."

"Well, however he did it, I'll be grateful to him for the rest of my life. Does anybody know where Walter Reed Hospital is?"

Mick, who had his own tale to tell about a World War I chest wound, knew all too well where it was. "It's in Washington DC, on Georgia Avenue. Shouldn't take more than an hour to get there by bus. I'd take you myself, only I have to work."

"Don't worry about it. I'll see if Hazel can go."

Despite Mama's advice not to rush off half-cocked, Lila and Hazel were on a Greyhound bus headed for DC by 10 am the next morning. By mid-afternoon they were back, with Hazel in obvious distress and Lila crying as though her heart would break.

"Did they turn you away?" Mama asked, anxiously.

"We got in all right. I pretended to be his wife," said Hazel, holding up her ring finger. "Nurses weren't the problem. It was Garret who turned us away." She glanced at Lila to see if she wanted to tell it her own way.

"The room was dimly lit, and I thought at first the bed was too long. But it wasn't the bed. His legs were missing below the knees..." Lila cried. "Worst of all - he doesn't love me anymore."

"He didn't say he doesn't love you," Hazel corrected her. "He said he can't bear for you to see him in that condition."

"It's his heart I care about, not his legs. He told me to go away and never come back. He was really quite cruel..."

"I'm sure he didn't mean to be," Lucille said, soothingly. "He's trying to be realistic with himself and merciful to you."

"But he turned his face to the wall," Lila cried. "I told him I wanted to take him home, but he said his future was a life sentence chained to a chair. He said if we went to a dance, I'd be forced to twirl him around in a wheelchair like a lame monkey. Then, he pleaded with me not to do that to him." Lila put her head down and sobbed for several minutes before continuing.

"I tried to take his hand, but he jerked it away and pushed the call button for the nurse. He told her to get us out of there and to notify the nurse's station if we attempted to get back in."

"It takes time to recover emotionally as well as physically from wounds that traumatic. The best thing you can do right now is be patient," Lucille advised. "If he loves you as much as you love him, he'll come around."

"What are you going to do in the meantime?" Mama asked, directing her attention toward more practical considerations.

"There's nothing I can do but wait until he wants me more than he doesn't want me to see him like that."

My sisters and I had not uttered a word, but our hearts were breaking for Lila and Garret. I decided to go find Cricket; I could count on her cheering me up anytime Lucille was too busy to do so.

**

Lila said it was because I had Libra rising, but Mama thought it was eleven years of sleeping between my older sisters and following them to school every day that caused my obsession with always having a best friend. "When she's not at their houses, she drags them here to play paper-dolls in the hallway. Can't stand to be alone. She even got attached to a little black girl at the playground named Cricket of all things. Then, she invited the kid's friends home to use the bathroom. A complete lack of gumption. Thank goodness Thurston put a stop to it before she did anything worse to embarrass us. But I'm afraid she'll never learn to think for herself."

When I heard Mama say that, I half expected God to smite me with swarms of crispy locusts for playing with Cricket. But instead of giving her up, I convinced myself that neglecting to tell my mother – so long as I didn't lie outright - was a misdemeanor forgivable by God, if not my parents. So I continued to spend my home-from-school hours playing hopscotch with Cricket in the colored playground, or sitting on the roof of the equipment building talking and giggling. I didn't have to worry about saying the wrong thing with her. It felt the same way roller skating did on cold mornings with the wind in my face. It felt like freedom.

There was a cost, of course, for the playground was visible to the kids who walked home from school through the alley. And there were comments about my choice in friends, including all the hateful labels of the day. But they were not enough to make me give up Cricket. Then, unexpectedly, the end came of its own accord. When I got to Cricket's house, hoping to be cheered up after Lila's encounter with Garret, there was a huge black Cadillac parked out front with Cricket's mother on the front seat holding a baby that looked brand new. Her stepfather was explaining to her grandmother that he had changed his mind and Cricket could move into their new house on North Avenue – exactly as Cricket predicted he would.

My stomach plummeted into a dark place and it took several minutes to absorb the blow. All at once, it seemed imperative that I give her something to remember me by. I ran home as fast as my feet could carry me, stinging as they slapped the sidewalk, and grabbed the doll I'd loved the longest, making it back just as her parents were climbing into their car.

I gestured for Cricket to roll down the back window and shoved my favorite doll into her arms. She looked surprised but said nothing, as her parents pulled away.

I never saw Cricket or my doll again. On the third day of sobbing inconsolably, my mother pronounced me pathologically emotional and my sisters poked enough fun to send the tears underground – but not the memory. It haunts me still, the depth of pain when your best friend moves away.

Feeling like a misunderstood orphan, I began a long running

fantasy of being kidnapped by my real parents, Tarzan and Jane, and taken to live in the jungle, where Cheetah and I would swing from vines, swim with crocodiles, and everything would stay the same forever.

Marjorie, Betsy, Silby and Garland

Chapter 13

Daddy had struggled six weeks and was winning the battle against alcohol but losing the war with sobriety. His nerves were raw as sandpaper, and he was gripped by a terrible urgency to make up for cruelties he could scarcely remember. In this distraught state, he somehow concluded it would be a good idea to ask my mother for a date.

"We've never really tried to hold a conversation," he explained to Lucille and Mick, who were slipping each other incredulous, sideways glances. "We were too busy escaping South Carolina, pregnant and frantic for employment, to focus on getting acquainted. If her sister Belle hadn't had to pee, we would not have met in the first place. Belle and I were playing badminton across the back fence when she ran in to use the bathroom. Suddenly, Claudia popped up - slamming the birdie back to me. What else could I do but return it?" Clearing his throat, he changed the subject. "I can't imagine what we're going to talk about tonight?"

"It doesn't matter – as long as it's not the children or money," said Lucille. "Just relax and act the way you feel."

"I feel old and filled with dread at the thought of talking to a woman, particularly the one I've lived with for fifteen years."

"That's because you've never tried it without a drink to boost your courage," Mick stated flatly. "Relax and be yourself tonight, and you might not wake up strangers in the morning."

"I've been drunk for twenty-five years. How could I possibly know who myself is?"

"You poor man," Lucille sighed. "You really are a nervous wreck. Well, I know something that will put your mind at ease. Turn around and look behind you."

Mama stood in the doorway, motionless as a moth, wearing a chiffon dress that caressed her slender body in gauzy folds of azure blue. For the first time in my life, it occurred to me that she had once been young. She went to the hall closet for her coat, and the sheer sleeves rustled against her narrow shoulders. Far from feeling more confident, Daddy began wiping his sweaty palms on his pants. Then he tried to stuff them in his pockets, but they'd grown to twice their awkward size.

"We'll be home early," Mama told Lucille, taking control of the evening before it started.

"Stay as long as you want. It'll give me a chance to spoil these hooligans," she grinned, patting me lightly on the head. "You know…I have a beaded handbag that matches your dress perfectly. It's in my bottom vanity drawer. Why don't you run get it?"

"This one will do," Mama insisted.

"You can't carry a boxy leather pocketbook in that fancy dress. It'll only take a minute."

Mama sighed impatiently and left the room. Mick reached in his pocket and handed Daddy a folded ten dollar bill. "You haven't worked in months, and I have more than I need."

"Ouch!" Daddy winced, torn between taking the money and clinging to the few shreds of pride he had left.

"Take her to Haussners," Lucille suggested. "The food's delicious and they have reproductions of Renaissance paintings all over the walls. If you run out of something to say, you can point to a picture and ask her what she thinks."

"Oh, yea; that's me being myself alright."

"It might be if you take the time to really look at them. Art's kind of like opera. You have to put a little effort into appreciating it."

Mama returned just as Daddy was pocketing the money. "Are you ready?" he asked.

"Ready as you are," she replied, a shade shy of sullen.

Later, in giving Lucille and Mick a blow by blow of their brief stay at the restaurant, Daddy said those were the last words either spoke before they got there. Once inside, with a table safe between them, Mama relaxed a little and began complaining in words as irritating as a paper-cut about the behavior of the children, the monotony of her job selling pots and pans, and the friends who cluttered their lives on weekends when she had mountains of laundry to catch up on.

As she droned on, Daddy said he took Lucille's advice and

studied the paintings on the walls, particularly the adult-faced children dressed like squat pilgrims. They reminded him of us, he said, patient beyond our years thanks to his drinking and Mama's habitual disapproval. He tried to imagine her nuzzling one of us affectionately but admitted he couldn't. That's when he realized he knew almost nothing about the woman he'd married. Had she ever needed him? And if not, was it because he hadn't been there for her, or had he not been there because she was too indomitable to acknowledge needing anyone for anything? At that point, he said Mama interrupted his pondering to accuse him of not listening. Overwhelmed by a sudden craving for a drink, he reminded himself he was guilty of any and all failures as a father and husband. Whatever she dished out, he had to take.

Mick interrupted to caution him against wallowing in guilt. "You need to keep your mind on future solutions, not past transgressions."

"I did everything I could to get her to leave the past behind, but she refused to talk about it. So I drove home, thinking being in familiar surroundings might help. Back to the battlefield," Daddy groaned, starting up the stairs. My sisters and I scampered to our bedroom, only steps ahead of him.

The first thing Mama said was "How come we start out talking about your faults and end up focusing on mine?"

"You're absolutely right. I'm sorry. Yell at me. Curse the day we met. Tell me what a bullying bastard I am."

"I wouldn't dream of holding anything you did while drinking against you. I've never been a grudge holder…"

"Oh, yes you have!" he shouted - then added less angrily, "You hold onto grudges the way Rockefeller hoards money. When Lucille's not around, you complain that she spoils the kids; Mick lacks ambition; Marjorie stomps when she walks; Silby is absent minded; Betsy's too much like your sister Belle; Belle is a floozy; your boss is a tyrant; Baltimorians say 'zinc' instead of 'sink;' and nobody, for Christ's sake, knows how to diagram a sentence anymore. Stone cold sober, you've become as tiresome as I was drunk. It's probably my fault; maybe partly your father's…"

Her voice grew steely at the mention of my grandfather. "You've been sober less than two months, and you've already figured out everything that's wrong with me. How clever you are without a drink."

"Then tell me! Tell me what I deserve to hear. List my crimes…"

"Oh, no you don't! I won't let you off the hook by making you feel guilty."

"I knew it! You're hanging on to every sin, so I have to pay penance in piddling portions for the rest of my life. You're incapable of forgiveness."

"That's not true!" she cried, fighting back tears.

"Then tell me. Tell me what I need to do for absolution so it won't fester like a boil between us."

"It's not my job to give you absolution. You want instant forgiveness for fifteen years of unhappiness. You accuse me of not being able to love. Oh…if you had only given me a chance in the beginning. Talk about stone. On that train ride from South Carolina, when I was pregnant and had just lost everybody who mattered to me, you were as unapproachable as a corpse. I couldn't even engage you in harmless small-talk. You had a pint in your pocket, but I didn't have anything to numb my pain. I needed you desperately and not once did you utter a sympathetic word. Your indifference froze my heart that day, along with any hope I had for the future of our marriage."

"I had totally blanked out that agonizing train ride. I really do regret my callousness. But what makes you think being drunk made our years together easier for me? Do you suppose there was enough whiskey on the entire east coast to keep me from knowing I was a nine-to-five cabinetmaker and always would be? That was somebody else's future; not mine. You and Belle cheated me out of a chance to do something important with my life. The two of you plied me with liquor then lured me into the bedroom. I may have planted the seed, but you-all set me up. Admit it!"

"All right. It's true. We did try to present me in a more appealing light. But why didn't you hold it against her the way you did me? She was slipping doubles to both of us all night. And for the record, getting pregnant was the last thing I intended. I just wanted you to make love to me. I was eighteen years old and over-the-moon in love."

His voice softened a little. "I didn't hold it against Belle because I didn't feel about her the way I did you. My relationship with your sister was strictly sexual – never personal. I assumed you knew that."

"It looked pretty personal to me," she muttered, choking back tears.

"Belle's most engaging quality is her willingness to settle for a good natured romp in the hay. You, on the other hand, are a nest-building blue jay, gathering your tiny twigs, never wandering far from the tree. I've been fighting the monotony of that since my first marriage, and burning myself out in the process. I tried to cool my anger with alcohol, but that only made it more combustible. By the time we got married, I couldn't face the droning days without it. I blamed all our problems on you so I wouldn't have to quit. I believe you're doing the same thing now; denying your anger, holding onto the hurt. Please don't add anymore years to the time we've already wasted on resentments."

"How convenient. We give up anger when you are no longer angry."

"I didn't choose the timing anymore than I understand it. All I know is I don't want to waste another minute of my life on bitterness. And I don't think the children should have to put up with it either."

She began to cry. "Why don't you ever talk about love?"

Daddy was speechless for the first time since my sisters and I began recording their arguments in our hearts. Like a blind man grasping at straws, he blurted out, "It's our first date."

"Damn you!" she cried. "You're a thorough cad. You manipulate with clever words to get what you want."

"I thought you knew," he whispered, more intimately than we'd ever heard him speak to her, "That's a drunk's most endearing quality."

Chapter 14

Mama had been expecting a visit from Aunt Belle for as long as I could remember. Finally, one Saturday morning in the spring of '44, it came to pass. As soon as I laid eyes on her, I understood why she'd left such an indelible imprint on my parents' marriage. She arrived in a taxi, and the first thing my sisters and I saw, our faces pressed eagerly against the front window, was a patent leather high heel, followed by a slender ankle and a long, silk-stockinged leg. Then she stepped onto the sidewalk and pulled her black beaver coat tightly around her shoulders. We inhaled in awe and sighed in one voice, "She looks like a movie star."

Instead of rushing outside to greet her, Mama waited for Belle to pay the driver and climb the front steps before kissing the air next to her cheek, remarking dryly, "Well, if it isn't my long lost sister." We followed Aunt Belle down the hall to the dining room, where she casually tossed her fur coat over the back of a chair and removed a pack of Pall Malls from her handbag.

My sisters and I were used to Mama focusing on us when company came, like flies one watches out of the corner of the eye at a picnic, ever conscious of their nuisance potential. Not so that Saturday. Every iota of my mother's attention was riveted to her raven-haired older sister. For Aunt Belle, the opposite seemed true. She ignored Mama and gushed over us like we were company and she the narrator of our unfolding little drama.

"I declare, Marjorie, you have the pious bearing of a nun. And Betsy, where did you get those striking green eyes? They sure didn't come from our side of the family," she laughed, exposing large white teeth with a tiny space between the front two. "And poor little Silby; don't you worry about those glasses, honey. You'll outgrow them, just like your mama did." Then she pulled Brother Boy closer, cupped his chin in her hand, and examined his features, a wrinkle forming between her sunflower brown eyes. "When are you going to name this poor child? He's getting too old for Brother

Boy."

"We named him Garland. I was waiting for you to squeeze us into your busy schedule before breaking the news."

"You named him after Daddy's favorite brother," Aunt Belle remarked, more an accusation than an observation. "Where's Thurston? The least he could do was take the day off after I spent seventeen hours on a train just to see you all."

"But it took you fifteen years to get here."

"Daddy knew I had a history with Thurston. If I'd come any sooner, he'd have cut off support for my girls. And I did send birthday and Christmas cards. Anyway, now that I'm married to Brice, I can afford to risk Daddy's disapproval."

"I can't believe Brice's infantry pay is going to keep you in cigarettes and fur coats."

"He won't always be a foot soldier. Every penny he doesn't need for toothpaste and shaving cream goes into war bonds, which he sends me for safe keeping." Mama snickered at the idea of Aunt Belle safeguarding a man's money. "He's going to open his own radio repair shop, and I'm planning to get a government job once this damned war is over. That's why I left the girls with Mama and Daddy, so I could apply for a secretarial position at Ft. Meade. I'm sure you don't remember, but I type like the wind."

"I remember, and it sounds like a sensible plan. Still…your first marriage was a financial disaster. What's makes you think this one will be different?"

"Harvey was a gambler and a drunk. Brice is a salt-of-the-earth farm boy from Oklahoma. He's used to hard work, and he doesn't gamble or drink."

"Not with money, maybe. What about you? Are you still drinking?"

"I haven't had anything stronger than iced tea since our second date."

"I'm impressed – skeptical, but impressed."

"You should be. This is the longest I've been sober since the eighth grade. I'm smoking three packs a day, but I haven't touched a drop of hard liquor."

"What do you consider soft liquor?"

"I occasionally have a beer, but I'd get too bloated if I drank enough to make me tipsy."

"Sounds like tempting the fates to me. What does Brice think about you drinking beer?"

"We made a deal. I won't touch anything stronger than beer – unless it's wine - and he'll drink the first one with me so I don't have to feel guilty."

"Good grief, Belle. Do you realize how crazy that sounds?"

A gruff voice interrupted from the doorway. "Hell's bells, she finally found time to visit her poor, displaced relatives." Belle threw herself into Daddy's open arms. Later, when I told Lucille I'd never seen him look that happy, she said it was because he hadn't been home in fifteen years, and Belle was as close as he was going to get to a visit. My grandfather's threat to shoot him if he ever showed his face in South Carolina again kept us firmly planted north of the Mason Dixon line.

Once the grownups sat down to cigarettes and small talk, Daddy confessed he'd been sober for three months. "It was hell, at first. Every nerve in my body either itched or tweaked me with prickly pain…"

"His hands shook so badly, I had to hold his coffee cup to his lips the first three days," Mama added.

Daddy changed the subject. "I'm taking you and Claudia out on the town tonight. Have you ever heard of *the block*?"

"I don't think so," Belle answered, wrinkling the flawless skin on her milky white forehead, brushing her jet black bangs to the side, a nervous gesture she frequently indulged.

"It's a section in downtown Baltimore famous for bars and burlesque, with some of the best jazz this side of New Orleans."

Mama's brows knit together in a thin line of disapproval. "I have no desire whatsoever to watch big bosomed women take their clothes off. Mick likes jazz. He and Lucille can go. I'll stay home with the kids…"

"She's become a martyr since you last saw her," Daddy explained, sarcastically. "It'd be easier to get the Pope to attend a bar mitzvah than to talk Claudia into having a good time."

"That's not true," Mama protested, but they continued to talk around her.

"She's been like that since childhood," Belle added, as if it were untreated rhinitis. "She used to walk around with a book of poetry in one hand and a wad of Kleenex in the other trying to get my mother to stop what she was doing and listen to her emote. I can still hear her," she laughed, "'Loveliest of trees, the cherry now, is hung with bloom along the bow,' sniffle, sniffle."

"Did you really read poetry to Granny?" I asked, with newfound respect born of Aunt Belle's allegations. But we were interrupted by Mick and Lucille returning from their walk to Wyman Park, filling the room with the sweet scent of fresh mown clover.

"Thurston wants to take Belle nightclubbing tonight, and he'd like for you and Mick to go along," Mama said, after introducing them.

"Wouldn't it make more sense for you to go? I'd be glad to mind the kids."

"I have a migraine headache," Mama complained, "so I plan to take an aspirin and turn in early. But I think you two should go, since Mick knows downtown Baltimore, and it will give you a chance to get to know Belle."

Lucille said she was willing to go to a nightclub for drinks but they could count her out if they were going to a trashy burlesque show.

"You've got the wrong idea," Mick said. "Burlesque is rooted in Vaudeville and the Ziegfeld follies – the best song and dance routines ever written. It's where most Hollywood hoofers and comedians got their start. Granted, there's a striptease element that didn't exist in Vaudeville, but it's done tastefully, by the likes of Gypsy Rose Lee and Blaze Starr."

Lucille grudgingly agreed to go as long as nobody took their clothes off.

Mick would later swear to Mama he had every intention of honoring Lucille's request until he turned East on Baltimore Street and Belle began waving her arms and shouting "Stop the car!" He jumped out and found her pointing to an animated sign, at least four stories high, with a neon girl kicking her leg in the air atop the marquee at the Gayety Burlesque Theater. World renowned, it held a thousand people, including fancy box seats for politicians and gangsters who frequented the nightspots on Baltimore Street in the thirties and forties.

"That's where I want to go," Belle cried.

Lucille continued to resist, until Mick told her there was a nightclub in the basement frequented by soldiers and sailors who just wanted a place to drink and meet girls.

When they got downstairs, however, there was a smoky stage where a comedian in baggy pants and a red and green tam o'shanter was delivering raunchy one-liners to a brassy blond as she walked and dipped to a draggy trombone. Half asleep in the corner, a drummer lazily wacked his stick every time she did a bump and grind. Lucille stomped out of the theater, with Mick close behind. By the time they got back to our place, she was still not speaking to him.

The first words out of Mama's mouth were, "You mean you left Thurston alone in a striptease joint with Belle?"

"I'm not his mother," Lucille cried.

"I'm sorry we let you down," Mick added, "but they can always take a taxi home."

"It's not their transportation I'm worried about," Mama sighed. "I'm going to bed. You kids need to do the same thing."

As we started upstairs, Mick grasped Lucille's arm and said, "There's something I want to talk to you about. It's been on my mind for some time, but I wasn't sure how you'd feel about it."

We waited until they reached the third floor then sneaked up the stairs to listen outside her door. Lucille was apparently preoccupied with watching out the window for a taxi to pull up with Daddy and Belle inside. "You're not listening to me," Mick complained, peevishly.

"I'm sorry. What were you saying?"

"I was trying to ask you to marry me."

My sisters and I collapsed in rapture on the stairs. It took a minute for Lucille to process what he'd said. "Did you ask what I think you did?"

"Well, darlin,' if you're not sure, maybe it's too soon to bring it up."

"No. It's just…you caught me off guard. It's not like anything about this evening set the stage for a proposal."

He pulled her to him and gave her a long, lingering kiss. "I really do love you, ya know. And I want more than anything to take care of you and your girls."

When Lucille heard that, she instantly forgave his unromantic timing and accepted.

She held out her hand so he could put the ring on her finger. But Instead of a ring, he pulled a manila envelope out of his breast pocket. "It's a deed," he explained. "There are rooms for Iris and Rose on the third floor, and one down the hall from ours for Andy. And its right around the corner on Maryland Avenue, so you can keep watching Silby and Bro…Garland as long as you want."

"This is all kind of overwhelming," she hedged, unable to hide her disappointment.

"Just say you will; that's all I need tonight. I'll get the ring later, I promise…" Before she could reply, a taxi pulled up and Belle and Daddy staggered out, singing "God Bless America" at the top of their lungs. Stumbling up the front steps and into the vestibule, they continued their slurry concert. My sisters and I raced back to our room only seconds before Lucille and Mick flew by on their way down to silence them. But it was too late. Mama stood like a high priestess on the second floor landing, just outside our bedroom door.

Aunt Belle giggled "whoops" and slithered down the hall to the living room, where she passed out on the sofa before Mama could finish telling her off. But we could hear her arguing with Daddy all night, which was almost as riveting. I eventually fell asleep with my chin on the railing at the foot of the bed, only to learn next morning that Mama had evicted Daddy from the bedroom, and he and Mick spent the night on the front steps drinking whiskey, consoling each other, and occasionally singing "Danny Boy" with an Irish lilt and a few tears of remorse.

Chapter 15

In an effort to get back in Mama's good graces, Daddy and Aunt Belle volunteered to take us to the zoo while she fixed Sunday dinner. Since Mama couldn't rely on Aunt Belle to keep Garland from wandering into the lions' den, Marjorie volunteered to take him to Sunday school. As it turned out, it wasn't Garland Mama needed to worry about.

Betsy and I were excited. We would not only skip Sunday school, we'd get to watch the streetcars turn around in the car-barn, adding a touch of local charm to our inconsequential, middle child existence.

We parked by the Druid Hill Park reservoir, and Betsy and I raced to the elephant house, leaving Daddy and Aunt Belle to feign an interest in the polar bears. We reconnected at the bright blue benches near Eutaw Street to wait for the clanging bell to signal a streetcar entering the car barn. In order to switch to tracks going in the opposite direction it was necessary for the conductor to make a complete circle and start over. Riding to the end of the line became a favorite Sunday afternoon pastime, as passengers poured from the streetcar to help push. When it was hot out, you could smell the oily iron tracks and leather seats, too scorching for little girls in dresses to sit on without a sheet of newspaper under them. We had watched for about an hour when Daddy suggested that he and Aunt Belle take a stroll around the reservoir. Betsy and I had no idea what we were supposed to do, but I could generally count on her to think of something.

"I know where there's a statue with a fountain. I don't think it's far from here," she said, optimistically.

As we ventured deeper into the shady foliage, I noticed that the roads were virtually deserted. "Are you sure this is the way to the statue?"

"Pretty sure," she said.

All at once, a black car pulled up and a man with a frizzy

gray beard leaned across and rolled down the passenger window. He asked if we wanted to go for a ride. It would be at least twenty years before *pedophile* became a household word. In our day, we had to rely on queasy stomachs to warn us of danger. Betsy huge green eyes turned dark hazel and I began to tremble.

Pushing the passenger door open, he said in an oily voice, "I'll give you candy if you go for a ride with me."

We stood frozen, waiting for instructions from on high.

He opened the driver's door, stepped out, and began walking toward us. I screamed *run*, and we took off through the trees toward the reservoir, hearts pounding, lungs on fire.

When we reached the reservoir, we spotted Daddy and Aunt Belle sitting in one of the picnic pavilions holding hands, their faces only inches apart. We both screamed "Daddy!"

"What is it?" he snarled, impatiently.

Betsy and I began babbling at the same time, fully expecting him to chase the bad guy and exact judgment in the name of his offspring. Instead, he told us to go wait in the car. By the time we got there, Betsy's hands were shaking so badly she had trouble opening the door. When it finally gave way, we hurled ourselves inside, crouching on the floor so we would not be seen.

"I can't believe Daddy didn't try to catch that man," I said, breathlessly. "Do you think we should tell Mama on him?"

"I think she deserves to know how careless they were in keeping an eye on us," Betsy said, in her sharpest grownup voice.

I was more interested in telling her about Daddy holding Aunt Belle's hand. It seemed the more compelling crime.

Nobody mentioned the man on the way home, and when we got there, Belle announced that we'd had a fabulous time at the zoo.

Dinner that night seemed ten years long and clearing the table, a life sentence. Finally, I cornered Mama alone.

"Daddy was holding hands with Aunt Belle in the park," I said, the words tumbling out as she washed dishes at the kitchen sink. She stopped and turned around, a dripping colander in her hand. "What do you mean they were holding hands?"

"They went for a walk around the reservoir and a bad man tried to make Betsy and me get in his car. We told Daddy but he didn't try to catch him."

"Did your Daddy and Aunt Belle do anything more than hold hands?" Mama asked.

"No."

"Good," she said, with relief.

"Aren't you mad at him for holding hands with her?"

"I'm sure it didn't mean anything. I want your word you won't mention it again – not to anybody."

"But she's not his wife."

"That may be true, but the smartest thing I can do right now is kill 'em with kindness. Guilt is a far more effective weapon than anger."

I couldn't imagine how kindness could kill anybody, but I did as I was told and didn't even tell Lucille, since she was sure to bring it up to Mama. I spent the next several days puzzling over Mama's form of revenge before concluding it would never work for me.

Betsy, Daddy and Silby

Chapter 16

It seemed to me, growing up, that what people did not say had more impact than what they did say. At least that's how it felt at our house for the next two weeks, with Mama casting threatening scowls and Belle drinking too much and laughing too loud. Daddy spent most of his time sipping whiskey in the cellar while Mick and Lucille pretended nothing at all had changed between them. My sisters and I could barely breathe for all the things not being talked about.

On the positive side, I could sit next to my parents' bedroom door after I was supposed to be asleep and if I listened long enough, overhear a secret. That's how I found out Mick and Lucille's engagement had only lasted one night. The news broke my heart, for I was counting on their marriage to provide a gateway of escape. Once Mama threw Daddy out and moved in with my grandparents - as she constantly threatened to do - Lucille could marry Mick and I would move in with them. It was the ideal solution to having parents and siblings. Unfortunately, relief does not always arrive in the form one expects.

More often than not, when there is a standoff in family communication, it takes the introduction of new blood – someone stumbling blindly in, completely unversed in the rules of the game - to initiate a shift in roles and alter group dynamics. Such a novice player was our new uncle, perfect for the position of game-changer by virtue of his utter lack of guile.

Uncle Brice showed up without warning after receiving a three week leave for a ruptured appendix en route to Germany. The minute he stepped through the front door, everybody else grew smaller in stature. He was six feet four, with the shoulders of a linebacker, and the large round face of a teddy bear. His eyes were translucent blue, soft and sympathetic; his mouth, wide and perpetually smiling; his hands, huge and protective; his laugh, booming and beautiful. I adored him on sight and never found a reason to change my mind, not even after Aunt Belle told him she'd blown their savings bond nest-egg on new clothes and jewelry.

Uncle Brice was so hopelessly in love, he treated the bad news as an opportunity to show how understanding he could be. Belle, in turn, called him "Sugar-bear" and cooed to him the way one might a new puppy. Brice had grown up an orphan, taken in by an elderly grandfather who had little to say. Each time Belle spoke to him, his facial features softened like a well-seasoned baseball mitt. Betsy and I voted him - next to Daddy and Mick - the safest lap to sit on in the neighborhood.

The payoff Uncle Brice received for his open-faced goodwill was permission to tell the truth without offending anybody...except Daddy, who could not believe there was a man alive who possessed no self-interest agenda.

The first morning after his arrival, we were sitting at the breakfast table when Uncle Brice asked if Mick and Lucille had set a wedding date. The grownups exchanged *how did he know* glances before Lucille stammered, "It's not really definite..."

"Oh. I thought Claudia said you bought a house for the children."

"Well, I did," Mick stammered, his fair Irish cheeks growing redder by the minute. "But I did it before checking with her..."

"I don't mind that," Lucille said, taking his hand in hers. "I'm just romantic enough to have wanted a ring to go with the proposal. God, that sounds so shallow..."

"No it doesn't," cried Mick. "I should have bought the ring before asking."

"Why don't you go get one now?" Uncle Brice suggested.

"I guess we could," Lucille said softly, the ridges lining her cheeks melting into a smile.

"I don't think it's wise to rush into marriage without thinking it over at least six months," Mama said, with authority.

"I think they should do it without thinking at all," Hazel countered, from her coffee drinking stance near the buffet, a broad grin on her freckled face.

"Let's ask the most sensible person in the room," Lucille said. "What do you think we should do, Marjorie?"

"I think you should buy the ring and get married today," she affirmed, with an uneasy glance in my mother's direction.

"The stores are open until five," Mick said, holding out his hand.

Lucille jumped up and kissed him full on the lips. "If it doesn't work out, we can always blame Marjorie."

I joined in cheering them all the way to the front door but couldn't help wondering what would happen to my parents without the calming effect of Lucille and Mick. Regrettably, it would not take long to find out.

**

Perhaps it was the mellowness of Brice's presence that created a temporary air of optimism, or it might have been the aroma of altar flowers when Lucille and Mick pledged themselves to each other's happiness and wellbeing for the rest of their lives. Whatever it was, nobody seemed surprised when my half brother Danny showed up on a quiet Sunday afternoon, looking forward to seeing his family and a pretty girl named Hazel he'd kissed goodbye in Pennsylvania Station only months before. He had kept his word and looked her husband Stanley up in San Diego, only to find she'd married a hard-drinking man with bad skin and a reputation as a love-em and leave-em cad, even among his shipmates. At that point, Danny must have realized seeing Hazel again was foolhardy, but desire slants reason when you are twenty-one and on your way to war.

"What the hell are you doing here?" Daddy cried, hugging the wind out of him.

"You can thank Great Britain," Danny grinned. "The British Royal Air Force recruited ten thousand Africans from Nigeria and declared war on Germany. Not only that, the Gold Coast King, Asantehene was so impressed with their bravery, he helped construct airfields and supply routes for the Allied forces. We were given unexpected leave while our ship is armed with guns powerful enough to sink enemy vessels approaching the African coast."

"You realize you'll be going head to head with Hitler's shrewdest general, the Desert Fox himself, Ervin Rommel?"

"Don't worry, Dad. Our boys in the air will give us all the

cover we need."

Mama had barely kissed Danny hello before reminding him how perfect he and Hazel were for each other, eliciting a mind-your-own business growl from Daddy. Lucille also did her best to keep Mama from interfering. "That marriage doesn't stand a ghost of a chance to begin with, and it's just plain wrong to try and hasten its demise." The issue reached a climax the following night, when the air was sweet and the stars twinkling.

Mama and Lucille had pestered Daddy and Mick into taking them to see Mrs. Miniver, a romantic drama about an English family coping with life in war-torn England. It starred Greer Garson and Walter Pidgeon, two of Mama's favorites. Hazel, who volunteered to keep an eye on us, had just tucked Garland into bed and was on her way downstairs when Danny appeared on his way up.

"Oh!" she cried. "I assumed you had gone to the movie with the others."

"I got word this afternoon that I have to return to my ship tomorrow, so I decided to spend my last night with the kids. I had no idea you'd be here, but now that you are, there is something we need to talk about. Come sit on the front steps for a few minutes."

Hazel glanced at Marjorie as though expecting rescue. When it didn't come, she said, "I'll be right back," and followed Danny out the door.

We turned off the living room lamp, eased open the floor to ceiling window, and jammed ourselves between the sill and the side of Daddy's overstuffed chair, where we could hear every word they said.

"First, I want to apologize for harassing you when we first met, even after you told me you were married. I was wrong to put you in that position. After I agreed to get in touch with your husband Stanley in San Diego, I told myself I would respect your commitment and quit trying to put the make on you. And I meant it at the time. Then I saw him face to face and thought he was a little rough around the edges for a wholesome Midwestern girl. But I was still willing to do the right thing...until Claudia wrote me about his other two wives. It was clear, then, that he did not deserve you. So...I'm here to say I love you and if I make it back from Africa in one piece, I plan to pursue the hell out of you."

Hazel had not uttered a word. My sisters and I held our breath.

"First of all, I'm shocked that you think delivering heartbreaking news about my husband's possible faithlessness is doing me a favor. Did you think not deserving it would make it less painful? And who are you to judge him after that performance you put on at the band concert last summer. Not only did you kiss me – a married woman – but you chased me all over the park trying to convince me that what you did was okay. I would have said all this then, but you were scheduled to ship out, and you seemed so lonely…I wanted to give you a happy memory to take with you. In addition, I never really expected to see you again."

"Well, if things turn out in Africa the way they very well might, you'll get your wish."

"I didn't say I never *wanted* to see you again, I said I didn't expect to. It would break my heart if anything happened to you. But that doesn't diminish my obligation to my husband."

Suddenly, everything grew quiet. I couldn't resist poking my head out the window. Danny's body was pressed against Hazel's, her yellow hair flowing across his right arm, lips consuming each other in equally moist measure, his left hand popping the buttons on her blouse one at a time… All at once, she pushed him off and ran up the street to her house. The last thing we heard was Hazel slamming the vestibule door and Danny forcing it open again. My sisters and I went to sleep that night drenched in sweet fantasies about their passionate night together.   .

.

Chapter 17

We were shocked when Lucille told us Lila and Andy were writing each other almost every day. I thought it was wonderful, but Lucille was not so sure.

"What if he gets his hopes up and Garret suddenly emerges from the past?"

"It's been close to five months since he left the hospital and nobody's heard a word," Mama reminded her. "He's probably gone to live with his parents – wherever that is. Lila said he always seemed reluctant to talk about them. She doesn't even have a contact address."

"She should forget Garret and keep writing Andy," said Brynn, with conviction. "Love by letter is much more romantic. The trouble with having a male underfoot is that every day's the same. I miss the stomach plunging doubts of dating: Is he or isn't he going to call?"

"Maybe you can talk Hugh into transferring to a combat zone in Germany," Lila hissed, returning from a tea-leaf reading guaranteed to shed light on Garret's whereabouts. "Then you'd *really* have something to wonder about."

"I don't think uncertainty is all it's cracked up to be," said Hazel, trying to lighten the tension between her friends. "I'm so impatient for a letter from Stanley I leap at the postman before he can get the mail in the box. He's the only person on the planet who's ever been afraid of me," she giggled.

"Better still," Lila continued, "why don't you join the WAVES and do something for your country. We could all use a break from your whining."

"For your information, I was already toying with the idea of signing up. I won't even have to cut my hair," she grinned, swishing her shiny brown bob from side to side.

"You can't be serious," Mama said.

"Why can't she?" Lucille asked. "It might be the perfect

solution to her chronic boredom."

"Have you mentioned this to Hugh?"

"No, and don't you mention it either, Claudia. I've always wanted to take a cruise to England, or a flight to Paris like Lucky Lindy. It's all that marching that worries me. I'm not sure I'm ready to give up high heels and satin slippers. The Navy blue uniforms aren't so bad, and the hat can be downright flattering when centered properly. It's almost tempting. Still, what would Hugh do without me?"

"Enjoy himself," Lila quipped.

"I don't think WAVES are assigned to ships unless they are also nurses, and then, only on hospital ships. And I'm positive they don't fly planes," Lucille pointed out.

"Well, what *do* they do?" Bryn cried, impatiently

"I think they mostly free up men for combat by doing secretarial work for various departments, although I recently read in Life magazine that they are branching out into communications. In fact, there are WAVES already working as tower operators at the Naval Air Station in Atlanta, Georgia."

"I could do that, but who wants to be stuck in an air tower all day?"

"Do you know how to type, take dictation, or decode messages in a foreign language?" Lila asked, already knowing the answer.

"I took French in high school and I have a good mind for detail. Hazel, you're a stenographer. How long would it take to learn to type?"

"Not long at all. But you realize the pay would be a pittance compared to the commission you make selling hats at the May Company."

"I don't care about the salary. I just want to serve my country."

"Oh, Lord," Lila groaned, rolling her eyes.

"I'll pay you fifty cents an hour to teach me to type, Hazel."

"I don't have a typewriter."

"That's okay. I'll get Daddy to bring one home from the office."

"I've got it," cried Lila, with malevolent eagerness. "You

could join the WACS; they're to the Army what WAVES are to the Navy. But they get to travel all over the world, from Paris to India. And you'd love the uniforms. They have several different styles, depending on the duty of the day."

"Are you serious? They actually get to wear a variety of dress designs? All I've seen are those mud-colored, two-piece, wooly ones."

"Not only that," said Lila, warming to her subject, "what they do isn't limited to ships and nursing. They can choose from a wide range of jobs, including espionage. I wouldn't be surprised if you ended up in Paris, typing for the underground."

"Now, Lila," Lucille cautioned, "you don't want to exaggerate the glamour."

"I like the sound of WACS more than I do WAVES. And the brown uniforms won't be so bad if you only wear them for marching. You probably change into something more sophisticated when you travel. And I'm good at keeping secrets. I could become a world renowned spy, like Mata Hari. Does anybody know how to get to the recruiting office?"

"I'll take you myself," Lila said. "We can stop at Maria's for spaghetti and make a day of it. In fact, why don't we all go?"

"I think you should talk to Hugh before committing to something you might later regret," Mama cautioned.

"Hugh doesn't care what I do as long as it makes me happy."

"Marjorie, your Daddy's in the cellar. Tell him we're going to talk to the recruiter about Brynn joining the WACS. Silby and Garland, play where Betsy can keep an eye on you. Do you think I should change into something dressier?" Mama asked, untying her apron, tossing it over the back of a chair.

"We don't have time. I want to sign up before I change my mind."

Lucille called a cab, and all four headed to the recruiting office by way of Little Italy. It was the last time my sisters and I would see Brynn before she boarded a flight to Fort Des Moines, Iowa for training as a teletype operator in the Women's Army Auxiliary Corps, with a rank equivalent to a private in the regular Army, but with significantly less income to spend on hats and high heeled shoes.

As luck would have it, Brynn began her career in espionage just in time to participate in one of the most significant wartime secrets every kept: the invasion of Normandy. To hear her tell it, victory by the Allied forces came about through a comedy of errors. The invasion needed to take place during a full moon if our troops were to recognize critical landmarks – thus, the carefully chosen date of June 6, 1944. However, on June 4th, a massive storm blew in blotting out the moon and causing waves too violent for small amphibious crafts to be launched from off- shore battleships.

Brynn said there was a desperate, last minute meeting between General Eisenhower, Britain's General Montgomery, and a meteorologist named J. M. Stagg. Stagg convinced them a break in the storm would provide a brief window of opportunity for a successful landing and Eisenhower decided to believe him. Underestimating the determination of British and American troops and overestimating poor weather conditions, German Field Marshal Erwin Rommel took the week off to celebrate his wife's birthday and allowed his troops to relax their guard, giving us a distinct advantage.

By July 24th, allied troops had successfully taken Normandy and Brittany, causing the Germans to retreat, and by August 24th, Paris would be liberated. Still, the War would drone on for another eight months before victory in Europe could be officially declared. In the meantime, little would change for those at home keeping track of the action by radio and newsreels at the movies.

Chapter 18

Hugh Pillstick grew bored waiting for Brynn to tire of her career as a decoder and volunteered for combat duty on the European front. Less than a month later, he found himself wading into the thick of one of the bloodiest campaigns in World War II, nicknamed The Battle of the Bulge. At about the same time, Stanley Polanski had another run of firearms good fortune. He was wounded in the second toe of his left foot - barely enough to provide a permanent limp, but more than adequate for entertaining his passengers when he returned to his career as a cab driver.

Germany was rapidly losing ground on the Western front, thanks to the combined forces of England and America following the Normandy invasion. In the despair of retreat, Hitler became convinced that splitting American and British troops would force them to negotiate separate peace treaties with Germany, freeing the Axis powers to focus on the Russians bearing down on them from the East. Believing its forest-like terrain to be of little value to the Germans, Eisenhower had begun using the Ardennes in Belgium for troop training and got caught with his defenses down.

Hitler ordered an attack on Antwerp, cutting off access to the seaport, severely limiting supplies to American and British soldiers.

Ground fighting began on December 16, 1944, with an attack by Germany's 5th Panzer Division. Heavy snowfall prevented the use of Allied aircraft, and we were forced to use trucks to maneuver in the battle for Bastogne. Once Eisenhower realized how severely outnumbered American forces were, he sent for General George Patton, who managed to move the 3rd infantry to Bastogne and contain the attack.

Hugh Pillstick was among the 20,000 Allied soldiers to lose their lives at the Battle of the Bulge, while another 43,000 were wounded and 20,000 more missing in action or taken prisoner. But the German offensive in the West was routed and by May, 1945, Hitler would be dead from his own tyrannical hand.

Just before the new year, Lila received a copy of an incomplete letter written two months before by Hugh and forwarded by a medic who found it in his pocket after he died. It read:

Dear Lila:

You once told me the cost to our boys at the Battle for the island of Betio was not worth the advantage of taking back the Philippines. I am deeply ashamed of my clinical analysis of the value of human life when you came to my office seeking information about Garret. Now, I find myself in the thick of battle, just as he was. All around me the world is crashing and exploding, with flying limbs and the moans of dying men.

You were absolutely right. There is no piece of land worth this terrible price. Turns out, though, this War is not really about territory, at least not for those of us on the defending end. It's about the right of an individual to choose the God he will worship and the truth he will follow in pursuit of his values and dreams – and the responsibility he is willing to assume by supporting laws that protect it from collapse at the hands of tyrants, profiteers, and foolhardy self interest seekers who would undermine its structure for their own ends.

We have just uncovered evidence of horrific gas chambers with millions of bones and open graves at a prison called Auschwitz. You've probably been hearing about it on the radio. Nothing you imagine could do justice to its depravity. And yet, I feel guilty every time I fire my rifle. War is an awful thing, but given the choice of saving people who cannot defend themselves, I guess one reluctantly chooses the lesser sin, gut-wrenching as it is for the guys who live it on the frontlines. Whatever you imagine combat to be, I can assure you it is far worse.

I haven't slept in three days, and we're expecting a German air attack at dawn. I'll try to finish this later. Just felt I owed you a better explanation than the one I gave before joining the fray myself, not that anything I say could make war less dreadful. What is it they say? 'War and taxes will be with us always.' Guess that's true. But so, thank goodness, will courage and sacrifice.
I'll finish this tomorrow."

Chapter 19

Daddy had sworn off liquor for a second time when he learned of Danny's death. Notification came in the form of a business letter from the War Department stating that Gunner's Mate, Third Class, Daniel Louis Dunn's death had been confirmed. At the request of my father or Danny's biological mother his remains would be transported from St. Vincent Island to the United States. They would ultimately send a Purple Heart and a Combat Service medal, but it seemed a meager consolation at the time. In what continues to be an unsolved family mystery, neither Daddy nor his ex-wife Ruby asked to have him brought home. The only evidence that he passed through this earthly portal is a small iron plaque on the ground between my grandmother's and my father's graves in South Carolina...and a handful of cherished memories.

When Mama read us the letter, we sobbed and denied and railed against the truth. Finally, after a period of mourning, we accepted that he would never come home again. The anger stage of our grief would come a few weeks later, when we learned how slim the margin between rescue and death had been.

Daddy's response to the loss of Danny was to sit in his living room chair guzzling whiskey and asking how God could have done this to him. He remained that way for several days before Mick got fed up and told him how ashamed Danny would be of his behavior. "Did you think you were immune to loss? Hell, man, there's a war going on."

"You don't get it. This time I really tried to do better. I quit drinking, got a job, did everything right - and this is how God repays me?"

"Maybe God wants you to see something you're still avoiding. True images never expose themselves without time in a dark room. Think back, Thurston. If you're honest, you'll admit that every important insight came after a loss or disappointment. That's why God created grief. I'll agree it's easier for Him, since He can see the finished product and all we feel is the present misery. But it's the way of everything in life to benefit from hardship, so long as we don't give up on ourselves or the others involved."

"You're full of crap," Daddy grumbled, continuing to drink until he passed out on the daybed in the dining room.

We were getting used to treating him like part of the furniture when he unexpectedly stood up, staggered to the dining room table, and announced that he was never going to drink again. Mama said she'd heard that before, and the rest of us kept on eating. Three days later, he was having full blown delirium tremens - shaking from head to toe, dripping with sweat, clawing at his arms with his fingernails. By the middle of that night, he was screaming at Mick to get the soldiers off his chest before they killed him. Mick calmly proceeded to shoot them one at a time with his forefinger, which brought Daddy surprising relief.

By the fifth day, he was able to sit up and sip from the coffee cup Mama held to his lips, and we began to hope he might really mean it this time.

The sick stage of Daddy's recovery was followed by a grouchy phase. Everything we did seemed to drive him crazy. We learned not to talk when he was in the room and to walk softly and not rattle dishes. The bellowing part of his sobriety lasted longest, and I was beginning to wonder whether it was worth it when he began experiencing brief periods of amiability.

Mama was completing her Sunday ritual, leafing through a week's worth of Hazel and Lila's old magazines before pin-curling her hair, having let it grow to a more fashionable shoulder length. Halfway through *World Events*, she spotted an article written by a sailor who survived the sinking of a ship named the SS Flashpoint. Her heart stood still, and her hands began to shake.

"On November 4, 1944 at 4:00 pm off the coast of Africa, the SS Flashpoint was hit by two torpedoes from a German submarine and within minutes sank to the bottom of the ocean. There was no time to launch lifeboats, but a wooden raft floated free, and eight sailors managed to hoist themselves on board. The sole survivor of those clinging to life was Elwood Gunther, a native of Pittsburg, Pennsylvania. Mr. Gunther wrote this about his experience:

"'Eight of us were adrift on a wooden raft without food or

water for twenty-three days. During that time, six mates died of thirst and infected blisters from saltwater searing their sunburned skin. Me and a young gunner named Danny Dunn lowered their bodies into the water, one at a time, and prayed for their hapless souls.

On the twenty-third day, Seaman Dunn could not stand it any longer. Sometime during the night, he drank saltwater and died. I could not bear to die alone, so I kept him on the raft until we were rescued - four hours later - by natives from a nearby Island. They gave me food and water and buried Danny's body next to a small Catholic mission.'"

"Thurston!" Mama cried. "Get in here. You've got to see this."

Daddy picked up the magazine and read the article through to the end. "Call him," he said, his voice flat with grief.

We gathered around the dining room table, hopeful spectators. Perhaps Mr. Gunther would tell us something better than we knew he could. He confirmed everything he'd written but added two things we may never have known. He said Danny was a great joke teller who kept the spirits of the wounded alive for weeks, when their final hopes were fading with every briny wave that ate at their flesh. When only the two of them were left, he said Danny talked endlessly about his family and how much he loved us. He also talked about a pretty blonde named Hazel he'd fallen head over heels for. Mr. Gunther knew all about Danny's mother Ruby and about my mother and father, and all of Danny's brothers and sisters. He said Danny made no distinction between those of us who were full and those who were half siblings, saying only that he was the oldest of seven. Until the last sane instant of his life, Danny never gave up believing he would see us again.

Knowing about his final days should have helped, but it only made us sadder – sadder and angrier. Why couldn't Danny have hung on another four hours? Why didn't Mr. Gunther keep a closer watch? Why didn't the natives spot their raft four hours earlier? And what could God have possibly been doing that was more important.

We sat silently waiting for our hearts to mend, afraid that speaking would shatter them permanently. Then, one by one, we drifted to our safe zones: Daddy to the cellar to hammer nails, Mama to the kitchen to bake bread, Marjorie and Betsy to the bedroom to read books and polish glass bluebirds, and me, to Lucille's house to cry.

Daddy

Chapter 20

Two weeks after Stanley's discharge, Hazel announced to the surprise of all of us, that she was pregnant. "I don't know why they call it morning sickness," she groaned. "The only time it stops is after I wolf down the banana split Stanley brings me when he finishes his evening shift."

"Being pregnant isn't all it's cracked up to be," Mama sympathized. "You would not believe what I went through. Marjorie wouldn't be here today if I hadn't kicked the nurse who was trying to keep her head from coming out. In those days, nurses lost their caps for a month if the baby came before the doctor got to the delivery room. It was a sign of shame, so they did whatever they could to slow down the delivery until he got there. But I have to give you the morning sickness, Hazel. Mine stopped after a couple of weeks."

"Do you have any Saltines," Hazel asked, her cheeks growing paler with every mouthful of crumb-cake the others shamelessly devoured.

"I'll get you some," said Lucille, who had baked the offending snack. "By the way, has anybody heard from Brynn?"

"Damndest thing!" Lila said. "She's written twice, telling me how much she loves her decoding job. Who would have figured Brynn for spending endless hours sifting through the tedious details of the occupation of Paris? It's like reading Funk and Wagnall's Encyclopedia as a romance novel. I guess it's anticipating what lies behind the words that makes them interesting. But why write to me? We weren't that close."

"She's trying to win back the respect she lost when she was harping on poor Hugh. The rest of us were more polite – or cowardly in our responses," Lucille concluded.

"Was I really that hard on her?"

"Yes!" Hazel and Lucille answered in unison.

"Well, she sort of had it coming. Instead of being grateful

for Hugh safely ensconced behind a desk, she complained about everything he did. How could I help resenting her when I'd have given anything to have Garret around to annoy…"

"Who could that be?" Mama interrupted, craning her neck at the sound of footsteps coming down the hall.

Without looking up, Lila recognized the lean, lopey gait of the boy from Louisiana, and her pulse quickened despite her measured breathing.

"Hey, Miz Dunn…afternoon ladies," he said to Hazel and Lila, his tone swiftly changing to frustration as he blurted out, "Mama! I can't believe you did that without talking to me first. What were you thinking?"

"I knew you'd never do it, so I decided to do it for you."

"But the choice belonged to me," Andy argued.

"It became mine when you couldn't make it."

"But I did make it. I decided not to…"

"Will one of you please fill us in?" Mama blurted out.

"I wrote to the Defense Department and asked that Andy be discharged early under the 'last living heir to carry on the family name' clause. I can't bear the thought of losing my only son to war."

"I told my commanding officer I didn't want to be discharged and followed that up with an official letter. But instead of granting my request, they sent me home on liberal leave until they decide what to do with me."

Mama sliced a piece of cake and handed it to him. "Eat this. It'll make you feel better."

"No thanks," he muttered.

"How about a Saltine," Hazel offered, sliding them toward him. "They make me feel better." Everybody laughed and breathed a sigh of relief.

I was still reeling from the idea that Lucille had made a mistake when I heard Lila ask, "When did you get back?"

"This morning; I came straight here from the train station. It's really good to see you," he smiled, soothing himself in the blue of her eyes. The adrenaline from his irritation seemed to bolster his courage and he blurted out, "How about having lunch with me?"

"It's only a little after eleven," Lila answered, caught off guard.

"Wolf's drugstore starts serving grilled cheese sandwiches at 11:30. If we leave now, we'll get there just in time."

"Go on, Lila," Hazel encouraged. "It'll do you both good."

"Any of you kids want to go along?" Lila asked, and to Andy's obvious disappointment, I blurted out, "I do."

My presence, along with the public exposure of lunch on a fountain stool, helped Lila feel less like she was betraying Garret. We'd eaten about half our grilled cheese sandwiches when Andy grinned and said, "This will give the ladies something to talk about – not that they ever run out of gossip."

"Silly, isn't it," Lila said. "It's not like we're on a date or anything."

"Would it be so bad if we were?"

"Of course not. Only…it won't be fair if I'm involved with somebody else when Garret gets home."

"What makes you think he's coming back?"

"It's not so much that, as…I simply can't imagine him *not* coming back."

"What would it take to convince you?"

"More time, I guess."

"That's the one thing I have plenty of. If I promise to keep it strictly platonic, will you go to the movies with me tonight?"

Lila took her time before answering, "No, but I'll go roller skating with you this afternoon if Silby comes along." She didn't need to ask me twice. Roller skating was my favorite pastime, and the thought of skating indoors to music made my heart dance all the way to North Avenue, where the rink was located.

They were exquisite to watch, Andy with his arm around Lila's waist, her hand in his, as they swooshed and swayed to the romantic notes of Benny Goodman on a 78 rpm, her flaming hair caressing his cheek, two moving as one to the hum of wooden wheels on polished pine floors. I could have watched them all day, but when the record changed to "Far Away Places," Lila suddenly stopped skating. I thought her skate was broken – until I realized there were tears in her eyes. She wiped them away with the back of her hand and hastened to the skate return counter. Andy kept asking her what was wrong, but she was past talking about it. I followed them home, a few feet behind. at a discreet distance.

As we neared the house, he tried to hold her hand, but she hurried inside without a word. Instead of following, he sat down on the front steps and put his head in his hands. I sat next to him and tried to be comforting. "She likes you a lot," I said.

"What makes you think so?"

"Her cheeks get red when she hears you coming down the hall, and she's always asking Lucille questions about you, like what time of the day you were born."

"That's more about astrology than me," he replied, not feeling much better.

"But she asks other things, like what's your favorite food," I exaggerated. She didn't so much ask about him as she focused intently whenever Lucille brought him up, which I figured was close enough.

He looked minimally relieved and said, "Thanks, half-pint. Guess I'll amble up to Mick's and see if he can talk Mama out of destroying my military career. Funny thing; the woman I want most wants nothing to do with me. And the woman I wish would let me make my own decisions is too involved. Don't think I'm one of those lucky in love guys you see on the moving picture screen."

Chapter 21

Bad news via the post office was as predictable as mood swings at our house, and the letter from Aunt Belle was no exception. My grandfather had financed a rambling white frame house in Buford, South Carolina for his favored daughter, and she and Uncle Brice invited my mother to bring the kids and stay as long as she wanted.

"What about Daddy?" I asked, feeling the bottom drop out of my stomach.

"He chose to drink again. He has to live with the consequences."

"It's for the best, darlin'," Lucille immediately added.

I knew she was right but still could not bear the thought of leaving Daddy behind. I took comfort in knowing Mama had threatened before without following through and put it out of my mind – until Lucille asked if I wanted to go with her to pack her suitcase.

"Are you going with us?" I asked.

"No, honey. I'm just moving back in until things are settled."

I followed Lucille to her house trying to figure out exactly what *settled* meant.

Mick was not at all pleased with her decision. "I can't believe you'd seriously entertain such a misbegotten notion."

"But this time she means it. She's finally had enough. Once she tells Thurston, all hell's gonna break loose, and I want to be there to keep things under control."

"You have no business being around a raging drunk with a gun in his bedroom - even if he is my best friend. If you're moving back, I'm going with you."

"You'll just make him mad. I can calm him down."

"That would only postpone the inevitable. As long as you're there to soften things, it'll be easier for him to convince Claudia to stay. The sooner he's confronted with the consequences of his drinking, the sooner he'll recognize the need to stop."

"But the children…"

"The children live in constant dread of the next blowup. Dragging that out can't be good for them."

"But I can reason with him…"

"Alcoholism is not an intellectual choice. It's a knee jerk reaction to a physical craving. You can't talk him out of it. His pain has to become more compelling than the physical need for relief before he can even hope to give it up. Trust me, I know firsthand."

"Well, if it has to get worse before it gets better, I want to be there to comfort the children."

"Honey, I know you mean well, but you've become part of the problem. Every time you make his drinking more tolerable to those around him, you keep him drinking that much longer. If you're not there, it won't be as easy to deny the damage he's causing."

"But…if he hurts Claudia and I could have prevented it, I would never forgive myself."

"That's exactly what he's counting on. As long as you and Claudia pacify him to keep the peace, he'll never stop. I don't know how to make it any clearer," he sighed, heavily.

Like weary battleships passing in the night, the two people I needed most pulled away from each other, she to pack her suitcase and he, to pour himself a drink.

By the time Lucille and I got back to my house, Daddy had found out about Aunt Belle's offer and his paranoia was in full swing. "Conspiring against a man in his own home, that's a new low for you and that conniving sister of yours. Well, you overplayed your hand this time. Those kids will never go with a cold-hearted bitch like you. Marjorie!" he bellowed. "Get in here and bring your sisters and Garland with you."

We inched into the dining room from the bottom of the hall stairs, where we'd been eavesdropping on the disintegration of our family. Daddy made us sit down at the table, while Mama and Lucille looked on, holding their breath, praying we wouldn't let them down.

"Your Mama is deserting me to go back to South Carolina.

You have to choose which of us you want to stay with.   Marjorie – which of us do you choose?"

An ashen-faced Marjorie answered, "Mama." Reeling from shock, Daddy staggered several steps backward.

Drawing courage from Marjorie's response, Mama left Lucille's side and moved closer to the table. "Betsy," she said, sensing an unexpected victory.

"Mama," she whispered, more timidly than Marjorie had.

"Garland," she continued.

"Mama," he answered, following his sisters' lead.

Daddy lunged forward and put his powerful hands on the table, palms down, a few inches from where I sat trembling and sick inside, appalled at my own ambivalence. Of the two, I actually preferred his company. Try as I might, I was never able to relate to the compulsive orderliness of Mama's symmetrical mind the way Marjorie and Betsy could. My father was more transcendental in his thinking. When I complained about getting lost on my way home from the zoo, Daddy stared dreamily out the window and said, "Always remember, the ocean is to the East." At that time I'd never seen the ocean and didn't know north from south, much less east from west. And yet – his answer sounded so profound, so filled with a truth beyond mortal understanding, I managed to find my way home from the park from that day on. Still…I hated him when he drank and bullied everybody in the house – most of all when he hit Mama.

I took a deep breath, convinced my answer was going to shake the foundations of the known universe. "Somebody has to take care of Daddy. I'll guess I'll stay."

"I told you!" Daddy brayed, as though my swing vote meant he'd won.

Lucille shook her finger in his face, forcing him to back away, and shouted, "Shame on you for putting these children in that position." She continued to back him down the hall and out the door, where he spent a full minute gaping at her with his mouth open. Then he stomped up 24th Street and disappeared for several hours - a period of shame for me but pride for my siblings who'd shown great courage.

When he finally returned, we were picking at the dinner

Mama insisted we eat. He sank into his chair at the head of the table, his hands shaking, and announced that he was never going to touch another drop. Mama said she'd heard that before and proceeded as though nothing was going to change. But she was wrong. My father died at the age of sixty-three from smoking induced lung cancer. But he'd managed, without the aid of Alcoholics Anonymous or therapy, to remain sober for eleven years.

Not long before his death, we were sitting on the front steps and I asked him, for old time's sake, what made the sky blue. He answered with the whimsical assurance of Peter Pan, "When man sees as far as the eye can see, he turns everything to blue."

Chapter 22

Mama and I were filling our shopping basket in Bernie's store when a distinguished looking gentleman wearing a blue suit, silk tie, and very shiny shoes stepped up to the cash register. After exchanging a few muffled words, he handed Bernie what was clearly a check and walked out the door. As we approached the cash register, Bernie quickly slipped the check into the drawer and put on his friendly face.

"Who was that?" Mama asked.

Torn briefly between discretion and camaraderie, Bernie chose the latter. "It's Mrs. Gardner's attorney. He drops by every three months to pay me for her groceries and ask how she's doing."

"I knew you'd been delivering her groceries but I assumed she paid you directly. I would never have dreamed she could afford an attorney."

"Oh, she's quite well off," Bernie said. "Her husband, God rest his soul, owned a lucrative saddle business which he was shrewd enough to sell about the time Ford was rolling his first car off the assembly line. When he realized he was dying of heart failure, he invested every dime in conservative bonds and hired Mr. Brinkstone – the man you just saw – to manage his estate. They had one son who was killed when his plane was shot down over Iwo Jima. I feel kind of sorry for her. She appears to be terrified of people and only cracks the door far enough for me to slide her groceries inside. I've had this store ten years and in all that time, I've never seen her leave the house."

I could hear the wheels beginning to turn in Mama's head, and I knew before the week was over she'd be on a first name basis with our reclusive neighbor. The following Sunday, before we sat down to dinner, Mama fixed a huge plate of roast beef, mashed potatoes, green beans and biscuits which she covered in several layers of waxed paper and sent Marjorie three doors up to deliver to Mrs. Gardner. She soon returned saying nobody answered the door.

Mama sent her back with instructions to call out, "Mama sent you a nice hot lunch. Keep repeating that until she opens the door. If it's been as long as I suspect it has, she won't be able to resist a home cooked meal." As usual, Mama was right.

My sisters and I had been taking turns carrying Sunday dinner up the street for several months, going back two hours later to pick up the empty plate, when Mrs. Gardner astonished me by asking if I'd like to come in. I was afraid at first because of the rumors the neighborhood kids spread about her being everything from a spell-casting witch to the ex-wife of Frankenstein. Well trained in the courteous thing to do, I slithered through the narrow opening between the door and the hallway and was astonished to discover she had light fixtures. Even on the darkest night, we'd never seen a sliver of light at her windows. Now I knew why. She'd taped the edges of the shades to the window frame to keep light from leaking out and sunshine from seeping in.

The furniture was quite old but well dusted and obviously expensive in its day. There were photo albums scattered on the sofa and the dining room table, and the buffet told the story of a boy's life in pictures, from infancy to the air force.

"Is that your son?" I asked, and her eyes instantly filled with tears.

"That's my Charlie," she said, wiping her eyes. "Would you like a cup of hot chocolate?"

When she returned with the cocoa, I was studying his baby picture. "He was born on Christmas day, 1920," she said, "and I knew right away he would do something extraordinary with his life." Then she walked me through his framed accomplishments, beginning with his first carriage ride and continuing to his certificate for winning the fourth grade spelling bee. Finally, she told me a story which I'd have thought made up if it hadn't been spun with such sincerity and motherly love.

"Charlie had dreamed all his life of pitching for the New York Yankees. He and his dad practiced every chance they got in the alley next to Bernie's store. Finally, when he was convinced he was good enough, his father took him to New York to try out for the Yankees. Impressed with Charlie's fast ball, they agreed to send him to Florida to work out with the team for six weeks. He performed so well they offered him a starting contract. It was the happiest day of his life," Mrs. Gardner said. "Shortly after his return, my husband died of a heart attack, and Charlie was beside himself with grief. He told me he wanted to honor his father's life by doing something for his country. I did everything I could to talk him out of it, but he enlisted in the Marines despite my objections.

"He ended up going straight from basic training to action in the South Pacific. In February, he took part in a battle to take back the island of Iwo Jima from the Japanese. You've probably seen the picture of six marines planting the American flag atop Mount Suribaldi. What you don't see is that three of the six marines who posed for the original picture were killed in action a few days later. My son didn't even make it that long. He was not a soldier, he was a baseball pitcher. He threw his life away on some misguided belief that it would make his dad proud. His dad was already as proud of him as any father could be. After the picture of the six marines won the Pulitzer Prize, the newspaper printed a story questioning whether or not the island was valuable enough to be worth the sacrifice of so many fine young men. I can tell you right now, the answer is *no*." She put her head down and cried as though her heart would break. I patted her awkwardly on the back until she said my mother would be worried about me and I'd better go.

I thought about all the mothers in all the houses in England, Scotland, Ireland, Wales, Australia, New Zealand, Russia, China, Canada, America, and countless other countries whose young people took up the cause so bravely. And I wanted desperately to say something splendid about forfeiting the lives of their sons to a noble cause. But all I could see was the woman in front of me and the lonely days spent resurrecting Charlie's life in black and white. Her private loss was too ordinary in a time of war to be considered profound and too profound to his mother to ever be ordinary.

She never invited me in again and after we moved, Bernie told us he had discovered her body after delivering groceries to her house. She had left the front door unlocked for the first time since he'd known her. I get past the sadness of her singular life by focusing on the kindness of my mother, who provided her with a hot meal every Sunday at a time when she had little to spare – except, perhaps, the desire to be a good neighbor.

Chapter 23

A few weeks before Easter, Brynn showed up without any notice. Her mother had contracted tuberculosis while visiting a friend who worked at a health retreat in Ashville, North Carolina, and she planned to place her mother in the same institution.

Daddy, who had turned into a chronic worrier without the numbing effect of alcohol, was convinced she'd contaminate all of us with the deadly disease. Mama ignored him and threw a welcome home picnic at our house.

"Anyone ever hear of the Manhattan Project?" Brynn asked, as we sat in a wide circle around the dining room table, balancing hotdogs and baked beans on our laps.

"Everybody has," Daddy declared. "It's where they're building the atomic bomb, in Los Alamos, New Mexico."

"Baloney," Stanley said. "That's a rumor FDR started to scare the Japanese into surrendering."

"That wouldn't have been a bad idea," Mick said, "but Thurston's right this time. We recruited German and Jewish scientists who wanted to escape Nazi tyranny to participate in its development."

"Doesn't anybody want to know why I asked?" Brynn interrupted, impatiently.

"Of course we do, honey. Hush and let her tell us about it herself," Lucille said firmly, as the men sheepishly grew silent.

"I told my commander this leave was to make arrangements for my mother. The truth is, it's to say goodbye before I head out for a new assignment in Oak Ridge, Tennessee. I'll be part of an elite group of women responsible for maintaining top secret files for the Manhattan Project. Only a handful of the best cryptologists in the country were chosen – quite an honor, if I do say so myself. My goal is to do well enough to be transferred to the Army Corps of Engineers in London."

"What's a cryptologist," I asked. With newfound patience

born of responsibility, Brynn answered, "Cryptology is a game played by two people who want to keep a secret. They invent a make believe language and give it meaning only the two can understand. Then they use it when writing to someone they don't like, so that person won't know the real meaning of the words."

Everyone was congratulating her on her contribution to the war effort when Lila suddenly said, "I was really sorry to hear about Hugh's death. You must have been devastated."

"Are you being sarcastic?" Brynn asked, having exhausted her quota of mellowness for the afternoon.

"Of course not. It's just... you haven't mentioned him, and I wanted to tell you how sorry I am."

"In that case, I'm sorry Garret ran out on you. Looks like it didn't take long to find a replacement," she grinned, glancing at Andy. Embarrassed by the attention, he stared down at his plate.

"You're jumping to conclusions as usual. Andy and I are just friends. I'm sure Garret will be back as soon as he adjusts to his...his handicap."

"Really? I hadn't heard - when do you expect him?"

Lila leaped to her feet, but Daddy grabbed her arm and pulled her back down. "This is a celebration of Brynn's success, not a cat fight about things that happened a long time ago." With that, Lila got up and stormed out the door. Andy started to follow, but a hard look from Lucille sent him back to his chair. After we finished eating, Brynn made a point of cornering Andy.

"I'm afraid I spoke hastily. I didn't mean to imply that you had jumped into Garret's shoes...no pun intended. It makes perfect sense for Lila to look for companionship after all she's been through. I felt the same way when poor Hugh died."

"How long were you married?" Andy asked, trying to fathom what manner of man would have chosen her.

"A little over two years. But it's not the length of time; it's the closeness that counts. My heart was broken when I had to leave Hugh to report for duty in Iowa, but I was willing to make the sacrifice for my country. Still, it's hard to get along without a man around the house. Now that my mother's sick and my father passed, I'll have to close up that three story mausoleum by myself."

"Let me know if I can do anything to help," Andy mumbled,

not knowing what else to say.

"I'll call you at Lucille's if I need manly assistance," she purred, playfully squeezing the muscle in his arm.

Lucille looked like she was going to be ill and asked Andy to help fold up the card table chairs.

I followed Brynn to the kitchen to help Mama with the dishes and said, "Your husband was really nice. He helped Lila find Garret when he got lost." But she wasn't listening. She was busy watching Andy from the doorway as he folded chairs. I was about to get my first lesson in romantic triangles – though not from her.

**

Andy Harrington was generally a laid-back kind of guy, but Brynn's snide remarks coupled with the threat of having to give up his military career had turned him into a man with a mission. He knew Lila would never risk loving him as long as Garret's ghost was looking over her shoulder, and losing her was beginning to seem preferable to becoming a lovesick lapdog. So he decided to find Garret himself and bring him home. If frivolous Brynn could decode messages from the Nazis, he should be able to find a missing comrade in arms. Using what little he knew about Garret's history, he asked Mick to drive him to Walter Reed Hospital.

Because Andy looked so young in his khakis and garrison cap, Mick convinced him he should do the talking. He asked to see the discharge nurse and after three cups of coffee and a little Irish charm, she provided them with Garret's sister's address in Saranac Lake, New York. It was the first any of us had heard about a sister.

Lucille tried to talk him out of going, fearing if he did locate Garret, it could easily end in Andy being the one rejected. I, on the other hand, prayed he would go and take me along. Cars were new and thrilling to ride in, and they fired my nomadic craving to see as much of the countryside as I was allowed. In the end, Lucille convinced herself that destiny had sent Brynn to light a fire under her complacent son and resolve the Garret issue once and for all. So she packed coca colas and tuna-fish sandwiches and stunned me by supporting my desire to keep them company. I think she assumed the presence of a child would prevent any conflict from erupting between Andy and Garret. She did add one final word of caution. "Son, you realize that meeting his competition may awaken Garret's desire to win Lila back."

"I know, Mama, but I feel like I'm adrift at the mercy of the women in my life. I have to get resolution in something, whether career or love, before I lose my mind." Lucille offered to withdraw her request to keep him out of combat, but he'd made up his mind to settle the Garret matter once and for all.

The drive took five hours, including, at Mick's request, a brief sightseeing trek through the teeming, boxed-in streets of Manhattan, its mammoth buildings casting shadows over preoccupied pedestrians below. Mick later told Lucille he'd never seen so many taxi cabs and pretty girls in his life.

Winding our way through New York State, we finally reached the low-lying hills of the Adirondacks near Lake Placid. Saranac lay only seven miles away. After asking the locals for help, Mick pulled up beside a spacious yellow frame house surrounded by blue spruce evergreens and vivid red maple trees, their mirror images reflected in the glassy stillness of its pristine water. Nearby, a girl sat in a wooden rocker, an unopened book in her lap. Her expression was so serene, her features so tranquil, I thought at first she might be an angel. Andy must have also been moved, for he lost his voice and stood staring down at her like a statue. Finally, she glanced up revealing eyes as hazel as autumn, and asked if she could help us.

Since Andy had not recovered his voice, Mick spoke for him, explaining that Andy was trying to locate an old military buddy named Garret Cummings. "The hospital said he has a sister named Amanda Cummings at this address."

"I'm Amanda," she said, enthusiastically. "My brother has never had a visitor; he'll be so excited to hear you stopped by."

Andy finally found his voice and stammered, "He may not remember exactly who I am. You know how it is in the trenches. All our muddy faces look alike." Mick nearly choked, but Amanda seemed to take his awkwardness in stride, telling us that Garret was at the rehab center and would be back in about an hour. She explained that he was having trouble adjusting to his prosthetic legs and might not be in the mood for company. "Could you possibly come back tomorrow?"

Mick told her we were just passing through and tomorrow would be too late. Then Andy surprised us by asking if we could wait there until Garret got home.

She invited us inside for something to drink, and Andy immediately asked if he could use the bathroom. He told us later he found four sparsely furnished bedrooms, but only two appeared to be in use. The first was clearly Garret's, for it had a tinted picture of Lila on the dresser along with dozens of track trophies from his high school running days. It wasn't until he entered Amanda's room that he saw Garret's face for the first time. He and Amanda stood side by side, he in dress uniform, she in a peasant blouse and full skirt, with a ring of daisies braided through her long wavy hair. In the frame next to theirs was a black and white photograph of a dignified, white haired couple wearing oddly outdated formal attire. He assumed they were the parents and hurried downstairs where Mick and I were struggling to make small talk.

"So it's just you and Garret," Andy commented, hoping he could generate more information.

She explained that their parents were missionaries who had just returned to China after a six month sabbatical to spend time with Garret. "My brother and I were born in China, but conditions were politically unsettled at the time, so we were sent to live with Mother's sister in Baltimore. This was her summer home, and it seemed like the ideal location for Garret's recovery. I worry about my parents all the time. China has taken such a horrific hit by the Japanese. But then, who would know more about the hazards of war than you? Are you on leave from some war-torn island in the South Pacific? I couldn't help noticing your tropical uniform."

Andy told her he'd recently been stationed in the Philippines and got to thinking about his old buddy Garret. "How is he, anyway?"

"You couldn't have come at a better time. He's so depressed I'm afraid he may be considering taking his own life. He has a girlfriend back in Baltimore he misses dreadfully but refuses to contact. He's convinced her loyalty is based on pity, and he'd rather be alone than live with that the rest of his life. You may have met her – Lila…gosh, I can't remember her last name."

Andy told her he had met Lila and she was utterly devoted to Garret - and not out of sympathy.

Amanda pleaded with him to tell her more about Lila. "All I have is a picture to go on. He used to talk all the time about her flaming red hair and horizon blue eyes. Now he doesn't talk at all. He just sits in a rowboat in the middle of the lake pretending to fish, pining away for her. He used to love music; he even taught me to dance. But now he makes me turn off the radio when music comes on. I think it makes him feel, and if he opens that door, all the agonies of the battlefield will come rushing in."

Andy assured her Lila was a lovely person, warm, funny, a bit obsessed with astrology. "To hear her tell it, Garret is the sensible one and she, a will-of-the-wisp, dabbling in every screwball idea that comes along…" Andy suddenly hesitated, then said, "You know…maybe we should be going. Our being here might upset him more than he already is."

She begged us not to go. "You are the only person I know who could talk him into contacting Lila."

But Andy was too awash with guilt to continue the façade. "Take my word for it. I'm the last person he'll want to talk to…" Just then, a Veteran's hospital bus pulled up. Glancing out the window, he saw the driver hand Garret his canes, then steady him as he started up the front walk. It was too late for escape. "Oh God," Andy groaned. "What have I gotten us into?"

I thought Garret was handsome but thin, with smoke gray eyes and light brown hair, almost to his shoulders. His jaw-line was boney and his cheeks sunken in. His lips were full and he had a slightly Roman, Charleston Heston appearance.

"Look who's here," Amanda cried. "It's Andy. He and Mick and Silby have come all the way from Baltimore to see you."

Garret stared at us blankly, unable to locate our faces in his memory. "Do I know you?"

"Well, you do and you don't," Andy answered. "We both have an interest in the same girl, which is practically the same thing?"

"Who the hell are you? And what are you doing in the house with my sister?"

Amanda assumed his wounds had made him forgetful and

reminded him, "You fought together at the battle of Betio."

"No we didn't," Andy blurted out. "I lied. You and I have never met, Garret. We just happen to both be in love with Lila, and I can't get to first base with her until you either come back or make it perfectly clear you never intend to."

At that point, Mick tried to nudge Andy out the door, but he was determined to play it out to the end.

"How could you do that, come into our home and pretend to be somebody you're not?" Amanda cried. "What kind of self-serving scoundrel are you?"

Garret lunged at Andy, dropping his canes, hitting him squarely in the face with his fist. Andy fell backwards against the hutch. Mick jumped up and restrained Garret as gently as he could. And that's when Andy delivered what Mick described as the longest speech he'd ever made.

"I had that coming," he said. "But there's something you need to think about. Nobody can deny your wounds are terrible and your life changed beyond imagination. But this didn't happen to you alone. Lila cries for what you're going through every day. You have to help her get on with her life - tell her it's okay to love again. If you're too pigheaded to go see her, write a letter, call her on the phone. But don't leave her with an image of poor Garret wandering the earth to mourn his wounds alone. She deserves more than that. So does your sister, for that matter. That's all I came to say." Having nothing to add, Mick and I followed Andy to the car, anxious to get back to Baltimore to give Lucille and Mama a full report.

Chapter 24

A mood of desperate optimism prevailed throughout the waning days of 1944, thanks to daily radio reports claiming Germany was losing ground to Russia. It was about then that Mama received a note from Brynn written in her left-slanted handwriting on rose perfumed paper - her initials monogrammed in silver at the top of the page. The entire message consisted of one sentence but its obscure tone made it read like more: "I know it seems the War will never end, but something unprecedented is in the works and I just had to be the first to share the news." We could only wait and wonder what was about to befall us.

Andy had been back from Saranac Lake about two weeks when he reached a compromise with the Army and accepted a transfer from the South Pacific to Ft. Meade, near Baltimore. By then, the catch phrase at our house had become "Has he told her about Amanda?" It didn't take long to figure out he wasn't planning to, especially after Lila agreed to go with him to see "Thrill of a Romance," with Van Johnson and Esther Williams. When Hazel teased her about their clandestine relationship, Lila insisted she only accepted because Van Johnson was a dreamboat, although she eventually admitted to letting Andy hold her hand in the darkened theater.

He considered it a major turning point and shortly thereafter, we began to notice the two rubbing against each other in the guise of reaching for something either could have accessed alone. Finally, Andy told Lucille she let him kiss her on a bench in Druid Hill Park one particularly starry night, when the dizzying smell of pine was in the air.

Next time Lila was at our house, Hazel and Mama demanded to know if it were true. "Well," she explained, "there was a cool breeze and he slid his fingers through my hair and before I knew it, he was kissing me."

"The important question is did you kiss him back?"

"I'm afraid I did," she giggled. "It was like a stomach plunging fall into the Grand Canyon. Every time I think about it, I throb all over. I can't sleep at night for fantasizing about his long beautiful fingers…"

"Little pitchers have big ears," Mama cautioned, nodding in the direction of my sisters and me pretending to play Chinese checkers at the table.

"Sorry, but I haven't felt this way since my first date with Garret, and I don't know how to turn it off."

"Why would you want to?" Lucille asked.

"Because it's Garret I really love, and I don't want to mess that up."

"Are you sure you haven't grown so used to waiting you no longer recognize a losing cause when you see one?"

"Absolutely not! If Garret walked through that door tomorrow, I'd fall into his arms as though he'd never been away."

"I'm really sorry to hear that," Lucille sighed. "Do you think it's fair to Andy?"

"I've never led him to believe otherwise."

"Maybe not in words, but recent changes in your actions could be sending that message," Mama pointed out.

As I listened to their grownup talk, I realized I could scarcely remember Garret, and I'd grown very fond of Andy. So I secretly prayed she'd marry Andy and bring their babies by for us to play with. I was just getting used to the idea when Lila rushed in to tell us Garret and his sister were moving back to his aunt's house in Baltimore. He asked if she would meet him the following afternoon in Wyman Park, on the bench in front of the Museum of Art. Hazel insisted he'd chosen that location to avoid climbing two flights of stairs to her apartment, but Lila couldn't help obsessing about the eerie synchronicity of meeting both men in her life on park benches no more than a week apart.

Cricket and I had spent countless hours on the hill in front of the museum building twig forts to protect our baby-dolls from air-raids. So I was perfectly at home crouching behind the bronze statue of Rodin's *The Thinker,* playing Lucille's little spy. It didn't take long for Amanda to pull into the parking lot. I watched as Garret got out of the car and dragged himself to a standing position, then I followed his eyes to Lila sitting on a green bench, her fiery hair glinting in the sun, the eagerness of Christmas morning on her face.

He approached the woman he'd dreamed of marrying since boyhood. She jumped up, ready to throw herself at him, but appeared to think better of it and sat back down. He painstakingly propped up his canes, then lowered himself onto the bench. Once he was safely seated, Lila threw her arms around his neck and kissed him on the mouth until he had to push her away to breathe. They remained seated for over an hour, his arm resting lightly on her shoulder. I couldn't hear a word they said, but it was clear he'd insisted that she leave first, which she did – but only after a long kiss goodbye. As soon as she drove away, Amanda hurried down the hill to assist Garret back to her car. As they rounded the wide curve toward Maryland Avenue, I cursed myself for spending all that time behind *The Thinker* to learn absolutely nothing. What was I going to tell Lucille?

Watching him struggle with his canes led me to switch my loyalty from Andy back to Garret. After all, who would take care of him if he didn't marry Lila? I needn't have worried. I'd barely walked the nine blocks home before she burst through the door crying like her heart would break.

Lucille wrapped her arms around her. "Don't worry, darlin;' you still have Andy."

"No!" Lila cried. "Garret's coming back…he's willing to give it a try. These are tears of relief…and anger. Did you know Andy located Garret weeks ago and didn't tell me. How could he do that and then cold-bloodily continue to pursue me as though nothing had changed. He knew how long I'd been searching for Garret. Every day I didn't find him was another century of despair. If I ever for one moment considered dating Andy seriously, his betrayal has closed that book forever."

"Don't judge him too hastily," Lucille pleaded. "I'm sure he was planning to tell you. It's just…you've been devoted to Garret for so long he wanted more time to even the odds…Andy actually tried to talk Garret into coming back to you. When he refused, Andy felt you were fair game."

"Fair game? I'm not a trophy to be bargained for. I can

picture all of you, now, sitting around the table, gossiping about us over coffee as the drama unfolded. Were you placing bets on the outcome? Who's ahead, Andy or Garret?"

"It wasn't like that. We just wanted what was best for you."

"The best thing for me would have been knowing Garret was safe and sound. I got more support from Hugh Pillstick – a military flunky who was reluctant to disclose Garret's whereabouts - than I did those of you who are suppose to care about me. This is the most insensitive thing you've ever done."

"I swear Andy was going to tell you. He was just waiting for the right time."

"After he tricked me into falling in love with him, right? Wasn't it enough of an advantage for Andy to have both his legs. You had to make it even harder for Garret by keeping his whereabouts hidden from me. You are monsters – both of you."

"I'm really sorry, but let's face it. You loved a brave, naïve warrior who went away to War and came back so deeply wounded, he concealed his whereabouts from the person who loved him most. All I'm saying is give it some time. Stop seeing Andy and date Garret exclusively for a few months if it makes you feel better, but don't close the door on Andy entirely until he has a chance to prove himself. He has a good heart, and whatever transpired between he and Garret must have convinced him he was justified in putting off telling you."

"I can't believe you're rationalizing his dishonesty. I don't ever want to see either of you again," she cried, darting out the door, her rosy cheeks ashen, her eyes filled with the pain of betrayal.

Lucille picked up the phone with motherly dread and told Andy Lila knew about Saranac Lake and did not intend to see him again. He immediately requested a transfer to combat duty, but Uncle Sam refused and he was doomed to endure the excited chatter on 24th Street after Garret cemented his and Lila's relationship with an engagement ring.

Chapter 25

It was a mild April afternoon and my sisters and I were sitting around the table doing homework. Mama suddenly burst through the door, looking as close to tears as I'd ever seen. "Is your father home?" she asked, breathlessly, but before I could answer, we heard his footsteps in the hall. To our astonishment my parents embraced in the dining room doorway, tears streaming down both their faces. As if that were not shock enough, Lucille and Mick hurried in behind Daddy, followed closely by Hazel, who was sobbing, and Lila, who put aside her anger and joined the mourners, repeating over and over, "I can't believe he's gone."

"It must be Garret," Marjorie whispered, and I burst into tears. Daddy walked to the mantelpiece and turned on the radio. The room grew silent.

"At 3:35 this afternoon, President Franklin Delano Roosevelt died of a cerebral hemorrhage. He had served three months of an unprecedented fourth term in office." The announcer's voice broke. "I'm sorry...the father of our nation, the hero who guided us through the aftermath of the worst Depression in history and this terrible War..." His voice broke again. "It will be up to Harry Truman to lead us to a final victory..." Then the national anthem began to play, and Daddy turned it off.

Recognizing the gravity of the loss, we closed our schoolbooks and listened to them talk. We learned the president had saved the banks by requiring insurance to protect depositors' money, while implementing Social Security to guarantee the financial future of seniors. He reduced unemployment by using federal money to create jobs and encouraged the expansion of labor unions to increase salaries. But of all Roosevelt's forward thinking solutions, the most popular was the repeal of prohibition, creating a huge tax base and much happier voters, not the least of which were Mick and Daddy. "We'd never have survived the economy and this damned War without him?" Mick said, wiping his eyes on his shirtsleeve.

A few weeks later, Daddy decided an outing on the water was the only way to shake off the gloom and sense of doom we were feeling. He reserved tickets at Mick's expense for all of us on the Bay Belle, a two story diesel replacement for the old steamship excursion liners, to transport us to Tolchester amusement park near the wide sandy shoreline of Betterton Beach.

Mama and Lucille prepared fried chicken, two dozen sandwiches, a small vat of potato salad, a dozen deviled eggs, a chocolate cake, and two gallons of very sweet tea. It was to be the grandest expedition we'd ever undertaken. Lucille insisted that Andy invite Amanda Cummings to go along. "Garret is all but living at Lila's and that poor girl is left to sit around the house by herself. It's the least you can do, since it's your fault she was uprooted from her lovely lakeside home." Andy relented out of guilt, and we picked her up on our way to the waterfront.

Unlike the refurbished waters of Baltimore's Harbor Place today, with its paved walkways and expensive seafood restaurants, the dock was a noisy mass of sweaty workmen loading and unloading cargo ships to and from Baltimore's aging factories. The first three piers were reserved for families seeking refuge from the city heat on excursion boats, and I could hardly believe we were among the lucky hundreds standing in line on Pier 2.

We started boarding the Bay Belle at 8 am and promptly at 9 o'clock the ear splitting wail of the smoke stack announced that we were pulling out. We hurried to the railings on the upper deck so we could watch her sluggish turn about, just beyond the Domino Sugar plant with its huge yellow sign and sand piles of dark sugar waiting to be processed.

I was instantly mesmerized by the bay water lapping against the hull and didn't budge from my day-dreamy vigil until we docked at Tolchester two hours later. Children poured off the ship, racing up the grassy knoll to claim a picnic table for their parents who were dragging containers of food behind them.

Despite the mild spring weather, Daddy decided to don his bathing trunks and walk down to the beach for a swim. Betsy and Garland and I begged to go with him. Garland immediately cut his foot on a seashell and Betsy got stung by a jellyfish. I was too excited about swimming with my father to miss the company of either. I danced around him, splashing and having the time of my life until a cramp sent a paralyzing pain down the calf of my leg and across the arch of my foot, causing my big toe to spasm downward and imbed itself in the sand. Terrified, I balanced on one foot while hanging onto Daddy's bathing trunks, yowling for him to fix my toe. But he pulled my hand away and snarled, "Don't be such a baby; it's only a cold water cramp. Walk it off." Then he dove headfirst underwater and swam away while I hobbled to dry land to realign my misdirected toe.

I got back just in time to join Garland, my sisters, Andy, and Amanda - with whom we'd fallen instantly in love - for a ride on the Whip. Tame by today's standards, it seemed like the scariest ride on the planet that day. We squeezed into a giant yellow cup and had our brains slung against our sculls for a few delicious minutes, as it spun in circles while lurching and dipping over humps in the floor. We rode until I was ready to throw up. Then the others went in search of the roller coaster while Betsy and I picked out pretty pink ponies on the Carousel, riding our steeds up and down to the shrill squall of the calliope playing a speeded up version of "Somewhere, Over the Rainbow."

We gathered back at the picnic table and stuffed ourselves on a feast of homemade food, while I made good on my vow never to speak to my father again. It is uncertain whether or not he noticed.

Toward mid afternoon, Lucille, Mick, Mama and Daddy climbed into a grownup wooden swing, operated by pushing the floorboards with your feet, and spent an hour or so dozing in the warm sun. Marjorie and Betsy took Garland to ride the train, and I followed Andy and Amanda to the dairy at the twin-towered dance pavilion for strawberry milkshakes. I spent the rest of the afternoon watching them dance to music from the jukebox. They made a lovely couple, she, with her long corn-silk hair and tiny waist - he, with his dark wavy hair and gentle way of holding her. Suddenly, the boat shrieked its shrill alert. We had one hour to board for home.

To this day, when I hear the warning wail of a ship in harbor, I smell the tinny, sea green waters of the Chesapeake Bay, hear the dozy exchanges of families overeating at sun-baked picnic tables, and hold tight to the reins of a pretty pink pony as it rises and falls to the screech of a calliope. Then I close my eyes and lose myself in the velvet voice of Nat King Cole crooning "I'm in the Mood for Love," while two wispy shadows who barely know each other twirl around the dance floor.

Marjorie at Tolchester

Chapter 26

On May 6, 1945, Hazel went into labor and on May 7th, Germany surrendered, although it would not become official until May 8th at 11:01 pm. The housewives of 24th Street poured out of their houses to celebrate, beating pots and pans with wooden spoons, sending balloons soaring into the bright spring sky, embracing neighbors and strangers alike. Hazel saw it as a good omen and named her baby Victoria Europa Polanski, doomed to be labeled the V-E baby for the majority of her formative years.

The surrender of Germany allowed America to focus on the war with Japan, and our air force was immediately reassigned to the Pacific Theatre, as naval and ground forces attempted to liberate the Pacific Islands. From the beginning, our number one problem had been a lack of access to the isolated island of Japan which meant there were no firsthand consequences motivating them to end the War.

Our first attempt to carry the battle to their front door had been in 1942, when we retaliated for the bombing of Pearl Harbor by launching an attack on Tokyo. Unfortunately, our inadequate B-25 bombers had to be launched from an aircraft carrier with less than enough fuel for their safe return. Lieutenant Colonel Jimmy Doolittle and his men were well aware it might be a suicide mission but idealistic enough to believe that miracles occasionally happen to the good-guys. While the attack on Tokyo was too small to inflict a great deal of damage, it did a lot to boost the morale of our fighting men.

With the advent of B-29 bombers in 1944, we were able to launch more strategic attacks, and on March 10, 1945, 300 US B-29 bombers dropped 1,700 tons of firebombs on Tokyo. It is estimated that 100,000 were killed, mainly civilians, during the three hour raid. Still, Japan did not surrender.

The dropping of the atom bomb on Hiroshima on August 6, 1945 would instantly kill 80,000, and leave 50,000 to die of injuries and exposure. The annihilation of Nagasaki three days later would cause the immediate death of 39,000. Still, all of that would not equal the total number of American service men killed while fighting two separate fronts for a War we did not want to enter. The majority of Americans had been opposed to getting involved prior to Pearl Harbor. Too bad Japan didn't realize that. But they thought our naval ships stationed in Hawaii would interfere with their sweep of the South Pacific Islands, thus they aroused a sleeping Goliath from its cozy isolation on the other side of the world.

It is difficult to imagine that in our passion to end the War, we were able to sit around the dining room table and discuss dropping an atom bomb on Japan as though it were just another battle strategy.

I think people could talk about it casually in 1945, because it was only an idea. Television was a technical gizmo of the future, and movies were made on backstage lots in Hollywood, more for entertainment than spiritual accountability. Now that we have instant visual replay, the victims of such tragedies are humanized, leading one to marvel at man's seemingly insatiable appetite for obliterating his own kind. I think naming the atom bombs "Little Boy" and "Fat Man" is symbolic of American innocence and naiveté at the time.

By European standards, with their two thousand year history of declaring war on each other, we were an idealistic, infant nation whose only claims to fame were the Constitution and the Bill of Rights. But for Garret and millions of scorched souls returning from the battlefield, everything after the war would seem profoundly superficial and far less invulnerable.

Chapter 27

One week before the start of school, Lila's sister Abigail asked if she would housesit her place on Assateague, a thirty-seven mile barrier island located on the eastern coast of the Delmarva Peninsula, the northern two-thirds in Maryland and the southern one-third in Virginia. While there were no residences allowed on the narrow strip of white beach, wild horses roamed freely, as did rabbits, squirrels, turtles, and snowy egrets. Abigail's house was located on one of a handful of saltwater marshlands with enough nutrients to support rich swampy flora.

My sisters and I were invited to go, as were Hazel and baby Victoria. We could not have imagined how different the experience would be from our daydreams of building sand castles on the shore and hurling ourselves into high-tide in the Atlantic Ocean.

On the first chilly morning in September, Mick drove us to the pier to board a ferryboat that would deposit us at the mouth of the Chesapeake Bay. The brackish smell of green waves slapping the sides of the boat sent our adrenaline into anticipation mode, and by the time we reached the other side, we were ready for a grand adventure. Abigail's car was waiting on the dock with keys on the seat, a list of directions for starting the kerosene heater, and an ad for a tour of an Assateague lighthouse, scheduled for the following afternoon.

"That's odd! Abigail's lived here three years and never once expressed a desire to see the lighthouse. Maybe historical landmarks take on more meaning as your body begins turning into one," Lila chuckled.

We parked the car near a marshy wetland overrun with wild Columbine; then picked our way across lopsided slabs of stone separated by tall stands of blue and purple monkshood, commonly known as wolf's bane.

"Don't pick those flowers, and wash your hands if you touch the stalks. They're poisonous," Lila warned.

All at once, the aroma of rosemary drifted across the moist air. "It's coming from the loblolly pines," Lila explained. The fragrant trees surrounded a two story frame house on huge blocks of cement – replacements for the wooden stilts that had failed to protect it from the vengeful Chesapeake-Potomac hurricane of 1933. The loblollies, in an effort to reach their full height of one hundred feet, had shed their lower branches, leaving scaly skeletal trunks with tangled masses of ten inch pine needles near the top, so irregular in design; they seemed to take on personalities of their own – especially when viewed on a dark night with a full golden moon suspended in the background.

There were two bedrooms upstairs - one with a guest crib - which Hazel and Victoria used, and one with twin beds that Lila and Marjorie shared. Betsy and I slept in a converted pantry downstairs, with a wall of can-goods at one end and a small, iron bed at the other. Although it had no windows, the room was drafty, and we could hear the brittle needles rustling against each other as the shrill wind snaked its way in and out of groaning gray tree trunks.

On the morning of our second day, we went in search of Assateague's lighthouse. Built just after the Civil War, its vivid red and white bands were fully visible from Maryland, despite its nocturnal watch on the southern tip of the Virginia side. My image of lighthouses was based on the terrifying thriller, "The Spiral Staircase," so I expected to see dingy, dripping concrete walls and floors. To my surprise, magnificent red brick arches overhung the windows. In the center, there stood a wrought iron spiral stairway with six separate landings. The original oil lamps at the top of its 142 foot span had been replaced months earlier by battery powered lights, four facing north and three facing south, from which we could see all the way to the Atlantic Ocean.

As we stood gazing out mammoth glass windows, a gaunt young man in crumpled khakis stepped up behind us and asked, "Have you seen her, yet?"

"Have we seen who?" Lila responded, taken aback by his unkempt appearance.

"Her," he repeated in a raspy voice. Just then, Marjorie pointed to a school of dolphins diving in sync not far beyond the breakers. By the time we turned back around, the soft-spoken man had vanished.

We took turns guessing who he might be, putting him out of our minds when we got close enough to smell French fries on the boardwalk in Ocean City, where we braved the chill to wade knee deep into the freshly washed sands of low-tide in search of starfish.

Later that evening, after putting Victoria to bed, we gathered in lawn chairs on the screened in porch to listen as night flying katydids competed with salamanders to lure unsuspecting insects onto wet tongues by rubbing their legs together. In front of us lay miles of salt marsh cord grass, hissing lightly in the breeze.

Just then, I saw the glow of a red lantern in the distance moving slowly through the watery grass. "Is that a boat?" I asked.

"Is what a boat?"

"That light out there."

"What light?"

"Don't you see it? It's red. Right over there," I pointed.

"I see it," Betsy said.

"Where?" Hazel asked.

Betsy and I pointed in the exact same direction. Marjorie pressed her nose against the screen and said, "You're making that up. There's nothing out there."

Lila peered more intently into the darkness. "Marjorie's right. You girls are seeing things. We've had a long day; let's turn in before we all start seeing things."

Once we were settled into our pantry-bedroom, I asked Betsy whether or not she had really seen the lantern.

"Of course I did. Didn't you?"

I secretly hoped she'd say *no* and I could chalk it up to my overactive imagination. Her confirmation meant the two of us had seen something invisible to everybody else, and that sent a chill down my spine. Could it have been a ghost on some midnight mission? I pulled the covers tight around my chin and wished I were at home, sleeping safely in the middle – between Marjorie and Betsy – with Daddy snoring rhythmically across the hall.

Sometime during the night, I awoke to see a figure in a flowing white gown standing in the doorway turning the light switch on and off – but without the usual clicking sound or any change in the brightness of the light that shown on her alone. It must be Lila making sure we turned off the light, I said to myself, before dozing back off.

The next morning, as we sat on the porch devouring Lila's homemade cinnamon donuts, she casually asked what Hazel was doing in her room the night before. Hazel looked puzzled and said, "I wasn't in your room – you were in mine, wearing a long white gown that floated around your body – which I just realized would have been impossible indoors.

I shivered and told them what I'd seen - my credibility handicapped by Betsy's having slept through the entire experience.

Then Marjorie asked the question we'd all been afraid to verbalize. "What if she's the "her" the man at the lighthouse asked if we'd seen. What if she's a ghost?"

"Don't be ridiculous. Ghosts only exist in Dickens's 'A Christmas Carol,'" Hazel assured her.

I wondered why Lila wasn't supporting the ghost theory, given her history of séance searching. "Maybe we should call Daddy," I suggested, nervously.

They looked at me as though I'd lost my mind. "We'd be better off calling Mama if we call anybody," Marjorie said. "She's more open-minded about bizarre happenings."

The idea of my mother evaluating the situation seemed to wake up Lila's pragmatic side. "We don't need to call anybody. It is not uncommon for two people to dream the same thing after sharing a common experience. That weird looking man planted a seed and we were gullible enough to take its possibilities to bed with us. Let's make a pact to put the entire thing out of our minds."

With the question of the lady in white resolved, we went to watch the ponies prance among the pines, convinced that a lack of interest would banish our ghostly visitor from the bedrooms for the duration of the trip.

We returned to the house at lunchtime so Hazel could nurse Victoria. Later, as we were enjoying grilled cheese sandwiches and tomato soup, she took the baby upstairs for an afternoon nap. We were talking about what we wanted to do next, when Victoria suddenly screamed. Recognizing it as no ordinary cry, we followed Hazel up the stairs and gathered around the crib as she tried to sooth her. Gentle words had no effect, so Hazel tried to pick her up. But that only made her cry harder. Suddenly, we felt a chilly breeze, and the baby looked toward the foot of the crib, in the direction of the doorway. A bright smile chubbied her cheeks and to our amazement, she said "Mama."

"Who is she talking to? I've been trying to get her to say 'Mama' for weeks." Hazel cried. She reached down and snatched Victoria out of the crib while we stumbled like nervous racehorses down the stairs.

"I want to go home," Hazel said, with more authority than she generally used.

"Let's be sensible," Lila responded, trying to calm the tremors in her own voice. "The baby was probably dreaming that it was you standing in the doorway."

"She's never done that before and given the lady we saw in the doorway last night, I'm not willing to take a chance."

"I'll admit it's a bit on the spooky side, but I'm sure there's a logical explanation."

Anxious to keep from going home before the week was up, I said, "I noticed a house within walking distance of this one when we first got here. Why don't we go ask if they've ever seen the lady in white? Maybe she lives around here." To my surprise, they did not reject the idea.

Lila and Hazel intended to take the baby and leave my sisters and me at the house, but we were too frightened to stay behind.

Lila knocked tentatively on the door and to our astonishment the pale man from the lighthouse invited us in. "I guess you've seen her," he said, in a dry, craggy voice.

"Who is she? Lila blurted out before we had time to sit down.

"Her name was Elizabeth Malloy. It was just before the war, and her husband was stationed on Guam, in the Mariana Islands. She became convinced she'd miss him less if she and their six month old daughter waited for his return at the beach house, rather than their home in Cambridge."

It suddenly occurred to Lila that he must be her husband. He denied it at first but recognized a fellow intuitive and lowered his guard. He told us he purchased the house he currently occupied for the sole purpose of making contact with his wife and infant daughter. "They were both killed in the hurricane of 1933. Elizabeth apparently left baby Alice in her crib while she ran next door for help, but there was nobody here. She raced back to Alice but only made it as far as the stairs. She will never rest in peace until she finds her. I couldn't bring myself to stay in the house that took their lives, so I bought this one after hearing that Elizabeth had been spotted in the cord grass carrying a red lantern, searching for Alice."

"When Abigail told me about your fascination with contacting the dead and your plan to housesit, I put the ad about the lighthouse in her car so I could be sure you and I would meet. My undernourished appearance seems to unnerve people, so I thought you might feel less threatened in a public place."

"Has my sister Abigail ever seen Elizabeth?"

"Not that she's admitted to. I think it takes an open mind to draw Elizabeth out of the marsh."

"Now that you've met me, what exactly do you want?"

"I thought I might convince you to hold a séance."

"Down here? That's not possible."

"Why not?"

"I work with a group of seers I've known for years. Not only would it scare the be-jeebers out of the people with me now, but I don't think it would work. Besides, inviting people to come back from the dead isn't without risk."

"Elizabeth would never harm us."

"As far as you know. What about the safety of baby Victoria if we are unable to reunite Elizabeth and Alice? She seems awfully drawn to her."

"I can guarantee the safety of everyone involved. Elizabeth was a good Christian woman. She'd never harm a child, or the child's mother."

"I'll help," I chimed in, anxious for the man to get his family back.

"I need time to think it over," Lila said.

"Take as long as you want. I'm not going anywhere."

We returned to Abigail's and sat around the dining room table discussing the merits of trying to contact the dead. I confessed to finding the challenge exciting, but Hazel and my sisters seemed repelled by the idea. After an hour or so, Betsy began to inch around to our way of thinking. "If that was her in the doorway, there's no evidence that she wanted to hurt us."

"You're being brainwashed," Marjorie said sarcastically, rolling her wide gray eyes.

"I don't think we should place the burden of making a decision on the children," Hazel said.

"I agree. You and I should do it."

"Do you guarantee Victoria will never leave my side and that you'll stop the instant I – or anybody else feels uncomfortable?"

"Given our inexperience, the chance of convincing Elizabeth to show herself is pretty remote, but if it makes you feel better, I promise."

"Since she clearly hasn't found her baby, how are you going to persuade her to give up the search?"

"I don't intend to. I plan to explain that it is she and not Alice who is stuck on the wrong side of paradise. Once she accepts that Alice is waiting for her on the other side, she'll go willingly."

"What if Elizabeth is an atheist and doesn't believe there is another side?"

"How could she not believe; she's here, isn't she?"

**

On Thursday evening, just as the moon emerged from a bevy of black clouds, we gathered around the dining room table, each with varying degrees of apprehension. Hazel had wrapped Victoria in several blankets and placed her in a huge wicker laundry basket on the chair next to her own. She believed the blankets would protect her from any other-worldly vibes that might find their way in. With the pale man at one end of the table and Lila at the other - as many candles as we could find lighting the room from the buffet - my sisters and I joined hands and pretended to take it seriously.

"If the spirit of Elizabeth Malloy is here, please give us a sign," Lila repeated over and over, to no avail. Finally, she asked, "Are you looking for Alice?" and an icy draft filled the room.

"I'm here my darling girl," the pale man shouted," and the candles flickered wildly. I grasped Marjorie's hand so tightly, she pulled away.

"Tell her Alice is not here. Tell her she followed the angels into the light."

We heard an ear piercing crash and the pale man seemed to lose his voice.

"Alice is not here," Lila called, in a loud voice. "She's in heaven, on the other side of the light. Go to Alice now. She's waiting for you,"

Suddenly, the pale man gasped, as though Elizabeth had passed right through him, and the candles flickered and died. Nobody moved.

After what seemed an eternity, Lila whispered, "I think she's gone."

The pale man grabbed Lila's hand and kissed it then dropped to his knees and began thanking God for releasing Elizabeth from her eternal maternal quest. The next day, we found a note in Abigail's mailbox thanking Lila for giving him back his life and saying he had returned to Cambridge.

Sleeping in the pantry was terrifying that night, so Betsy and I played twenty-questions until daybreak. When Hazel declared she was not spending one more day on Assateague, we packed up and drove home that very afternoon. I expected we'd jabber about our ghostly experience for the next three hours, but a strange code of silence seemed to permeate the car. Even after we got home, aside from Lila filling Mama and Lucille in on the basics, the subject seldom came up. That was my first experience with group denial and minimizing an experience nobody could explain without feeling foolish. Over time, my sisters and I lost our certainty about how much was real and how much a product of chilly drafts and flickering candles. Still, I suspect amid the shadows on windy moonlit nights, when loblolly needles rub and hiss together, it comes back to haunt their dreams. I know it does mine.

Chapter 28

None of us knew much about Garret, and Mama made up her mind to put an end to that right quickly. The following Sunday, when we got home from Church, she told us not to change out of our good dresses. "Garret and Lila are coming to dinner and so are Lucille and Mick." My sisters and I were ecstatic. Company meant Mama and Daddy would talk sweetly to each other…at least Mama would.

Sunday dinner, except during the hottest days of summer, was always the same: roast beef, mashed potatoes, green beans, buttermilk biscuits, and banana pudding for dessert. Only the substitution of store-bought glasses for jelly jars was a sign somebody special was coming – that and my mother's extraordinary coconut cake sitting on a stand on the buffet. She made it from scratch, splitting a coconut in half with a hatchet, then chiseling out the sweet meat and grating it on a handheld shredder. Not only was it tedious, it left tiny cuts all over her knuckles.

Unlike the swash and swagger of Stanley Polanski, there was a stillness in Garret that made one think of rusting chapel bells in abandoned churches that no longer had a reason to ring. A small, compact man with sad gray eyes, he expended as little energy as possible on conversation – as though his capacity for interaction had been consumed by the violence of war and lay dormant on the battlefield.

"What are your plans, son?" Daddy asked, sensing a need in the stoic young man for guidance.

"None at the moment, sir."

"What did you do before you signed up for the Marines?"

Garret stared off into space as though vague recollections from boyhood were drifting across his mind.

Lila answered for him. "He wants to open his own commercial airline."

"Does he know anything about airplanes?" my pragmatic

mother asked.

"Hell," Daddy said. "Nobody does. Even Howard Hughes hasn't figured out how to build an aircraft big enough to carry more than a handful from here to Paris."

"But he's rich enough to hire people to find out," Mick reminded him.

"The point is, the boy sees a future in flying and ought not to give up his dream. Do you have any rich relatives who could provide you with start up cash?"

Garret was beginning to perspire and glance furtively toward the door. "Why don't we let him relax and enjoy his dinner," Lucille suggested.

Garret managed to make it through the meal but he and Lila left shortly thereafter.

Mama was so worried about him, she invited Andy and Garret's sister Amanda to supper to talk about how we could help him start his own airline business.

"You are talking millions of investment dollars," Andy pointed out. "Only a handful could afford to build the planes and buy enough land for runways."

"How did Hughes learn to build airplanes? Is there a school for that?" Mama asked, with her uncanny ability to strike at the heart of the matter when it concerned people she barely knew.

"Actually," Daddy admitted, "that's exactly what he needs, an engineering degree in aeronautics."

"He looked into the availability of aeronautics training a few years ago, but everyone said the best way to learn was to join the Air Force. Unfortunately, he had his heart set on being a Marine and assumed there would be time enough to do both. Now it's too late," Amanda sighed. "Even if there is such a school, it would cost a fortune. I guess we could sell the house at Saranac Lake, but I don't think he'd agree to it. I do know Albert Einstein recently bought a summer place not far from ours. That might help it sell…"

"You don't have to sell the lakeside house," Andy interrupted. "He can go to college anywhere he wants on the GI Bill – and get a federal stipend to cover living expenses while he goes. We need to investigate good engineering schools with aeronautics programs."

"I can tell you right now, he won't agree if it means leaving Lila."

"Well then," said Mama, "we'll have to talk him into marrying her so she can go along."

"I hope it turns out to be that simple," Amanda sighed.

"Have a little faith, Baby. If I'm willing to talk your brother into marrying Lila, the least he can do is agree to it." We realized at that moment Andy was more involved with Amanda than we suspected.

"Now, let's decide who's going to do what. I know Mama and Mick will be glad to help. Hazel will too, for that matter. She can type letters to major universities asking who has the kind of program he needs."

Having plotted a course for rescuing Garret, we set about devouring Mama's ham and green pepper Spanish spaghetti. To cap our success, she served Daddy's favorite dessert, lemon meringue pie.

**

"It's a non-profit school in Miami, Florida, established in 1939, according to the Dean's secretary. It's called the Embry-Riddle School of Aviation and it has a civilian pilot's training program. There are also alternatives for those who don't actually intend to fly, in case Garret's handicap rules it out, such as air traffic management or the building and maintenance of airplanes. It sounds ideal to me," Hazel said, enthusiastically.

"Now all we have to do is convince him he wants to go," Amanda said. "I think Lila should be the one to tell him. She'll do anything to help Garret, even if it means a temporary separation."

"I disagree," Daddy retorted. "She'll get it all tangled up with female feelings. No! Mick and Andy and I should approach him in a businesslike manner."

"Don't be ridiculous," Mama said. "We should all be there so he feels supported."

"That many of us might spook him," Lucille said, sensibly. "I think we should limit it to no more than two people – preferably Lila and Amanda."

Mick agreed, as did my sisters and I, though we were pretty sure our vote wouldn't count.

The final decision was to invite Lila over and ask her opinion. She came as soon as Mama called, telling Garret, who'd grown uncharacteristically possessive, that she was going to help Mama with a recipe. Her expression became apprehensive when she saw us sitting around the table like a grand jury, and she demanded to know what we were up to.

"Don't get defensive. This is for your own good, as well as Garret's," Mama assured her – instantly arousing Lila's suspicions.

"We think we've found a way for Garret to pursue his dream of owning an airline. There's a school in Miami that offers a degree in aeronautical engineering. Money is no object thanks to the GI bill."

"Have you lost your mind? I just spent six months trying to find him. Why would I encourage him to go away again?"

"That's the best part," Lucille assured her. "You can go with him. All you have to do is rent a cozy little apartment nearby. He'll be through before you know it, and once his career is established, you'll never have to worry about him going away again."

"I don't know…I need time to see what's transiting his 10th house of career…"

"Great God!" Daddy roared. "Don't you recognize a golden opportunity when you see one? Forget about the stars and think about Garret. I've never seen a boy more in need of an avocation."

"I can make him a lot happier than owning his own business," Lila countered, shaken by the force of Daddy's words.

"It could mean a wonderful future for both of you," Mama added, more diplomatically. "As soon as he finishes school, you can start a family. You've always said you wanted children,"

"I see the logic in what you're saying, but what if his dream requires more hope and energy than he can muster. The last doctor he saw at Walter Reed said he's shell shocked and could easily become suicidal if he enters the work-a-day world before he's ready. I think we should give him more time. Hell, it's hard enough for him to adjust to living with me, much less the two of us packing up and moving to Florida. Give him another month to rest and if he shows any sign of improvement, I'll present the possibility of going to Embry-Riddle to him. But I will not, under any circumstance, pressure him into going."

"That sounds fair to me," Amanda said, relieved for her brother's sake.

Everyone else agreed, so Daddy had no choice but to go along.

Chapter 29

Lila was getting rid of a ten year collection of metaphysical paraphernalia to make room for Garret's belongings in the three story house they'd recently rented. She invited my sisters and me to sort through a stack of exotic Indian outfits intended for psychic readings but which she'd never had the nerve to wear. We were sitting on her living room floor, luxuriating in brightly colored tulle and silk when we heard Garret come in from his physical therapy session. At first, we paid little attention – until the volume suddenly escalated. Garret had apparently brought in the mail.

"Why is there a packet from Emory-Riddle Aeronautics School addressed to me?"

"I was sitting around talking to Claudia and Thurston the other day, and the subject of you investing in a commercial airline came up."

"Came up? I barely know those people. The only way it could come up would be for you to bring it up."

"If you must know, it was Amanda who encouraged them to look into schools for you. By the time they let me in on it, Hazel had already suggested Emory-Riddle. I don't know what you're making such a fuss about. All they want to do is help."

"I don't need their help – or anybody else's."

"You may not need help, but you do need something positive to focus on. All you do is sit around complaining about things you can't fix. You need a project - a goal to work toward. There's so much you're still capable of."

"Thanks for noticing. I'd never have figured it out for myself."

I expected Lila to burst into tears, but instead, she said, "Do you really think you can experience the loss of your limbs and not need assistance from the people around you...at least in the beginning?"

"When I need help, I'll ask for it. In the meantime, I'd

appreciate being allowed to manage my own affairs."

"Are you asking me to tell them never mind about school?"

"What does it sound like I'm saying?"

"There's no need to be sarcastic."

"Sarcastic? Furious is more like it."

"Well, what *are* you going to do for a living?"

There was a moment of dead silence – then the slamming of a door.

We tiptoed into the kitchen. "Maybe we should come back later," Marjorie suggested, in keeping with our conflict avoidant natures.

"No. I'm tired of walking on egg shells. He doesn't have to go to school if he doesn't want to, but he does have to allow me to suggest it. I can't spend the rest of my life afraid of saying the wrong thing. Come on. Let's bundle up the stuff you want."

We were shoving our treasures into paper bags when the door opened and Garret walked in. "I'll see you girls later," Lila said, literally shooing us out the door.

**

In September, 1945, Garret enrolled in the Embry-Riddle School of Aviation, and he proposed to Lila. My sisters and I felt more sad than happy, for the move to Florida meant they'd be joining Danny and Hugh Pillstick as absentees from our group around the table.

Garret still woke up sweating, shaking, and searching for his legs, but Lila convinced him the cure was to immerse himself completely in building airplanes and raising a family. Mama insisted on giving them a reception after their brief, private ceremony at the Justice of the Peace. Amanda baked a two tiered wedding cake using Mama's coconut icing recipe, and Lucille contributed dozens of chocolate raspberry petit-fours.

I was sitting on the front steps listening to Garret and Daddy talk about incidentals when Garret suddenly blurted out, "How do you make it enough?"

As though he'd expected the question, Daddy responded, "The first thing you have to do is get over expecting it to be.

Nothing ever is. Marriage is dreary days of riding a streetcar to the same dull job and coming home to noisy kids and the odor of Clorox from damp laundry drying near the furnace in the cellar. It's watching a woman with thickening ankles shuffle around the kitchen in scuffs, listing the crimes committed by the children as though you were actually interested."

Garret was speechless and I was heartbroken to learn how intolerable we noisy kids made Daddy's days. The positive part of sitting on the front steps with my father was his assumption that I was not only invisible but hard-of-hearing, making me privy to a plethora of adult secrets. The bad thing was that it almost always made me cry.

"Still..." he continued after a ponderous sigh, "every now and then she'll put on that blue chiffon dress and rouge her cheeks and we'll walk to North Avenue to see the latest Errol Flynn swashbuckler, and you'll imagine you're that hero on the screen - until she spoils it all by talking about Garland's runny nose on the way home. And you'll desperately want a drink - but you know you can't have one. And just when you decide there's no way you can do this the rest of your life, one of the kids needs help with arithmetic or a jar needs opening, and you suddenly realize they need you and there's nothing you can do about it. Once you surrender to that, it somehow becomes enough."

I found myself wishing Daddy had gone away to war. It might have helped him appreciate his family a little more. For Garret's part, he seemed at a complete loss for words. Fortunately, they called us in so he and Lila could cut the cake, but I couldn't help wondering whether Daddy's talk had dampened Garret's tenuous belief in the merits of marriage.

Chapter 30

Betsy and I volunteered to help Lila and Garrett pack for their pilgrimage to Florida. She was in a lighthearted mood, humming cheerfully, sensing that her lifelong dream was within her grasp. She had baked scones and made weak coffee with lots of cream for Betsy and me to build up our energy.

"Are you excited about going to school," I asked Garret, who sat at the table picking at his plate, wearing an expression that would have passed for utter indifference had it not been for his tormented eyes. He slid them toward mine in slow motion.

"What did you say?"

"Are you looking forward to learning to make airplanes?"

"Make airplanes? Yes. I suppose so."

I immediately looked at Lila, expecting her to react to his peculiarly vacant response. But she was so caught up in the excitement of the move, she didn't seem to notice. "I don't mean to rush you girls, but we have tons to pack before the sun goes down. We'll be driving all night as it is to get there by tomorrow."

I wolfed down my scone and followed Lila and Betsy as they picked their way through stacks of astrology books all over the living room floor. In a slightly elevated position on the sofa sat a King James Version of the Bible and an Episcopal hymnal. Mama once told me Episcopalians were allowed to do whatever they wanted. I guess that's why Lila could dabble in astrology without feeling guilty. "When you finish the books, you can go to work on the linen closet. I wish Mick would hurry up with those boxes. I'm ready to start on the kitchen."

Betsy and I had just filled the few we had left when Garret come upstairs from the cellar, where he'd been packing tools. He asked Lila if she'd run to the store for a bottle of aspirin.

"There's a brand new bottle in the upstairs medicine cabinet. I'll run get it for you."

Garret managed to avoid eye contact with Betsy and me until

Lila returned. "I guess you're right. The bottle's empty. I could have sworn it was full."

"Maybe the girls should ride along with you to the store," Garret mumbled, woodenly.

"No need for them to do that – unless they want to go," she said, glancing toward us.

"That's okay; we'll keep working," Betsy said, much to my disappointment.

Having filled our boxes, we were struggling to tuck in the flaps when we heard what sounded like a chair falling over in the cellar.

"What was that?" Betsy asked, her green eyes widening. Neither of us felt comfortable alone in the house with Garret - not that we thought he'd harm us. We were afraid he'd do something we wouldn't know how to handle.

"It sounded like he fell down," I whispered.

"He didn't fall," Betsy said. "And why are you whispering?"

"I don't know," I said, raising my voice to a shrill squeak. "It sounded like a chair falling over. One of us should go check on Garret."

"Lila can check on him when she gets home. We're supposed to work on the linen closet."

"But if he fell and hurt himself, Lila will be mad at us for not helping him."

"Well, you can go if you want, but I'm staying here."

"I'm not going by myself."

"Don't be silly. There's nothing down there that can hurt you."

"Then there's no reason for you not to come with me."

"I don't like cellars," Betsy admitted, defensively.

"Neither do I, and if you don't go with me, I'll tell Lila you made me go by myself."

Betsy heaved a sigh. "Okay, but you go first."

"You're the oldest," I reminded her. Marjorie and Betsy were first in line to get diphtheria shots, so it seemed reasonable that she be ahead of me on other scary occasions."

"It was your idea, so if you want me to go, you'll have to go first."

I tiptoed to the cellar door and slowly turned the knob. The staircase was dark as pitch. "Why did he turn off the lights?"

"How should I know? Maybe he's taking a nap. He did say he had a headache."

"Nobody takes a nap in the cellar. There's no bed."

"When were you in Lila's cellar?" Betsy asked.

"I wasn't, but I've never seen a cellar with a bed in it."

"Let's get this over with," she grumbled, anxiety fueling her impatience.

I started down the steps, carefully holding onto the crusty plaster wall, each step creaking like brittle bones. When we reached the bottom, I called softly to Garret. There was no response. Glancing around, I saw a coal bin on the left, blocking the light from a tiny window used to send sooty chunks of anthracite swooshing down the shoot. Just to the right stood a fat, asbestos wrapped furnace. Next, we came to rows of wooden shelves filled with shiny gray tools. "It doesn't look like he packed a single thing," I whispered to Betsy, who was by this time trembling.

"Hurry up," she whispered back.

We were inching our way to the far end of the cellar when we saw the shadow of something swaying side to side. That was followed by a raspy groan, like a rope swing stretching under a child's weight on a windy day. We'd just marshaled the courage to take another step when we heard a dull thud. We both screamed and began trampling each other, clawing our way up the stairs. At the top, we slammed into Mick and Lucille, who'd been calling our names, but we were too frightened to hear them.

Betsy rattled off everything we'd seen and heard in a taut, anxious voice, while I clung to Lucille's dress, shaking so hard my teeth chattered.

"Stay here, all of you," Mick said, hurrying down cellar steps, expecting to rescue Garret from the rafters.

We cackled like nervous chickens as Lucille did her best to calm us down. "Where is Lila?" she finally asked.

Before we could answer, Mick called, "All three of you, get down here." Lucille led us down the stairs, now dimly lit by an overhead bulb in the back of the cellar. Hanging from a piece of clothesline thrown over a wooden plank in the ceiling were two hams swaying ever so slightly as they cured in the dry, drafty basement. They'd been dangling there since long before Lila moved in and a third one had just fallen from its mooring.

As we struggled to get over our humiliation, Betsy and I asked at the same time, "Where's Garret?"

"I was hoping you'd be able to tell me," Mick answered. Just then, we heard Lila and Daddy calling our names from the top of the stairs. He had rented a truck, and she was in a hurry to start loading it.

"Don't either of you mention what you thought you saw in the cellar," Lucille cautioned. "We don't want to scare Lila for nothing."

"Yes, ma'am," we answered, relieved to be deserting the scene without discovering a body.

"Garret," Lila called down the cellar steps. "I brought your aspirin."

"I don't think he's down there," Mick said.

"He must have gone upstairs to lie down. I'll be right back."

When she returned, she still had the unopened bottle in her hand. "The only thing he packed was a suitcase full of clothes. His half of the closet is empty..." she cried, cupping her hands over her mouth, trying to hold back tears. Lucille did her best to be comforting. The question on all our minds was why he'd taken off with such a bright future in front of him. Daddy suddenly took a leadership role, perhaps because he'd initiated the idea of Garret enrolling in school and felt responsible. "We can check with Embry-Riddle to find out whether or not he shows up for registration. If he does, I'll drive you and your belongings to Florida myself."

In the weeks that followed, Amanda and Andy appointed themselves the official investigative committee. My sisters and I were assigned the task of taping up descriptions of Garret in grocery and drug stores windows, as well as the lobby of all three theaters on North Avenue. A dark movie house seemed like the ideal place for him to spend lonely afternoons. Even Stanley Polanski rose to the occasion, pinning one of our descriptions to the sun visor on the passenger's side of his cab.

By the end of the month, Lila was losing hope. As a last resort, she approached Amanda about renting the Saranac Lake house for a year in case Garret showed up there. Amanda agreed but insisted that she pay nothing. In early July, she and Andy borrowed Mick's car and drove Lila to the empty yellow house on the lake.

Chapter 31

On the three month anniversary of his most recent sobriety, Daddy put four hundred dollars down on a used 1940 Chevrolet sedan – the first car he'd owned since marrying Mama. It had wide cloth seats and looked more like a fat red beetle than the square Model Ts we were used to. Like most factories in the '40's, Daddy's shut down for a week's vacation during the month of July. Since we'd be out of school, Mama decided the time had come to go home again.

When Aunt Belle heard the news, she invited us to stay at her mini mansion in Buford, South Carolina. She even talked my grandfather out of shooting Daddy if he dropped us off on his way to Leesville to visit his mother, about fifty miles south of Aunt Belle's.

Lucille bought us new shoes so Mama wouldn't have to cover the holes in the soles with cereal box cardboard. Lila contributed the material for Mama to make new skirts and blouses for my sisters and me. Even Garland got a new pair of short pants that buttoned onto his shirt, thanks to Hazel. The only problem was the war induced shortage of gasoline. Cars were gas gobblers in those days despite the 35 mile an hour speed limit on most highways.

Bernie taped a sign to the front of his cash register asking anyone with leftover gas to let him know by Friday afternoon. Between that and Stanley's extra taxi supply, we were able to get enough to fill the tank plus several cans for refills. Uncle Brice assured us he had enough contacts to provide fuel for the trip home. My sisters and I felt a little guilty, having been told by our teachers that conserving gas and other resources was not only important to winning the War, it was critical to the clean up and rebuilding efforts in Europe and the Pacific Islands. But I thought about all the fudge we'd missed because of butter and sugar rationing and was able to sooth my conscience.

We headed south on Route 1 and by the time we crossed into

North Carolina, we were choking on the dry top soil that blew in the windows as we droned along endless ribbons of hot highway. Finally, after eight hours, including a restaurant and bathroom break, we entered South Carolina, where fields of corn and cotton separated patches of pencil pines as high as the darkening sky. By the time we pulled into Buford, crickets were chirping and a million lightning bugs twinkled like golden night-lights in our faces. We were sweaty and exhausted but still excited.

Aunt Belle was suffering from a bout of cirrhosis of the liver, and her milk white skin had a decidedly yellow tint. Uncle Brice was warm and welcoming but smelled noticeably of alcohol – which I found disturbing. He'd been transferred to duty at the local recruiting office following a shrapnel wound while stationed in Germany.

Their house sat on twenty acres of old plantation and had four white columns and a porch that ran all the way around. The rooms were huge, high ceilinged, and beautifully furnished in elegant Victorian – thanks to the former owner and not anything Aunt Belle was interested in. There was a maid who served breakfast after which Daddy left for Leesville to see his mother.

Too sick to make the trip, Aunt Belle went back to bed and we headed for Spartanburg, where she and Mama had grown up. Uncle Brice talked all the way there about Aunt Belle's decline into alcoholism and her three admissions to the hospital for cirrhosis flare-ups. I wanted desperately to remind him of his own drinking but instead, added it to a long list of things I would one day regret not saying.

We pulled up in front of a modest but beautifully gardened single story house. Standing in the doorway of the screened in porch was a commanding figure, six feet two, lean and tanned, with a hawk nose and snow white hair. It was T. W. Silby in person. He shook hands with Uncle Brice, gave my mother an awkward hug, and was formally introduced to his grandchildren. As angular as he was, my grandmother was soft and round - four feet nine inches tall, soft spoken and gracious.

While Mama got reacquainted with her parents, Garland and I took ourselves on a tour of the back yard. To our amazement, it was filled with chickens. A wire barrier separated the hens and their egg-laying coups from the biddies – baby chicks who needed to be protected from the rooster. I made an immediate impression on my Grandfather by opening the gate, allowing the biddies to mix with the hens, sending the rooster into a clawing, screeching fit. Garland tried to save the day by catching the rooster and got soundly pecked for his trouble. Granddaddy spent the next hour re-separating his chickens.

We made our way back to the house and found Marjorie and Betsy admiring the Bavarian china and sterling silver knives and forks. The tablecloth and napkins were pale peach linen, and the glasses were crystal. Betsy whispered, "You'd think they were entertaining the Queen Mother and the King of England."

My grandmother had selected two small chickens for dinner and we covered our eyes when the maid chopped off their heads and plucked out their feathers. Dessert consisted of fresh sugar-figs picked by Marjorie and Betsy from bushes in the backyard. After dinner, we were astonished to learn we were expected to lie down for an hour while the maid cleaned up the kitchen. Having no concept of household servants, Marjorie and Betsy kept getting up and trying to talk the maid into letting them do the dishes.

Garland slept in the guest room with Mama, and my sisters and I slept in my grandmother's four poster bed. Before joining granddaddy in his room, she sat down at her vanity, unpinned the bun at the nape of her neck, and began running a silver brush through her knee length brown hair – which she swore had never been cut. Then she pulled it over one shoulder and plaited it into a thick, glossy braid. It was like watching a scene from "Gone With the Wind."

About mid afternoon the next day, my mother's oldest sister Enid arrived to take us to her place for dinner. They lived in a wandering L shaped house that was so long, I had trouble finding my way back from the bathroom. Aunt Enid had married a land wealthy real estate broker with a huge belly and a bombastic voice. Since those most interested in buying houses were overseas, he simply sold a few acres when they needed money, or borrowed from my grandfather - which we later learned all his children did from time to time…except my mother.

Enid and Mama seemed more like distant cousins than

sisters, greeting each other in a friendly but formal manner. Aunt Enid had a son who would grow up to be a gifted screenplay writer and a daughter named Gloria, who formed an instant attachment to Marjorie, insisting that she spend the night. After dinner, we sat on the front porch and ate boiled peanuts until our ankles swelled from the salt and heat.

It was well past dark by the time we returned to my grandmother's, but it didn't matter. We were too excited to sleep, for Mama was taking us to meet our Lee County grandmother the following day.

**

If you blinked, you would miss Leesville altogether. It had one locally owned restaurant but no store large enough to require a sign to identify its location. There was a Methodist Church which Daddy attended as a child, an opera house, a row of mansions - one of which had been designed by my great-grandfather - several blocks of ordinary houses, and a cemetery with a bronze plaque listing soldiers who'd lost their lives in World War I.

We turned down a dirt road that ran along the train track until we came to a weather worn house that had not seen a paint brush since Daddy went away to school. I immediately thought of the posters we'd seen on telephone poles asking for donations to the poor people of Appalachia.

We stepped directly from a tiny front porch into a tinier living room. In the far corner, sitting in a creaky wicker rocking chair, was the oldest woman I'd ever seen. Her hair was snow white and her face, wrinkled as seersucker. Seated next to her was my Aunt Lorena, alternately waving a cardboard fan in my grandmother's face and her own.

There were two characteristics that set Aunt Lorena apart from our other aunts. She was morbidly obese, gasping every time she stood up, and she bellowed when she talked. She had spent the last twenty-five years taking care of my grandmother, her own brother Felix, whom we'd yet to meet, and two younger sisters who escaped to Charleston for better job opportunities as soon as they were old enough. We later learned Lorena had made a deal with my father whereby she would work to pay his tuition through business school in Poughkeepsie, New York, and he would come back and help support Uncle Felix and their two younger sisters. Instead, Daddy married a red-haired beauty named Ruby who immediately got pregnant with my half-brother Danny, leaving Aunt Lorena to support her entire family on a pittance of a teacher's salary.

Daddy came in from the back yard with an unusually short man whose thick black hair appeared never to have been combed. His facial features were asymmetrical and his black/brown eyes harbored a blank history. He held up a bottle Daddy had apparently bought him and said, "Coke." He was introduced to us as Uncle Felix, and we soon discovered he'd been born with a cleft palate. Although his words were barely discernible, he had a generous grin and a warm handshake. My brother Garland, whose heart of gold I was too young to appreciate, instantly became his adoring shadow, keeping my uncle entertained throughout our visit.

There was one other malady Uncle Felix suffered from which was not as easy to work around. He'd been run over at age six by a horse and buggy, and it left him with chronic epileptic seizures.

Aunt Lorena insisted we each chat with our grandmother who was partly blind but mostly deaf. We had to speak through a hearing horn attached to a tube with an ear piece on the end. Betsy and I were never able to get more than a shrill "huh" in response to telling her our names and ages. Aunt Lorena finally hollered "These are bubba's girls," and that seemed to satisfy our familial obligation to be sociable.

Daddy took Betsy and me on a tour of the house and we were horrified to learn their only source of water was a back porch pump. Even worse, the bathroom was a backyard outhouse filled with spider webs and wasps, and we were expected to sit on a board with a hole in it. I vowed I would not drink water or go to the bathroom for as long as I was required to stay.

Unexpected relief came in the form of Mama's sister-in-law who picked me up that afternoon to spend the next two days at her house. If I'd known what disquiet lay in store for Betsy, I might have refused to leave her – but then again, my revulsion for the pump and outhouse may have led me to forsake her anyway.

My mother's only brother Tom had incurred my

grandfather's wrath by marrying a model from New York he met while stationed in Paris. She had a daughter named Linda exactly my age, with whom I spent the next two days riding bikes to the Elks Club pool to swim. Aunt Millie only ate two meals daily: a Hershey bar for breakfast and scrambled eggs for supper, so determined was she not to lose her seventeen inch waist. I thought she was cooler than cornbread and hated having to return to Aunt Belle's to reunite with Daddy for the trip home.

On our way back to Baltimore, my sisters were uncharacteristically quiet, each processing the strangeness of our first look at a world beyond 24th Street. Mama suddenly asked Marjorie what she enjoyed most about the trip.

Marjorie thought for a minute and said "The lives they lead. Aunt Enid calls her friends every afternoon just to chat. Gloria and her friends get their licenses at fourteen and drive brand new cars up and down Main Street barefooted, laughing and waving to each other. They swim at the Country Club and have Birthday teas for each other where they play Bridge and Canasta. They walk uptown to the picture show and stop at the Dry Goods Store to see if anything new has come in since they last rummaged through the racks. From there, they walk to Lawson's Drugstore for a chocolate malted milk shake. They sleep in shorty pajamas and have their hair done at the beauty parlor. That's the way I'm going to live when I grow up."

"What about you?" Mama asked Betsy. "What did you enjoy most at Grandmother Dunn's?" A flood of words poured out of Betsy's mouth. "It was awful. They have enamel chamber pots they keep under the bed in case you have to tinkle during the night. They have no running water, so you have to brush your teeth at the back porch pump. The house is hotter than Hades and you can't take a bath to cool off. The next-door neighbor installed the electricity and the light switches shock you when you turn them on. I woke up in the middle of the night to a loud crash and found Uncle Felix lying flat on his back, foaming at the mouth, shaking like he would fly to pieces. Aunt Lorena took us swimming in a muddy pond that smelled like algae and my ear's been hurting ever since. You have to drive all the way to Sumter if you want to see a picture show, and Uncle Felix sleeps in his under drawers. When I grow up, I want everything they don't have at Grandmother Dunn's."

"Well," Mama stammered, "next time we'll make sure you spend more time in Spartanburg with Mother and Daddy."

She didn't ask me what I liked best so I pondered the question in my mind and said to no one in particular, "Most of all, I loved trying on my cousin Linda's toe-taps and dancing on the kitchen linoleum. When I grow up, I'm going to be Debbie Reynolds."

Grandmother Dunn

Chapter 32

Front step rumor had it that the 1936 version of the movie "Show Boat" was about to be re-released. Mama's favorite actress was Irene Dunne, and she deeply regretted missing her in the role of Magnolia "Nolie" Hawks, daughter of the show boat's owner, the first time it played in Baltimore theaters. The theme of the movie was race, and it brought into focus the laws that prevented blacks from participating in activities that might alter their status – such as performing before a white audience or marrying a Caucasian.

Set in 1887, the movie opens with the lead singer of the Cotton Blossom learning that the town sheriff is on his way to arrest his wife, Julie La Verne, a beautiful bi-racial woman, for miscegenation. Reminding the others that it takes only one drop of Negro blood to call a white man black, her husband takes out his pocket knife and slashes Julie's hand, swallowing the blood that would legally render him a Negro. The sheriff cannot arrest Julie, once Cap'n Andy and his wife Parthy swear her husband has black blood in his veins.

The high point in the movie is the song "Ol' Man River," sung by Paul Robeson. The words reflect the river's complete indifference to the injustices born by the black man. Based on Edna Ferber's book, the words and music were written by Jerome Kern and Oscar Hammerstein. Nothing bordering on the subject of race relations had ever been presented in a Broadway musical, and it unquestionably opened the public's eyes to the tragic stigma of being black in America. Because of this, Mama concluded that Vera Washington would be thrilled if she took her to see it.

Like public schools, movie theaters were segregated in the 1930's and 40's, as were hospitals, restaurants, swimming pools, and drinking fountains. This meant that Vera would have to be smuggled into the picture show disguised as a white woman. Despite Mama's conviction that Vera would appreciate the opportunity, common sense whispered that she ought to run it by the girls before bringing it up.

Raised on a cattle farm, Hazel's only contact with blacks had been Saturday morning trips with her parents to Kansas City for supplies. Still, she intuitively sensed that Vera would view disguising herself as demeaning. She labeled the idea a bad one, and my sisters and I, who were only partially contaminated by racial biases, agreed with her.

Brynn, who happened to be home on leave, instantly bought into the challenge of creating the perfect outfit for Vera and voted that it would do no harm if Mama presented it as an adventure she could tell her grandchildren about.

Lila was almost as cursed as I was when it came to getting trapped between the merits of two points of view. "First and foremost," she said, "Vera is a Leo, so anything that threatens her pride, like dressing up to hide who she is, will be met with fierce resistance. On the other hand, her Mars in Sagittarius makes her a perpetual student of human behavior. If she decides to go it will be for the sole purpose of better understanding what leads white folks to draw such arbitrary lines between races. I think Vera will be equally torn between both options, wanting to see the movie and preserving her innate dignity."

Lucille supported Lila's opinion but couldn't help adding, "The average American thinks of Africans the way Hollywood portrays them in Tarzan movies, as a land of foot stomping savages with shrunken heads around their necks. We do not question it because it's Hollywood, and Hollywood can sell us any fabrication – until we know better. But they have also given us Hattie McDaniel, Paul Robeson, Nat King Cole, and Lena Horne, opening our lily white souls to the warmth, grace, and power of the human spirit when viewed from the heart rather than skin."

"So, are you saying I should or shouldn't invite Vera to go see "Show Boat" when it comes out?"

"I don't have the slightest idea what you ought to do," Lucille laughed. "But I don't think I would, if it were me."

**

Surrounded by her children, Mama walked up Lorraine

Avenue to Vera's homegrown ice-cream store to invite her to the picture show.

Once we were ensconced on the front steps with our ice-cream cones, Mama said, "Remember when you told me your life's dream was to see Paul Robeson perform "Othello" at the Savoy Theater in London?"

"I remember," Vera said, disappearing momentarily into hero worship and wishful thinking.

"Well, if I told you there was an opportunity to see him on the screen singing "Ol' Man River," would you be interested in going?"

"Would I be interested? I'd like to see anybody stop me," she laughed.

"Well, I can make it possible. All you have to do is agree to go."

Suspecting it was too good to be true, Vera said, "Tell me more."

"The movie "Show Boat" is being re-released sometime this summer to a handful of theaters in the Baltimore area, and I want to take you to see it."

"It's not possible. You can go see it, and I can go see it, but we can't both go see it in the same theater."

"That's the best part," Mama laughed, warming to her subject. "All we have to do is disguise you as a white woman, and we can go see it together. Brynn will help design your outfit. A high collar, a wide-brimmed hat, and a little peaches and cream make-up, and you'll be set to go."

Vera appeared dumbstruck. She stood up and began pacing up and down the sidewalk in front of us, making soft guttural sounds. "Uhm-humn, uhm-humn." Every now and then, she paused and gaped at my mother as though she were from an alien planet. Finally, she stopped and stared her straight in the eye.

"Are you crazy?"

"I thought you'd like the idea."

"You must be crazy."

"It's a really good movie, and you love Paul Robeson."

"Tell you what I'll do," Vera said, enunciating as distinctly as Winston Churchill. "The day you paint your face black and go with me to see Cab Calloway at the Cotton Club in New York City is the day I'll don a blond wig and go to see "Show Boat" at an all white movie theater."

Mama looked shocked, then confused, then deflated, and I couldn't help feeling sorry for her. She was guiltier of insensitivity than she was malice. But that didn't make Vera feel any better. Finally, in an effort to cheer Mama up, I said, "Maybe Vera doesn't like peaches and cream make-up."

Chapter 33

On Tuesday morning, my history teacher told us we were going to have a test the following day. History was my favorite subject, so I went to school Wednesday despite a mild pain in my right side. She began the day by postponing the test until Thursday, at which time the pain had progressed from severe to relentless.

On Thursday, she rescheduled the test for Friday, and by that evening, the pain was so intense, I burst into tears when Mama fussed at me for not eating my peas. At Daddy's urging, she called the doctor who diagnosed it as a probable hot appendix and told her to take me to the hospital. Mama tried to convince him she could cure me with laxatives, but the doctor suggested she only try that if she wanted to kill me.

Daddy drove us to Sinai Hospital where they wasted no time prepping me for surgery. After it was over, the surgeon told Mama my appendix was gangrenous and I would have died within two hours if she had not brought me in. My mother looked at him with as much forbearance as she could muster and said, "Oh, surely not."

Daddy had an irrational fear of hospitals and only visited once during my five day internment. He handed me a Wonder Woman comic book, asked if I needed anything, and hurried out the door.

Since Lucille and Mick no longer occupied the third floor, Mama banished my sisters to their vacated rooms to make sure they couldn't accidently kick me in the side turning over. I had to stay on the same floor as the bathroom for a week, so I got to sleep in their room all by myself. Hazel and Amanda took turns stopping by each day to fix my lunch and help me hobble to the bathroom to wash up.

On the fourth day of my in-home recovery, Aunt Lorena called to say Grandmother Dunn was dying and Daddy needed to come right away. It was so quiet in my newly privatized room I could hear my parents discussing it without having to crawl to the foot of the bed.

"This will make the third time you've gone to South Carolina for her funeral," Mama reminded him. "Do you think she means it this time?"

"I thought she meant it last time," Daddy said, defensively.

"I know you did. Men just don't have good intuition when it comes to life and death – not the way women do."

"I'm not a mind reader. All I can do is trust Lorena's evaluation of the situation."

"I'm not blaming you. I just don't want you to waste another trip. If you do decide to go, take Silby with you and kill two birds with one stone. Amanda and Hazel are running themselves ragged checking on her every day."

"A funeral's no place for a twelve year old."

"Neither is lying around an empty house all day. If it gets to be too much for her, she can lie down in Lorena's room."

"But it's a ten hour drive. Surely the doctor won't give you permission..."

"I'm not planning to ask him. We can make a comfortable bed for her on the back seat. She'll probably sleep all the way there."

"Maybe she won't want to go," Daddy reasoned, optimistically.

Next day, when Mama asked what I thought, I expressed horror at the idea. "They have an outhouse with spiders in it."

"Not anymore. Lorena put in a bathroom and indoor plumbing right after our visit. And your Uncle Felix is in a nursing home thanks to the generosity of his Charleston sisters. It would just be you and Daddy, Lorena, and her cats."

I weighed the negative side of Aunt Lorena's house against the benefits of getting to spend all day riding in the car with Daddy and decided I wanted to go.

We set out around 5 am, hoping to reach Leesville by sundown. Daddy kept the car radio on so he only had to talk to me during bathroom pullovers. Since I couldn't bring myself to ask him to stop, I spent much of the trip with a bursting bladder praying he would have to go soon.

Mama was right about the outhouse. Aunt Lurena had added a pea-green bathroom with a tub and a shallow metal sink with separate spigots in the kitchen. The funeral home had picked up Grandmother Dunn's body that morning, but there was no way to let Daddy know she had passed. He seemed to take it casually and put his suitcase in Uncle Felix's room. I followed mine to the foot of Lorena's bed and saw Grandmother Dunn's hearing horn lying on the pillow like a shrine.

"Is that where I'm supposed to sleep?" I blurted out. "I can't sleep where a dead person slept." When they both ignored me, I resolved to sleep on top of the covers until Aunt Lorena dozed off then sneak out of bed to the living room sofa. My next big challenge was the funeral itself.

Short of a threat to my life at the hands of my father, I resolved not to look at Grandmother Dunn's body. To my dismay, when we got to the funeral home, the crowd parted like the Dead Sea to make way for my father and me nearer the casket. I grabbed my side, screwed up my face, and pretended to be in pain. Daddy took me to the secretary's office on whose lounge I curled up for the remainder of the service.

"Don't be embarrassed about not wanting to look at the dead, Sugar," said a cheery bleached-blonde with bubble-gum pink lipstick and huge aqua eyes. "I can't look at them either."

"But you work here," I reminded her.

"That's right," Sugar. I work right here in this office. You won't find me roaming around where I might stumble onto one of them."

"I'm afraid she'll look dead," I confessed, not even certain what I meant.

"I know what cha' mean. They make up their faces, but it doesn't make them look alive. I think it was brave of you to refuse to look."

"I didn't. My appendix was just taken out, so I pretended my side hurt. I wish I could tell people the truth about what I want, but I'm afraid they'll be disappointed in me. I used to disappoint people all the time – until I learned to lie. I'm ashamed of doing it, but it's better than feeling wrong, which I always do when I want something they don't."

"Oh, Sugar. You need to get over that. How will anybody know who you are if they never know what you want?"

I pretended to be asleep because I didn't know the answer. Finally, the funeral was over and Daddy came to get me.

The ladies at my grandmother's church had prepared an elaborate meal and set it up in the lobby of the opera house, across from the funeral home. Daddy bumped into an old high school buddy named Roger, who happened to be Director of their Shakespearean performances. While they chatted, I studied the posters in glass cases on the walls. My grandfather Dunn, whom I'd never laid eyes on or heard anybody talk about, appeared on almost every placard. Not only had he written a humorous weekly series for the local newspaper, he had appeared in the majority of their plays until his death in the flu epidemic of 1918.

I wandered back just as Roger was telling Daddy that Rut Rutledge had called out sick and he ought to fill in for the role of Polonius. "You were a pretty good actor if I remember correctly."

"I'm sure you don't," Daddy laughed. "But I do love Hamlet." He wrestled with temptation for several minutes but concluded there was no way he could learn the lines by show-time.

"As often as you watched your dad play Hamlet, I can't believe it wouldn't come back to you – at least the gist of it. Besides, you're leaving town tonight and Mrs. Dunn has gone to meet her maker, so it's not likely you'll pass this way again. It's a golden opportunity to play a delicious part without worrying about what the local critics think."

Daddy finally accepted the script, and we drove to Aunt Lorena's to pack the car and say goodbye. We planned to head back to Baltimore as soon as the curtain came down."

Daddy sat me in the front row of the theater and went back stage to put on his costume. An elegant looking lady with bluish hair and the scent of moist lilacs sat down next to me and before long, the Leesville Opera House was buzzing with people. I asked the sweet smelling lady what the play was about.

"The King of Denmark dies under suspicious circumstances and his brother Claudius marries the king's widow and takes over the Kingdom. Hamlet, the king's son, gets so upset about it, he sees the ghost of his father and loses his mind. Later, while arguing with his mother, Hamlet thinks the man who killed his father is listening behind a curtain. He runs him through with his sword only to find he has killed a man named Polonius by mistake. Polonius has a son named Laetes. Laetes avenges his father's death by killing Hamlet with a poisonous sword, and that's about it."

"It sounds like a very sad story," I said.

"It is, honey. Maybe next time you can see one of Shakespeare's comedies. They are as funny as this one is tragic."

A few minutes later, the curtain went up and I immediately fell asleep, waking up just long enough to hear Polonius, played by Daddy, give his son Laetes advice as he is preparing to go away to college in France. After telling Laetes "Neither a borrower nor a lender be," Polonius adds one final word of advice: "This above all: to thine own self be true, and it must follow as the night the day, thou canst not then be false to any man."

The next time I woke up, the theater was cold, dark, and utterly empty. I was petrified and thought Daddy had returned to Baltimore without me. The odd thing is that it would not have surprised me. Despite the fact that I adored him in his sober moments, when he entertained us with mystical tales about life near the cypress swamps of South Carolina, I knew I figured very little in his everyday interest at home. Sad and afraid, I decided I would never be rescued if I sat in the dark crying. So I tiptoed cautiously to the far side of the stage and was relieved to see a stream of light, followed by my father's voice saying, "Don't be that way, Ruby."

I sat down in the hall floor beside the half opened door and heard Ruby reply," How do you expect me to feel. Separated less than a year and you get a teenager pregnant."

"I didn't go looking for her. Her sister Belle set me up."

"The only thing that would have surprised me less would be your getting Belle pregnant."

"It wouldn't have happened if you'd let me come home when I wanted to."

"You were still drinking and running around with night floozies. You gave me no reason to take you back. You think I wanted to raise three kids on my own?"

"That's the one thing we did right," Daddy said, his voice softening. "Danny made me proud everyday of his life." My daughter Marjorie is my Danny now. That girl has a gift for knowing the right thing to do. And she does it with grace and dignity. She's going to do something exceptional with her life."

"Well, I'm glad it worked out well for you and your teenage bride. Truth be told, I'm actually pretty happy myself these days. I've got a husband I can trust. Alvin found a job as a disc jockey on the radio, and Delores graduates from the University of South Carolina this year – not that you've ever indicated you cared."

"Speaking of caring, I've got a kid asleep out front and we have an all night drive to Baltimore. How about a kiss goodbye for old time sake?"

I could tell she'd let him kiss her. She walked out the door without saying goodbye or noticing me sitting on the floor, a lace hanky over her mouth, tears streaming down her cheeks.

The next thing I remember is waking up near Washington DC, with streaks of golden lightening ripping through dark clouds. "You want to sit out the storm having breakfast?" he asked. The only thing that might have thrilled me more would be a conversation with God.

As I dabbled in the oatmeal Daddy made me eat before the jelly donut, I asked him what false meant. It had troubled me since the play, when Polonius gave advice to his son Laetes.

"You know what false means. It's the opposite of true."

"Not that kind of false. The kind of false one person is to another person, like you told your son Laetes in the play?"

"It means what is says. If you are true to yourself, you'll find it impossible to be untrue to others."

"But…how can you be true to yourself and everybody else at the same time?"

"I don't know what you're talking about."

"Well, suppose somebody lies to keep somebody else from being disappointed in them. Are you being true to yourself as long as you know it's a lie?"

"Of course not. To be true to yourself, you have to be as honest as you can with the people around you. Otherwise, they'll think they know you when they don't, and they'll keep making the same mistakes over and over, until you think they're never going to understand you. Then you'll quit being friends with them, and they won't have the slightest idea why. It's like wearing a mask and expecting people to recognize you anyway. It sounds to me like the person you are talking about wants to be liked more than she wants to tell the truth."

"I guess it is kind of unfair. It never occurred to me that I'm not helping them know what I want if I keep lying about it. So that means I have to be true to them so they can be true to me so I can be true to myself."

"Something like that," Daddy laughed.

"Then I'm right back where I started. I still have to tell them I want something they may not want, so I'll still be wrong – at least to them."

"But what if they are wrong and you are right? Most everything people disagree about is a matter of beliefs taught by parents, teachers, preachers, and friends, which means they could just as easily have been taught the opposite. People take themselves and their opinions far too seriously and see right and wrong where it is only a matter of early influence and personal desires. You can spend your life pretending to agree with everybody around you – which means they get to live their life and yours too. Or you can tell yourself you are entitled to want something else because you are you and they are not. That is being true to yourself. When you can do that, you won't have to spend all your time keeping up appearances and false fronts. Do you understand?"

"I think so. I'm just not sure I can do it."

"What the hell is wrong with you?" he shouted. "Don't you have any gumption?"

That unexpected flash of impatience took me back to his drinking days and an episode that occurred when I was five or six. I was sitting on the cellar steps watching him turn splintery wood into fine grained furniture when he suddenly picked up his hatchet and a tiny piece of wood. He stood the piece of wood – about the size of my index finger - on the step next to me. Then he told me to hold it while he split it in half with the hatchet. I blindly followed directions, trusting his carpentry skills completely. He slammed the hatchet into the step, missing my fingers by about an inch. I didn't flinch.

"What the hell is wrong with you?" he bellowed. "Only an idiot would have held that stick seeing the ax coming. Do you have to do everything people tell you to do? Why can't you stand up for yourself?"

Suddenly, I was reliving that shameful experience all over again. I sank deep into the car seat and spent the rest of the ride trying to figure out what was wrong with me. It would be years before it dawned on me that Daddy and Polonius were trying to explain the same thing to their offspring. The difference is that one of them was sober at the time. From that trip onward, I developed a distrust of happiness - a sinking feeling in the pit of my stomach whenever I caught myself laughing with complete abandon.

Chapter 34

We had stuffed ourselves with turkey and dressing and were waiting for pumpkin pie when the phone rang. Daddy answered and called, "Its long distance." Mama left the table and walked down the hall, lowering her voice. After several minutes, she returned and sat down.

"That was Brynn's mother. Her tuberculosis is in remission but she's decided to remain in Ashville for the clean air." Mama hesitated then quickly added, "Brynn's request for a transfer to the Army Corp of Engineers in England was finally granted. She was on her way to London when a thick fog set in. The pilot missed his landing, and the plane went down killing everybody on board. Brynn is dead."

The lag the brain goes through when it receives news it doesn't want to hear stunned us into silence.

Marjorie and I were deeply saddened - but Betsy was inconsolable. She and Brynn had shared the creative language of fashion and fourteen year old Betsy could not imagine who would fill the void. She continued to sob until Daddy suddenly said, "Put on your coats." Ignoring our questions about where we were going, he led us to the #10 trackless trolley. We got off when we reached Lexington Street and walked several blocks to a scene of utter chaos. They were dismantling the Thanksgiving Day parade floats and letting the air out of over-blown cartoon characters, the final one being Santa Claus and his elves. Their lifeless rubber eyes gaped at us from the still, cold sidewalk. We watched as they folded and stuffed yards of rubber bodies into crates for interment in a downtown warehouse.

I was wondering why he'd brought us to such a morbid scene when he suddenly started walking again. After several blocks, we reached a crowd of parents and children in front of Hochschild Kohn's Department Store, staring expectantly at the storefront window. The shade slowly began to rise, exposing an oversized, mechanical Santa Clause sitting in a giant chair, laughing uproariously as "You better watch out, you better not cry…" blasted through the loud speaker. The laughing Santa Claus was resurrected every year on Thanksgiving Day to attract shoppers who needed a place to park their children while they went inside to shop. It could be that Daddy was simply trying to take our minds off of Brynn's death, but I choose to believe it was a clumsy effort to help us understand death and resurrection - although I only faintly made the connection at the time.

Brynn's mother returned to Baltimore long enough to bury her daughter in Greenmount Cemetery, next to her father. The mourners included the commander of Brynn's WACS unit, our family, Lucille, Hazel, and Lila. Daddy, Mick, Andy, and Stanley served as pallbearers. It was the first funeral my sisters had ever attended and the first where I looked at the body. Seeing a ceramic-faced Brynn lying in a wooden casket caused a shock it would take years to get over.

Mama invited everyone to our house for a post burial lunch. Betsy knew Brynn's mother better than Marjorie and I did from countless afternoons watching Brynn create exotic outfits. Like Brynn, her mother was a bit of a clothes horse – though not as classy - and she had draped a shabby fox fur across one shoulder, with its sharp, shiny nose dangling over her bosom. When she saw Betsy, she rushed across the room and threw her arms around her, crushing her face into beady fox eyes. Betsy let out a yelp and pushed her away, only to be re-embraced when Brynn's mother mistook her reaction for sorrow and hugged her all the tighter. Once Betsy finally escaped, she spent the rest of the afternoon ducking behind chairs and peeking around door facings to avoid contact with the creepy fox face.

Despite Daddy's puzzling Thanksgiving parade tutorial on death and resurrection, there was one question that remained unanswered – one I was sure even he could not explain away. It haunted me all that night and for countless nights thereafter. Why had God allowed Brynn to die when she was on the verge of achieving the very thing she wanted most in life? It was a question that had troubled me when my brother Danny missed survival by four measly hours. Had they committed some unpardonable sin that caused them to deserve a premature ending? I could not for a minute accept that as true. Perhaps each had completed the central task for which they'd been born? But with all the hopes and dreams that get replaced in the face of disappointment, that seemed pretty unlikely. Was death pure random chance after all? At twelve years old, that is too frightening a possibility. I decided I was going to read the King James Version of the Bible from cover to cover – except the begats – once a year until I found the answer. I'm currently rereading the Book of Romans.

Chapter 35

The return of men from the battlefield meant women were no longer needed in munitions factories, rolling out jeep and airplane parts. Many opted for clerical positions, while others returned to the kitchen, but not for long. Economic prosperity would soon draw them into retail sales and assembly line production requiring a fine touch, such as placing pins in the hinges of metal compacts. The sale of beauty products flourished as women dressed for the office rather than the kitchen, and baby food in jars streamlined mealtime for those who had celebrated reunion with their wounded warriors by making love.

Coca Cola was in, rationing was out; butter and sugar were in grand supply. Every neighborhood soon had a bakery, relieving working mothers of the time consuming task of baking bread, cakes, pies, and cookies. The American Can Company tripled its output as the food industry rose to the demand for quick and easy meals. Frozen food would soon be as convenient as the nearest Acme.

The production of automobiles had ceased during the War due to the military demand for rubber and metal parts. But Ford and Chevrolet were soon pumping out moderately priced cars for the average working class household. Oil companies bought up the old streetcar lines and replaced them with diesel fueled busses, allowing transit to include more remote areas of the City, opening the door for an affluent, middle class suburbia.

Daddy was still recovering from his bungled attempt to guide Garret down the untested path of the post war entrepreneur, when he decided Andy should sign up for a course in economics at the University of Maryland. He resurrected his own degree in accounting and convinced Stanley they could make a fortune if they established a private taxicab chain. All they had to do was convince Mick and Lucille to put up their house as collateral to pay for a second cab and a dispatch system Amanda could operate from her house on Calvert Street.

I had reservations about the plan since it would increase contact with Stanley Polanski. I'd never forgiven him for not coming to Mama's rescue when Daddy was drinking abusively. But once I saw how tenderly he attended to baby Victoria I decided to forgive him – as long as he was good to Hazel and never saw his two make-believe wives again.

For Mama, the best part was being dropped off every day by Stanley at her new job as receptionist at the library, only one block from the school my sisters had attended and Garland and I still did. She paid Stanley back by laughing at his jokes – which had grown no funnier over the years. I loved it for I got to visit her every afternoon on the way home from school, when I returned yesterday's books and checked out new ones. The library had never held the magic for Garland it did for his sisters.

Every moment not devoted to homework, reading, or helping around the house was spent with Hazel, mailing descriptions of Garret to police departments up and down the East Coast. Once or twice a month, Daddy and Mick would take over Andy's route as second cab driver so he could run up to Saranac Lake and check on Lila. More often than not, Amanda went along, but she'd been nagged by private customers into starting her own wedding cake business when she wasn't busy dispatching cabs, and she found the five hour drive to New York increasingly tedious.

Then, one cold February morning Amanda received a phone call saying a body had been discovered in the swampy Florida everglades that resembled Garret's description, and they would like for someone to come identify him as soon as possible. Lila, Amanda, and Andy set out on their morbid journey the following morning, and I walked with Daddy to Bernie's to ask if he knew anybody who could temporarily fill in as cab driver until Andy got back. A swarthy, second generation Greek named Nicholas Darius Carras happened to be standing nearby, drinking a coke and eating a moon-pie. He appeared to be in his mid twenties and was oddly dressed in shiny black pants and a white shirt with a satin bow tie at the collar.

"I can do it," the young man bragged.

"Do you know anything about driving a cab?" Daddy asked, trying to sound professional.

Nicky grinned. "I know how to drive and pull over to the curb. What else is there?"

"I'll keep you in mind," Daddy said, turning back to Bernie, brushing off the brash young man. He would later tell Mama he found his answer a touch condescending but decided it would be unwise to reject their only applicant.

Nicky finished his coke and hurried home to tell his family what he'd done, giving Daddy a chance to ask Bernie what he really thought.

"Nicky's a good boy. He comes from a hardworking, second generation Greek family. If you want to know more about the Carrases, you should drop by their restaurant for supper one night. Everybody in the family works there, and they must enjoy it for it takes very little to get them to break into song – and sometimes dance. But the best part is they serve braised lamb with honey and almonds, which is my Gertrude's favorite."

**

The name above the door read simply "Carras Brothers" and it was located near the corner of Charles and 22nd Streets. We could have walked but Mama made Stanley take us in his taxi, insisting the six of us resembled a funeral procession. I rode with Mick and Lucille in their car.

The minute Daddy entered the restaurant Nicky rushed over in his black bow tie with menus. We threaded our way to the back, where he pushed two tables together and welcomed us enthusiastically. Betsy leaned over and whispered to Marjorie, "He's cute."

With the exception of Mick, we had all grown up on southern cooking, so words like baked moussaka and chicken souvlaki were Greek to us. Daddy knew what a gyro was, but that was as close as we came to deciphering the menu. Mama finally stumbled onto spinach pie and suggested we all order that. But Nicky insisted we let his father make a family serving of his famous lamb and vegetable stew, with cinnamon rice pudding and fresh dates for dessert.

While we waited to be served, Nicky introduced us to his

father, three uncles, a dozen cousins, and two beautiful olive-skinned sisters, Athena and Alexandra. Each family member seemed friendlier and more exuberant than the one before. "You give my boy a job driving your taxi, I send you a warm tray of baklava every day for a month," his father Spiros promised, with a proud pat on Nicky's back. Daddy rose and lifted his glass of water, announcing that Nicky had the job and could start first thing in the morning.

The happy news led to an uproar of good will and the sweet resonance of lutes and lyres being played somewhere near the kitchen. I decided a gathering of Greeks was the warmest place to celebrate good news and vowed right then and there to grow up and marry one.

As the restaurant began to empty and more and more Carrases gathered around our table, Spiros poured two glasses of Orpa and slid one toward my father, saying, "We toast my son and his new boss." My sisters and I stopped breathing and prayed Daddy would say no. We looked toward Mama, hoping she would intercede and rescue Daddy from his social snare. But she sat as motionless as the rest of us.

Finally, Daddy placed his hand over the top of the glass and said, "I don't drink."

"Come on," Spiros persisted. "You have one drink to celebrate my son."

To my utter amazement, Daddy said, "I can't drink just one."

Good man that he was, Spiros drank his own, then held Daddy's up and said, "I salute you for your resolve," and drank that too.

Chapter 36

Andy and Lila dropped Amanda off at our house on the way back from Florida so she could fill us in on the details about the body that turned out not to be Garret's. She seemed a little shaken from the experience, telling us how horribly decomposed a body is after several weeks in steamy swamp water. "The only way we could be certain it wasn't Garret was a ring from a high school in Bedford, Indiana on the third finger of his right hand. Garret graduated from Baltimore Polytechnic Institute."

"How awful for you and Lila to have to go through that," Mama said.

Amanda collapsed into a chair at the table, put her head in her arms, and began to cry. Mama stroked her hair, repeating "Don't you worry. He'll turn up sooner or later."

Once she was able to stifle her sobs, Amanda confessed that it wasn't just Garret she was crying about. We leaned forward, expectantly.

"I think Andy is falling back in love with Lila."

Lucille, who'd been there for Sunday dinner, tried to put her mind at ease. "He's so used to checking up on her, it probably appears he's more involved than he is."

"Garret looked out for me from the day I was born. It wasn't that kind of concern," Amanda insisted.

"Andy's not the type who'd fool around behind somebody's back. He'd tell you straight out if his feelings for you had changed," Lucille argued.

"Maybe you're right. I'm probably just worn out from the trip. I think I'll go home and sleep the rest of the day. How did Hazel make out subbing for me? Victoria probably loved the scratchy voices on the two-way radio. On second thought, I'm too weary to walk home. Would you call and ask Thurston to come give me a lift."

"Good grief; I forgot to tell you. We hired a new second

driver, so Thurston and Mick don't have to fill in for Andy anymore. They're down at the docks watching the ships come in. It's just until Andy comes back fulltime," Mama added.

"Why didn't he tell me you were hiring somebody to fill in for him?"

"He didn't know. It was Thurston's idea, so he can spend more time on the books and Mick and Lucille can do a little traveling, now that they can afford to."

Amanda felt like an outsider for the first time since moving back to Baltimore. Of course their first loyalty would be to Andy…including covering for him if need be. Had she been blind all these months, encouraging Andy to spend as much time as he could comforting Lila? She was beginning to feel ill and left the table to lie down on the daybed, where my sisters and I recuperated when we were too sick to go to school.

On impulse, I dragged my chair to the foot of the bed. I was sure Mama and Lucille had not conspired to replace Andy so he could move in with Lila – and yet, their voices seemed to have whispers behind them, as if they knew more than they were allowing themselves to consider.

Before long, I heard unfamiliar footsteps coming down the hall. It was Nicky. Mama had called him to pick up Amanda. Without waiting to be introduced, he strolled over to the daybed and held out his hand. "You must be Amanda."

She sat up slowly and brushed her hair back from her face. "And you must be Nicky," she whispered, forcing a halfhearted smile.

"I've come to take you home," he said, and my romantic soul expected to hear choirs of angels singing the Halleluiah chorus. They looked perfect together, like the couples on top of Amanda's wedding cakes - he, with soot black hair and shiny mahogany eyes, she, with yellow hair and delicate pink skin. I was certain God had sent him to shield her from whatever Andy and Lila might be up to, and I was fully committed to serving as His assistant if necessary.

It turned out not to be. After dropping Lila off at Saranac Lake, Andy drove back and spent the weekend courting Amanda. The timing could not have been more perfect. It was her birthday. Not only did Andy plot with Mama and Lucille to bake her a cake, he took her to see a matinee showing of "Anchors Aweigh" with Gene Kelly and Kathryn Grayson. By the time they got back, they seemed as happy as they'd been weeks before.

"Did you enjoy the movie?" Mama asked, lighting the candles on her cake.

"It was wonderful. Kathryn Grayson has the voice of an angel," Amanda said.

"I agree," Lucille responded, enthusiastically. That was the first in a series of short, dead-end conversations, until she asked Andy outright how Lila was feeling after the trip.

"How do you expect her to feel? She's still legally married to Garret and she just identified a corpse that might well have been his."

From then on, conversation grew even more stilted – until Amanda reached over and took Andy's hand. He lifted hers to his lips and kissed it tenderly, dissolving the tension in the room.

"Is everything going to be alright?" I asked, when Lucille was telling us goodnight.

"Of course it is, darlin.' It's just…men can be kind of distant sometimes and it makes the women who love them feel less important. But they generally work it out and live happily ever after."

"I love happily-ever-afters," I said, snuggling down under the covers.

"Me too," she smiled, turning off the light.

**

Amanda's house was equidistant from school and 24th Street, so I often stopped on my way home to watch her dispatch Stanley and Nicky to their appointed taxi routes. Since Stanley was the head driver, he got the first call-ins, leaving Nicky to ride around looking for passengers. To avoid burning up gas, he occasionally dropped by Amanda's for a coke. If I happened to be there, he'd make a game of pretending not to remember my name, calling me Silly instead of Silby.

Now and then, he'd send me to Bernie's for Almond Joys, one for each of us. When he consistently failed to eat his, I concluded he was more interested in being rid of me than he was candy. Anytime Amanda wanted him out of her hair, she simply gave him the next call – even if it was supposed to go to Stanley. Then she and I would spend the afternoon giggling about what a catch he'd be for seventeen year old Marjorie in a couple of years. And everything might have remained that playful if it hadn't been for the blizzard.

Betsy and Marjorie had moved on to high school, leaving me behind to complete the seventh grade on my own. I had walked several blocks in saddle oxfords and bobby sox when the sleet and snow began to make my toes ache, so I stopped by Amanda's to warm them. Since it was Friday, she cleared it with Mama and invited me to spend the weekend. I put on a pair of her fuzzy slippers and a warm flannel nightgown that dragged the floor and perched at Amanda's elbow to watch her work.

At first she was flooded with calls but before long, people were too busy shoveling to need a taxi. Stanley clocked out early and Nicky parked his cab in front of Amanda's in case there were any calls. After an hour or so, we decided he must be freezing, and Amanda radioed him an invitation to supper.

The son of a restaurant owner, Nicky insisted on cooking for us. Using a tomato, a bit of basil, and a little pasta, he came up with a luscious casserole and dessert - which he created by turning flour, butter, and brown sugar into pastries. He even did the dishes while we set up the Monopoly board. By seven o'clock, I was falling asleep, so I curled up on the sofa while they continued to play. Every now and then, I'd turn over and catch a casual exchange between them.

"It was lonely having my parents away in China for most of my childhood…"

"I'd have welcomed a little loneliness at my house. It was overflowing with brothers and sisters, cousins, aunts and uncles, grandparents…"

"How wonderful," she sighed.

"Do you ever get lonely now?" he asked.

"Not really…except when Andy's been away for a long weekend – sometimes I do."

"Why is he away on weekends?"

"My sister-in-law Lila is going through a really tough time. My brother Garret disappeared right after they were married, and she's been searching for him ever since."

"That's really sad, but I don't get why her unhappiness is your boyfriend's responsibility? You must be as worried about Garret as your sister-in-law is. Maybe more…"

"He feels responsible because he talked my brother into going back to her…it's a long story…"

Just then a call came in from an elderly woman who had run out of coal and needed to be driven to her sister's for the night. After Nicky had gone, Amanda went to bed, but I could hear her crying softly until she fell asleep.

Chapter 37

Andy had been in Saranac Lake over a week without so much as a phone call when Lucille first considered the possibility that Amanda's intuition might be correct. She called him and insisted that he drive down the following weekend to explain any impropriety on his part.

It was evident from their averted eyes that Andy and Lila were guilty of something. Mama invited the grownups to sit down at the table for coffee and pineapple upside down cake - which Lucille said was uniquely appropriate for the occasion. My sisters and I lined up on the stairs, within earshot but out of sight for what we were sure would be a showdown in the name of love.

Marjorie, the family moralist, thought it was wrong of them to get involved before telling Amanda; Betsy, who viewed herself as more avant-garde thought they had the right to fall in love with whomever they pleased; and I secretly hoped Amanda would fall for Nicky so she'd never have to leave Baltimore – at least until she finished teaching me to twirl the baton.

Lucille opened the conversation by confronting Andy. "You went through this once before with Lila and she bolted as soon as Garret appeared on the scene…"

"Whoa!" Andy shouted. "You're convicting us without a trial. Lila and I have not broken any significant vows. The most we've done is discuss the possibility. I'm still as fond of Amanda as I ever was and Garret will hold a special place in Lila's heart forever. But romantic love is not the most important consideration at the moment."

"I know you want to rescue Lila from loneliness, but…"

"Excuse me!" Lila interrupted. "What Andy and I do is nobody's business but our own. The fact that I'm willing to discuss it at all is evidence of my gratitude for all he's done. I adored Garret. I still do. But the man who skipped out on a future paved with happiness is not the brave, sensible guy I fell in love with. If he showed up tomorrow, I'm not sure I'd take him back. Beyond wounding his body, the War has killed his spirit."

Turning to face her son, Lucille asked whether he had already committed to taking Garret's place.

"Mama!" he snapped, uncharacteristically. "You need to stop while you're ahead."

"The boy's got a point," Mick couldn't help adding. "I'm not comfortable giving them the third degree. Andy's a thoughtful boy. He'll do the right thing."

"It's not Andy I'm worried about," Lucille mumbled.

"How can you say that after all the years we've been friends? Will it help if I promise not to lure your son into a love affair until Garret comes home and I can reject him in person? Would that prove Andy can trust me with his heart? Damn you, Andy! I should never have let you talk me into doing this."

"You don't have to prove anything to anybody," Andy said. "The truth is, Lila was pregnant with Garret's baby when he walked out on her."

There was a collective gasp.

"I think you owe Lila an apology, Mama."

Lucille's face was so red I thought her head might explode. But she inhaled deeply and said, "I'm so sorry. I had no idea."

"And it's my fault for going to Saranac Lake and stirring things up in the first place. If I'd left well-enough alone…"

"Don't be ridiculous," Daddy said, speaking up for the first time. "There's no way you're responsible for Garret getting her pregnant – much as you apparently want to believe you are."

"We can't be sure he wasn't a contributing factor," Mama muttered, under her breath, flashing back to her sister's role in her own pregnancy.

Lila addressed Lucille directly. "The Garret I cherished no longer exists – except in my memories. The love we shared is a casualty of war…"

"Does that mean you've decided Andy would make the better father?"

"We're just trying to do the right thing," Andy said. "We want to provide the child with a stable home, with parents who won't run away when things get tough…"

"Then do it," Amanda suddenly cried. "Have the courage to act on what your conscience tells you instead of splitting yourself between Lila and me – and breaking my heart in the process. The truth is, it's not that difficult to forgive both of you for following your feelings. But what I can't forgive is you talking about my brother's child as though I had no stake in the outcome. You should have called me the minute you knew about it and invited me to be part of the solution. How could you think I'd act in other than the baby's best interest - even if it meant giving you up, Andy? Whatever you two decide about parenting, I'd like to be a part of. You can stay in the Saranac house as long as you want. If you're financially strapped, I have a little nest-egg I'd be happy to contribute to the baby's care."

"Thanks for the offer," Lila said, "but we still have several months before making any final decisions. I'm not even sure what I'd do if Garret came back. He *is* the baby's father, although he may have no interest in acting like it. Andy and I need time to consider all the pros and cons before committing to anything permanent."

"What?" Andy cried, clearly not on the same page as Lila. "That's it. We're leaving before you people gum up everything we've spent weeks working out."

Still reeling from the news about the baby, nobody tried to talk them into staying. Once they were gone, the grownups sat around the table swapping opinions until long after I was in bed asleep.

Chapter 38

The end of the War created an unexpected novelty on 24th Street - extra cash to spend. That Christmas, Daddy bought Mama a wider wedding band and a watch with a pinpoint diamond in the face. Then he shocked us all by bringing home enormous stuffed Panda bears for Marjorie and Betsy and an accordion pleated camera for me, with flash bulbs that blistered when you snapped a picture indoors. For Garland, there was a Lionel train with tracks that wound halfway around the living room.

The taxi cab business was booming, so we no longer hauled Bernie's fifty cent bags of coal home in Garland's wagon. We could now order enough to fill the coal bin via delivery truck. By the time hot weather set in, Mama had an electric sewing machine and a refrigerator with a built in freezer. Daddy had our telephone converted from party-line to private, and my sisters and I took turns talking to our friends in the hall coat closet, so we wouldn't disturb Daddy listening to George Burns and Gracie Allen on his floor model Philco in the living room.

Everybody seemed happy except Amanda, who was still struggling to get over Andy, and Nicky, who couldn't get to first base with her. When the direct approach failed, Nicky talked his sister Athena into hiring Amanda to make her wedding cake. It was stunning, with seven individual cakes in graduated sizes atop sparkling crystal cylinders. Each cake was trimmed in white roses with silver ivy around the sides, culminating in more white roses and figures of the bride and groom at the top. The cake was such a success Spiros Carras hired Amanda to do all the cakes for the restaurant, keeping her too busy to moon over Andy.

Lucille and Mick were working off her chocolate Easter weight gain by walking around the reservoir at Druid Hill Park when she suddenly became short-winded. They sat down on a park bench in front of the old streetcar barn where Andy had kissed Lila the first time. There were no cell phones in those days and no 911 operators to send an ambulance, so Mick tried to comfort her into feeling better. When that didn't work, he stopped a lady pushing a large black baby carriage and asked if she would sit with Lucille while he went to get his car, parked a mile away.

By the time they reached the emergency room at Sinai Hospital, Lucille was no longer conscious, and by the time Mama and Daddy got there, Mick was sitting in the hallway with his face in his hands, sobbing, "She's gone."

Mama called to tell Marjorie what had happened, and she passed it on to the rest of us, adding that we should set a place at the dinner table for Mick.

"What do you mean, she's gone?" I cried, icy panic sucking the wind out of my lungs.

"There's no sense getting emotional," Marjorie said, trying her best to parent in Mama's place. But I was no longer listening. I had bolted out the door and was in the race of my life to outrun death, heart slamming against my chest, my bronchial tubes on fire. I ran as far and as fast as I could, until I collapsed in exhaustion on the stone gray steps of the First Methodist Church.

I tiptoed inside and went straight to the sanctuary, where I sat down in an aisle seat and began praying to the star speckled ceiling for God to bring her back. I used every bargaining tool I could think of, from promising to be nice to Garland, to taking a tub bath every Saturday night whether I needed one or not. As I sobbed my way through desperate pleas, Mr. O'Leary, the Irish caretaker who lived in the church tower with his wife, walked quietly in and sat down across the aisle from me. At first, he didn't speak, and I tried as hard as I could to turn off my hicuppy blubbering.

Mr. O'Leary was barely five feet tall, thin and dry as a leaf, with a million wrinkles around his twinkling blue eyes. He'd known me since I was seven and he took my sisters and me to the top of the tower to see Baltimore City from all four sides. "Something wrong?" he asked, softly.

I immediately launched into an hysterical description of Lucille's passing and how utterly impossible it would be for my family to get along without her.

"I see, I see," he said, rubbing his deeply crevassed chin. "I think I may be able to help you."

I doubted that completely but my southern roots required that I humor him by pretending to believe he could.

"You know anything about leprechauns?" he asked, in the lyrical meter of a natural storyteller.

"I know they wear green hats and live in the woods where they leave pots of gold at the end of the rainbow for poor Irish people who lost everything in the potato famine."

He couldn't help chuckling. "Who told you that?"

"My father - and he has Celtic roots - so he ought to know."

"Aye, he should at that," he smiled. "But there's a whole other part to the story you may not have heard, born in the Colonies as you were." Then he reached in his shirt pocket and handed me a handkerchief made of fine Irish linen – which I accepted but didn't use because I couldn't bear to get it dirty.

"There are several kinds of leprechauns living in Ireland today, the most beloved of which are the teaching leprechauns."

"I've never heard of a teaching leprechaun," I said, suspiciously.

"Aye, it's true. They are popular because they don't play tricks on the people they help, although they have been known to hide the true value of their teaching in the hope that people will figure it out for themselves – which, as you know, is the very best way to learn anything."

I glanced at him apprehensively but decided it wouldn't hurt to listen a little longer, since it kept my mind off of Lucille.

"In the year 1845, just after the potato famine wiped out half the population, the leprechauns got together to express concern about the people of Ireland not being smart enough to plant more than one crop, such as carrots or rutabagas. When nobody could come up with an explanation for the oversight, they decided right then and there to appoint a teaching team to help farmers and housewives think beyond the potato.

"Now there was a head leprechaun named Luther whom the others trusted more than the rest when it came to giving sound advice. 'What we need,' Luther told them, 'is a committee of volunteers to knock on the doors of worthy families and teach them to solve everyday problems – the most important of which is how to cope with the loss of loved ones following the potato famine.'

"They voted unanimously to disguise themselves as wise old women – since wise old men, being map followers, only show up for miraculous births with a star to guide them. They would go out on Halloween and offer guidance to needy families. You may know such a person yourself."

"Lucille came to us on Halloween. Could she be one of them?"

"I wouldn't be a bit surprised," he chuckled softly. "The good news is that leprechauns never die, although they sometimes appear to, especially when it's time to move on to the next family. If she is one, and I'm not saying she is - though I'm not saying she isn't - there's nothing to do but let her go. She'll live forever in your heart and that, after all, is the real gift of the teaching leprechauns."

Chapter 39

In 1933, Katherine Hepburn and Marlene Dietrich shocked the world by wearing trousers in public for the first time. Once the War broke out, housewives began wearing their husband's casual pants to clean house, since their husbands were overseas and would not panic about the risk to their femininity. It didn't take New York designers long to recognize a fertile market, and by 1945, trousers without flies were available in every department store in the country.

Hazel's mother had sent her a ten dollar check for her birthday, and she was wrestling with the moral issue of buying a pair. Stanley was not the kind of man who could appreciate progressive fads in fashion – particularly for his wife.

"Baloney," Mama said, when Hazel told her she was worried about what Stanley would think. "If I were younger, I'd be wearing them myself. They keep your legs warm and you don't have to worry about getting a run in your stockings."

"Would you mind taking care of Victoria long enough for me to run downtown? Stanley has a long distance fare to Washington today, so I can be sure of not running into him. I have to account for every penny I spend, and the last thing I want is to get caught buying slacks."

"I understand completely. Your best bet is Epstein's in Highlandtown. That's where I bought the girl's Easter dresses. Their prices are reasonable and the quality is on a par with Hutzler's."

"Would you like to keep me company, Silby – if it's all right with your mother?"

"Yes ma'am," I answered, thrilled to be going anywhere with anyone as nice as Hazel.

We took the number 10 trackless trolley down Howard Street, and I managed to avoid my usual bus-sickness all the way to Pratt Street, where it zig-zagged through several turns before dropping us off on Eastern Avenue.

Epstein's had a grand array of blousy, cotton trousers in gray, black, and navy blue. Hazel tried on all three pairs in size ten. She strutted around like a peacock in front of the mirror, empowered by the exhilarating freedom of not having to sit like a lady and keep her skirt pulled demurely over her knees. I could tell she'd fallen in love. Still, she couldn't get the image of scowling Stanley out of her head.

"My husband would kill me if I bought a pair," she sighed.

"Come now," the saleswoman responded, her forehead furrowed by a frown. "They're all the rage. I heard in California women wear them to church."

"You don't say." Hazel pondered for several more minutes before promising to think it over, reluctantly handing them back to the clerk.

Seeing my disappointment, she said, "Come on, Silby. Haussners is only two blocks from here. I'll treat us to a piece of their famous strawberry pie."

I tried to be cheerful, knowing she wanted them as much as I thought she should have them. The waiter led us to a small table in the far corner. Just after we placed our order, Hazel began ducking down, trying to hide her head behind mine. "Don't move," she cried. "What is it?" I asked, automatically turning around to see what lay behind me.

"It's Stanley," she cried. "He's not in Washington at all. He's with another woman, having a glass of wine."

I wanted Hazel to tear across the room, snatch him out of his chair, and send the woman on her way with a stern lecture. But Hazel was stuck somewhere between pain and shock, and confrontation was the last thing on her mind.

I ducked my head and peeked at Stanley and the woman every chance I got without exposing Hazel's head. Finally, they stood up and walked to the door, his arm tightly around the woman's waist, she gazing into his eyes like a new puppy.

The wind had gone out of Hazel's sails, and she sat staring ahead, not saying a word while I finished my pie. I didn't really want it but was afraid her feelings would be hurt if I didn't eat it. Finally, she paid the bill, and we walked as silent as wooden soldiers back to the bus stop. On the ride home, I asked her what she was going to do, and she said, "I'm going to insist on an explanation." In my heart of hearts – based on Mama's response to Daddy's behavior during the drinking years, I thought that meant she was going to do nothing.

Less than a week later, Hazel sought advice from Mick, Daddy, and Mama about the best way to get Stanley to give up his lady-friend. My sisters and I were at our usual post, on the stairs outside the dining room doorway.

Mama told her some things never change and if a man is a runner, it is likely that he will always be - no matter how many promises he makes.

Mick added that although it was generally true of men in their twenties, Stanley had recently experienced fatherhood and might have a handle on the ability to see things more maturely. "At least, give him a chance to give the woman up."

"That's ridiculous," Daddy said. "No man's going to give up a playmate for his wife unless he has to. What you need to do is make him more afraid of losing you than he is of losing her."

"How do I do that?" Hazel asked.

"You make him so obsessed with what *you* might be doing he loses interest completely in what he could be doing with her. You're an attractive woman, Hazel, but you have the sex appeal of a door latch. The first thing you have to do is create a little mystery; learn to be less predictable."

"I'm not sure I know how. I got married too soon to learn to be seductive."

"You don't need to. You start out in little ways, upsetting the balance of his expectations. You get home from the grocery store just late enough to be a little breathless and giddy. Never answer his questions directly. Appear to be bird-brained and vague. It will drive him crazy. Before you know it, he'll be trailing everywhere you go, trying to catch you doing something you shouldn't. Next, you start giggling and hanging up the phone as if you've been talking to a man. You insist it is a new friend named Claire you met at Bernie's waiting for steak. When Stanley points out you never cook steak for him, you pretend to be surprised and ask if he's sure. The minute he begins to doubt himself - which is how he's kept you obsessing about him throughout your marriage - you pull out the big guns. You ask him for a divorce."

"What?" Hazel cried. "That's the last thing I want."

"You and I know that, but if you allow him to find out, I can promise you'll end up losing him to another woman. You have to want him enough to play a little dirty pool, or you'll end up the victim of women who'll stop at nothing to steal your man. Stanley is clearly a player at heart. You have to make the game too risky if you want to hang onto him."

"I don't know," Hazel mumbled. "I don't believe in an eye for an eye. It seems a little two faced."

"Then you'd better get used to him fooling around on you."

"What do you think?" Hazel asked, turning toward Mick.

"I'm afraid the average marriage supports Thurston's theory. Only one person at a time can be in control of a marriage, and the one unwilling to take risks will be the one constantly looking over his or her shoulder - like you're doing now."

Hazel reluctantly agreed to give Daddy's method a try and within three weeks, she had become so adept at making Stanley wonder where he stood, he bought her a fur coat, a dozen roses, and a romantic card swearing to be true to her alone for the rest of his days. Best of all, she went back to Highlandtown and bought all three pairs of slacks.

Mama suggested that Daddy start charging 24th Street brides for advice on how to keep their husbands insecure enough to be loyal. But by then, he'd lost interest and was focusing on expanding the cab company to include Washington DC, an idea he got from Stanley's alibi the day Hazel caught him cheating.

Chapter 40

The leaves were just beginning to turn when Nicky nagged Amanda into going to the annual harvest fair. She agreed to go if my sisters and I went along. Mama had lectured Nicky about trying too hard, so he did his best to be casual and lighthearted when speaking to Amanda.

We spent hours roaming up and down rows of farm equipment and homemade jars of pickles before finally reaching the funnel cake. Sitting down at a picnic table, we watched children passing by with cotton candy in one hand and spinning pinwheels in the other. Amanda's relaxed laughter seemed to indicate that Nicky's strategy of treating her more like a friend than a date was working. We tried to talk them into riding in the tunnel of love, convinced they'd go in as friends and come out mad about each other. But their courtship was destined to bloom slowly, the way steady warmth causes dough to rise.

On New Year's Day, Nicky and Amanda agreed to supervise us riding our sleds down the steep hills at Wyman Park. Amanda stood at the top, making sure we were securely anchored, while Nicky stood guard at the bottom, ready to body slam any of us in danger of crashing into the stone wall..

We had each ridden several times when the frozen ridges created by the sled tracks caused Garland to accelerate faster than he could control. Recognizing the danger, Nicky hurled himself on top of Garland and crashed the sled into a tree, knocking himself out cold.

We ran screaming down the hill, straight into a patch of red where Nicky had split his head open. Marjorie raced home and rode back with Mick and Daddy. They carried him up the hill and into Daddy's car then drove to the nearest hospital where his head was x-rayed. He had a concussion and the doctor ordered him to rest for twenty-four hours, holding an ice-pack on his head at fifteen minute intervals.

Amanda insisted he spend the night on her sofa so she could keep an eye on him. I was invited to join them for the sake of propriety. By the time Mama dropped me off, Amanda had turned her work area into a nurse's station, with a thermometer, alcohol to clean his cut, gauze, adhesive tape, and an ice pack sitting on top of her radio transmitter. She did everything a mother hen could do except lay eggs.

On the following day, I checked in on my way home from school. Nicky had recovered and Amanda was back at work. I'm not sure whether it was my presence at the bedside during his recovery or my passive personality, but in the weeks that followed, they began treating me like a mascot and taking me with them to the movies, where they held hands throughout the feature.

By far, my favorite thing to do was sit on the front steps and listen to them talk. He spoke of the warmth and closeness of his noisy Greek family, while she focused on the enforced quiet growing up with her maiden aunt. "If Garret had not been there to provide companionship and humor, I don't know what I'd have done. He could always make me laugh. But once my aunt passed away and he joined the service, I was so lonely I read every romance novel in the library."

"It's hard to believe a pretty girl like you could ever be lonely. What about the friends you made in high school?"

"They were actually very nice. It was my own lack of confidence that led me to turn down invitations. I was always more comfortable with books. After a while, they quit asking me."

"How did you get involved with Andy?"

"I think I won Andy by default. He was head over heels in love with Lila, but she only had eyes for Garret. So he transferred his affection to me. Once Garret disappeared, Andy did his best to comfort Lila and over time, she accepted him as an adequate substitute. I'll never believe she loves him the way she did Garret. But I do think she's convinced she can make him happy if only because he's wanted her so long."

"Is that how you feel about me – someone to transfer your affection to in Andy's absence?"

"Of course not…Well, to be completely honest – maybe I did in the beginning."

"Ouch!" he said, wincing.

"I'm sorry. I'm trying to be honest. I don't feel that way anymore. Do you think love that grows gradually can be as powerful as passion that strikes like lightning and makes you crazy with desire?"

"I don't know. You knocked me off my feet the first time I laid eyes on you, lying on that daybed at Claudia's, pining away for Andy. You reminded me of a delicate flower in danger of wilting, and I wanted to kill the guy who broke your heart."

"I didn't know you knew about that."

"If you hang around Claudia long enough, you find out everything. Do you think your feelings for me are strong enough to develop into love?"

"They already have," she said, softly.

He stared into her eyes, brimming with emotion, and confessed, "I worship you." Then he kissed her like it was the first and last kiss on earth.

**

Two months to the day after Nicky's accident, he dropped to his knees in our dining room and asked Amanda to marry him. To boost our joy, she invited my sisters and me to be bridesmaids and Garland, the ring-bearer. Hazel would be the maid of honor. But best of all – Amanda's parents were returning from China after twenty years of missionary work and would be moving into the yellow house at Saranac Lake. Unfortunately, it meant Lila and Andy would have to leave.

"I can't believe my father will be here to give me away," Amanda cried joyfully.

"The reception will be at the restaurant," Nicky added, "so it should be a rowdy affair."

"The only thing that could make it more perfect would be Garret coming home. But then, he doesn't even know about the wedding. If only there were some way to get a message to him," Amanda sighed.

Lila had taught me not to reject any spontaneous idea, no matter how farfetched, so when "the obituaries" popped into my head, I blurted it out.

Everybody in the dining room dismissed my out-of-context comment as meaningless. But Amanda had the gift of open mindedness, and she allowed herself to consider the possibilities before eliminating it entirely. "If I were traveling far from home and wanted to remain incognito, I'd check the obituaries in the hometown paper to keep track of family and friends. Nicky, doesn't one of your cousins write obituaries for the Baltimore Sun? Do you think he could slip an announcement of our wedding into the obituaries?"

"You can't put your wedding announcement in the obituaries," Mama cried, horrified.

"This time I have to agree with Claudia," Daddy said, lamenting the need to do so.

But Nicky, whose ancestors were steeped in Greek Mythology, was less insistent upon a discreet line between life and death. "I don't think it could do any harm – except to my cousin's income when The Baltimore Sun fires him."

"Well," said Mick, "maybe he could insert it as a classified ad on the same page as the obituaries with Garret's name in large print and hope it catches his eye?"

"It's okay with me if it's okay with Amanda," Nicky grinned.

**

On April 24th, 1946, my sisters and I floated down the aisle in our homemade, aqua satin dresses, with one eye on Nicky, waiting at the altar, and the other on the handful of people seated on the bride's side, hoping Garret would be there.

Amanda wore her mother's wedding gown, laden with antique lace and a graceful flowing train. The formal service was sweet and both of Amanda's parents cried, mostly for her happiness, but also because Garret had not found his way to the ceremony.

After Daddy took pictures with the camera he'd given me for Christmas, we made our way to the reception, down St. Paul to 22nd Street and up Charles to the restaurant. It was not uncommon in those days to see wedding parties in their ceremonial garb walking between home and the neighborhood Church, since ordinary income households were just beginning to purchase cars.

Nicky's relatives had pushed back the tables and cleared a space for dancing in the middle of the room. His Uncle Gus served as DJ, playing 78 rpm's of the big band sounds of Glen Miller and Tommy Dorsey, with his uncles entertaining during breaks with their lyres and lutes and a circle of men with locked arms dancing as their ancestors had since the beginning of civilization.

Amanda's parents had spent twenty years in China surrounded by a mostly quiet race of people, and to them the reception resembled New Year's Eve in Times Square. My sisters and I loved it, for there were dozens of beautiful Greek boys polite enough to dance with us.

By the time Amanda and Nicky left for their honeymoon in Niagara Falls, the sky was pink and purple twilight. Guests were beginning to trickle out, on their way back to simple routines and the everyday obligations that busied their ordinary lives.

My sisters and I, high on sugar and our first romantic adventure, went to bed early. Marjorie and Betsy now had separate third floor bedrooms, and I rotated between the two, depending on which I thought had been nicer to me that week. Garland inherited our old second floor bedroom. We all three piled into Marjorie's bed so we could giggle about the boys we'd danced with.

The wedding ushered in a major milestone for my sisters – boys on the front steps. It started when Nicky's Greek cousins began dropping by to strut their studly stuff. Mama embraced the concept fully and constantly invited them inside for cokes and her four sticks of real butter pound cake. Daddy took a somewhat dimmer view, stationing himself in his living room chair next to the floor to ceiling window where he could monitor every word they uttered.

Chapter 41

Amanda and my sisters and I were painting Mama's kitchen walls a warmer shade of battleship gray, when the doorbell rang. "Who could that be?" Mama asked.

Marjorie went to answer it and was astonished to see Andy and Lila with a baby in her arms. She invited them in and we stood like shocked statues with dripping paint brushes in our hands.

"Well, my goodness," Mama said. "What a beautiful baby…in yellow. Let's go in the living room."

"It's a boy," Lila said. "We named him Garret Andrew Harrington."

Amanda made a little sobbing sound and asked if she could hold him.

"Of course," Lila answered, handing the chubby baby boy to her sister-in-law.

Amanda inhaled the sweetness of his baby scent and studied his features. He had Garret's wide gray eyes rather than Lila's bright blue ones, but his hair promised to be auburn, if not red, like his mother's. "I don't suppose Garret has seen him," Amanda said.

"We don't know where he is. We went ahead and listed Andy as the biological father on the birth certificate. It seemed in the best interest of the baby."

"Where are you living?" Amanda asked, anxious to keep in touch with her newborn nephew.

"We've been staying on the base since Garret's parents' returned. Andy has applied for a transfer to Alaska."

"I'll bet my parents were ecstatic about little Garret, especially since he so clearly resembles my brother."

"The thing is," Andy said, clearing his throat, "Garret's future involvement is doubtful, so we've decided to treat this like a legal adoption. We've named Lila's mother and father as godparents and they'll serve as his grandparents as well."

"Well, that should break my parents' hearts. Are you

planning to tell him I'm his aunt?" .

"The truth is, we intended for this to be a one-time visit."

The color drained from Amanda's face.

"But Amanda would be the world's greatest aunt," Mama said. "Are you sure you want to deprive the baby of her influence?"

"We didn't make the decision lightly..." Lila said,

Amanda ran out the door, and I ran after her, not realizing Andy was following close behind.

When we reached the sidewalk, Andy grabbed her arm. "Please try to understand. We want the least complicated life for the boy. It isn't like we'd turn you away if you came to visit. But we're hoping you'll appreciate the wisdom of our decision and act accordingly. I know some of what you're feeling is related to my walking out on you..."

"I got over that a long time ago. Do you think I'd have married Nicky if I hadn't? All I want is to stay in touch with my brother's child – and I pray that someday Garret will want to be involved, too. But I suspect that's not feasible given your current mind set."

"I appreciate your understanding. You know, to be perfectly honest, I did not expect to miss you as terribly..."

Before he could finish, Lila and the baby joined us.

She gave my sisters and me a huge hug, then started to say something to Amanda but changed her mind. As they got into the car, Amanda leaned down and said, "Silby. Say goodbye to Andy and Lila. It's not likely we'll be seeing them again."

Chapter 42

Marjorie, Betsy, and I were invited to spend a week at the Saranac Lake house papering the walls in spritely greens and pinks, which Amanda felt would make it less nostalgic and more cheerful for her parents. Mama and Daddy had driven up for Sunday dinner, and we were just sitting down to Nicky's homemade chicken pot pie, when Daddy made an offhand comment about what a blessing it was that the United States, England, and Russia had been able to set aside their differences to defeat Germany in the War.

Amanda's father grunted, his scarlet cheeks revealing a significant rise in blood pressure, which aroused Daddy's curiosity.

"You do agree that the alliance was critical to winning the War, don't you?"

"You know," Mr. Cummings began, choosing his words carefully, "the average man on the street believes the Allies consisted of the United States, England, Russia, and France. Very few remember that the fourth ally was China. The Japanese first invaded China in 1937, and by the time the War started, 600,000 were occupying the country. But none of the World War II allies volunteered to send troops as they did when European countries were under attack by Hitler. Mark my words, the day will come when the United States regrets failing to market its democratic principles more vigorously to the Chinese when it had the chance. Do you have any idea how huge China is – and what Chiang Kai-shek's alliance with Russia will mean to the spread of communism?"

Daddy seemed thunderstruck but quickly rallied to say Pearl Harbor is what led us into the war with Japan, and anything that happened before that did not involve us.

"And it was Pearl Harbor that convinced China to join the allied forces in their fight against Fascism. We were sympathetic to your plight. Why have you never been sensitive to ours?"

"We have been, overall," Daddy said, back-peddling. "We supplied troops and arms to China – maybe not as early as we should have, but remember, we were fighting two wars at once, one in Europe and the other in the Pacific. And our entire naval fleet had been destroyed at Pearl Harbor."

Mama interrupted at this point to say she thought it would be more thoughtful to everyone at the table if we changed the subject. Daddy was about to ignore her when we heard a knock on the front door. "Who could that be?" Amanda asked, as she made her way down the hall.

A seedy looking man with a grayish beard and long, unkempt brown hair stood in the doorway. The only clue to his identity was the cane he leaned against. "I'm looking for the girl who advertised her wedding in the obituaries."

"Garret!" she cried, throwing her arms around his neck.

Daddy jumped up and offered him his chair, for the man was painfully thin, with skin as pale as unbuttered bread. After suffocating him with hugs and kisses, Mr. and Mrs. Cummings sat on either side, each holding one of his hands.

"Where have you been, Son?" his mother asked gently, not wanting to pressure him.

"Here and there," he answered, his voice hoarse from lack of use.

"It doesn't matter," said Mr. Cummings, whose favorite Bible verse was the story of the prodigal son. "You're here now, and that's all I care about."

Garret studied Betsy's face and mine, trying to remember where he'd seen us.

"Are you sure you're all right, son? You look awfully thin," Mrs. Cummings commented, picking lint off of his faded flannel shirt.

"Where are you living?" Mr. Cummings asked.

"Mostly in California. I've taken a couple of classes at Berkley."

"What's your major," Mama asked, relieved to have something concrete to inquire about.

"I don't have a major. I've taken a little philosophy and psychology, but mainly religion: Hinduism, Islam, and Buddhism. Right now, I'm studying with a group of Buddhists exploring the Tao."

The War Brides of 24th Street

"I noticed you left out Christianity," Mr. Cummings said. "Any particular reason?"

"I'm not interested in joining a church."

"Well, son, you can't just pick a religion out of a collage catalogue."

"I don't want a religion. I want peace of mind. Buddhism teaches you to let go of worldly attachments – those drives and ambitions that make you feel desperate when you can't achieve them. If you buy a house, you think you own your home, when in reality your mortgage owns you for the next thirty years. If you own nothing, you won't feel compelled to barter your soul to keep it. I have no aspirations, so I need no inspiration – only freedom from obligation. That's why I couldn't go to Florida with Lila. She had a head full of fantasies about having children and buying a home in the suburbs, with me making it possible through the building of airplanes. Well, I can't live my life for things – or even people. There is a wellspring of incongruity churning inside my head, and meditation brings a form of uncluttered release only one who has been to War can appreciate." Then he wiped perspiration from his forehead and said, "I'm going to step outside for a smoke."

Daddy and Nicky went with him and would tell Mama on the drive home that he'd brought his own marijuana cigarettes wrapped in a bandana that smelled of damp leaves. The only person Daddy knew of who smoked pot was a drummer named Gene Krupa, and he was fairly certain he'd served time in jail for doing so.

When they came back in, Mr. Cummings picked up where he had left off. "It's all well and good to make the Self the central focus while you're trying to sort out your slot in the universe, but it's another to permanently go against everything that's natural in a man. Every species in the universe operates within some family framework, even if it's only a spider, bent on eating its young. There are stages of life we all go through, and adulthood means learning to care about somebody besides yourself. Now, I'm all for you taking as much time as you need to get over what happened to you, but I draw the line at you deciding to become a Buddhist vagrant without a home to call your own."

"Well, Papa, if you're determined to cling to the idea that I must have a family and home, I can only say that the quicker you let go of it, the happier you'll be."

"I don't give a hang about you owning a house. This one will be yours after I'm dead. But I can't sit by and watch you throw away the joy of having a family because of old war wounds. Every man needs loved ones who care whether or not he makes it home at the end of the day, someone with whom he can share his hopes and disappointments - someone like your mother..."

"I tried that with Lila. It's too exhausting. Face it, Papa. We're different generations. I've seen things you could not imagine from your cozy little American life..."

"Wait just a minute," Mr. Cummings shouted, slapping the table. "Your mother and I have spent the last twenty years caring for widows and orphans amid squalor and starvation in a country torn apart by war. We did not think about ourselves..."

"Nor about Amanda and me..." Garret blurted out.

Amanda looked horrified and scrambled to put a stop to the discussion. "You two are never going to agree, so before we end up losing Garret again, I suggest we talk about something else."

"I will, if Garret promises to pray about his future and ask the Lord for guidance," said Mr. Cummings.

"I can't pray to a God I don't believe in – a God who lets war happen."

"It is man, not God who causes war."

"Papa!" Amanda cried. "Please drop the subject."

"I think it will be better for everyone if I leave," Garret said, softly.

"You're not allowed to speak for everyone. I think it would be better if you stayed – and I suspect the others do to," cried Amanda. "Besides, there's something I want to talk with you about, but not today. We need to lighten up and enjoy being back together again."

**

Marjorie and Betsy and I were sitting on the front porch gazing at the lake when Garret came out and joined Amanda in the swing. "Lila has had a baby," she said gently. "She and Andy – Lucille's son – have moved to Alaska to raise the child in a place less complicated than here."

"I'm happy for her," he said.

"You may not be for long. The baby is yours."

"It can't be. She'd have told me…"

"She intended to as soon as you got settled in Florida. She saw it as part of your new beginning – new home, school, and fatherhood. She had no way of knowing…"

"Is it a boy or a girl?"

"You have a son. They named him Garret Andrew Harrington."

We heard a wrenching sob, and then the terrible sound of a grown man crying.

"Andy is willing to raise him as his own, but the question is should he?"

"Of course he should. It would only muddy the waters if I got involved."

"I've lived with you most of my life and this much I know – baby Garret could only be a better person for having you in his life."

"I don't think I can," he whispered. "Just the thought of it…the sheer weight of it…"

"At least take the time to make a considered decision. I know you'll do the right thing. By the way, I haven't told Mama and Papa the baby is yours. I think that should be your decision. I've written down Lila's address in Alaska. The rest is entirely up to you."

Three weeks after we returned to our mundane routines, Amanda stopped by with a letter from Garret. She asked that Hazel and Stanley be there when she read it.

My dearest sister, Amanda:

Thank you for having the courage to tell me what I didn't want to hear but needed most to know. I have rented a log cabin a few miles outside of Juno, where Lila and Andy live. As you can well imagine, they did not welcome me with open arms but gradually became convinced I meant them no harm. After much deliberation, we have decided that my role in little Garret's life will be that of the trapper who lives down the road and occasionally takes him camping and gives him advice. Since I have no interest in the rest of what goes along with parenting, it is the ideal arrangement. Even better, I get to be near Lila without any expectations on her part.

I can carve out a life for myself which allows peace and privacy while maintaining a relationship with my son. It is far more than I deserve or have a right to expect.

I'm enclosing my address in case you and your Greek Adonis ever want to stop by. Feel free to let Mama and Papa know where I am and why.

Your loving brother,
Garret

Chapter 43

It seemed to be a rule of life that when one thing got fixed, another got broken. We had been basking in the satisfaction of a happily-ever-after for Lila, Andy, and Garret, when Hazel dropped by unexpectedly. My sisters and I were sitting around the table doing homework when we heard her ask Mama if she could speak to them privately. She foolishly believed there was such a thing in a house where children had grown up without television to provide emotional entertainment.

We dutifully left the dining room to resume our usual ease-dropping position on the stairs. It is quite likely they knew we were listening, since parents in those days had a grittier view of reality and thought it beneficial for children to be aware of the adult struggles awaiting them.

"I left Stanley," Hazel said. "Or rather, he's leaving me."

"Another woman?" Mama asked, more sympathetic than surprised.

"In a manner of speaking. Her name is Victoria."

""Little Victoria? Can't stand the hassle of a noisy child in the house?" Daddy asked.

"Nope. I found lipstick on his collar and a woman's phone number in his jacket pocket. So I told him to get out. He immediately began trying to sweet talk me into forgiving him. That's when it struck me. By giving him second and third chances, I was teaching Victoria that women are duty bound to put up with infidelity for the sake of the family.

"When I told him again he had to leave, he became verbally abusive, saying he would take Victoria someplace I'd never find her. I was terrified and blurted out the truth: 'Victoria is not yours.'"

Daddy suddenly became furious. "Girl," he bellowed, "don't you lie about a thing like that."

"Calm down, Thurston," Mama said. "Are you absolutely sure? Whose is she, then?"

Sitting in the hallway, I suddenly remembered the night Danny followed Hazel to her door – the night my sisters and I found so romantic. That would explain why Victoria's eyes were the color of autumn leaves, while her mother's were blue and her father's, grass green.

"She's Danny's. It was the night you went to see Mrs. Miniver. He followed me home, and it just happened. It was not intentional – or more accurately, not planned. Don't look at me like that. It's unnatural for wives to sit and wait while husbands go away to war. The stress itself makes you vulnerable and in need of comforting."

"Men have been going off to war since the beginning of civilization, and most could count on the loyalty of the women they left behind," Daddy said tersely.

"Why are you so angry?" Mama asked. "You have a little piece of Danny back. You should be overjoyed."

"I know how you women operate. Sooner or later she'll take her back to Kansas to be with her family, and I won't get to see Danny's little girl grow up. I always suspected. Hell, she looks exactly like Danny did at that age. I wish you hadn't told me, Hazel."

"I have no intention of going back to Kansas, except for occasional visits. I have good friends in Baltimore, including you two, and I don't plan to give that up. Besides, Victoria has three half sisters here and a half brother who adores her. Why in God's name would I take that away from her?"

"If that jackass Stanley gives you any trouble about being tossed out, call me and I'll give him a personal escort out of town," Daddy told her.

"Thanks, but I think Stanley is secretly relieved to be unshackled."

As Hazel started down the hall, my sisters and I followed close behind, pretending we didn't know, while dancing in circles around her feet.

Chapter 44

We were lying on our stomachs across Marjorie's double bed listening to *The Adventures of Sam Spade* on the tiny radio that sat on a trunk Lucille had left behind, when we heard fire trucks screaming outside the window.

"Somebody's house must be on fire," Marjorie said.

"Long as it isn't ours," Betsy giggled, and we went back to listening to the mesmerizing voice of Howard Duff as he solved baffling mysteries with the greatest of ease.

More deafening fire trucks pulled up and we could see flashing lights reflected on the ceiling. My mother suddenly appeared in the doorway and said, "Put your clothes on, girls. They want us to go outside."

Daddy bellowed over her shoulder, "You don't have time to dress. Jump up and run outside as fast as you can." Leaping out of bed, we ran downstairs barefoot in the blousy cotton petticoats and underpants we slept in on hot summer nights. Only Garland was wearing pajamas, blue, with Superman figures flying all over them.

We were ordered out of the way as firemen ran in and out, dragging a hose attached to the hydrant down the street. White smoke billowed from the downstairs windows. Before long it was black and seeping through the windows upstairs.

The fire department blamed faulty wiring for the inferno, not that the cause mattered much. Most of our furniture suffered from water warping and would have to be replaced, along with our clothes which reeked of tinny smoke.

Amanda, who heard about the fire on the dispatch radio, drove to our place and took all four of us home with her. We were thrilled, for she let us stay up half the night playing board games. The worst part of the ordeal was getting over the embarrassment of being seen by neighbors and firemen in our petticoats.

Mama and Daddy spent the night at Mick's. He helped her convince Daddy the time had come to buy a house and move his family to a better neighborhood. Crime had begun creeping across North Avenue from the crowded inner city streets, and we'd started locking the front door for the first time. When I stumbled over the body of a drunk passed out in the alley next to Bernie's store, Daddy caved in and agreed that Mama was right.

They applied for a Federal Housing Administration loan and bought a house on Guilford Avenue, a major step up in residential status. Instead of three stories of bright red brick with white marble steps that required weekly scrubbing, we now had two stories of peach colored brick, with a wide front porch painted blue. Although the houses were conjoined like the row houses on 24ᵗʰ Street, there was an eerie absence of mothers gossiping across porch railings. Nor was there the sound of children playing outdoors. It was as if the roomy, impersonal porches absorbed the sound and unconcerned neighbors never showed themselves. I felt lonely and invisible and utterly unfamiliar with the cooler, more sophisticated world I was thrust into.

Mama and Daddy enclosed the second floor back porch and for the first time in my life, I had a room of my own. But it was poorly constructed, and the wind howled mercilessly, scaring my brains out on nights when Marjorie and Betsy were socializing at church dances. Before long, I developed night terrors and lay awake for hours, too paralyzed to move. Only the sound of Daddy's snoring provided comfort.

That September, I started Junior High School and met my best friend, Patricia Ann. Soon, everything began to change. We no longer played outdoors or roller skated in the alley but spent most afternoons giggling about boys - or watching *Your Show of Shows* on our ten inch black and white television screen.

Patricia Ann taught me to smoke and bleach my bangs blond, for which Mama threatened to shave my head. That autumn, while climbing a steep hill at Harper's Ferry during a Methodist Youth Fellowship retreat, I suddenly developed a phobia of heights and threatened to throw our preacher over the side if he didn't stop trying to help me. Hands reaching out in elevated places became inexplicably terrifying, and I was sure they'd cause me to fall if they got too close. Soon, I began retreating to 24ᵗʰ Street with old friends who seemed less complicated, and before long, I had fallen for a fourteen year old boy who gave me a ride home on his shiny green bike. Daddy insisted that I quit seeing him after rigorous interrogation revealed that he was Catholic - and I experienced my first broken heart.

It seemed like nobody gathered around the dining room table to talk anymore, except Marjorie's and Betsy's boyfriends who wanted to pump Mama about the secret to winning their affections. Even Hazel and Victoria reduced their visits once Daddy's health began to fail and his heart and lungs made talking too tiring.

Mama kept her position at the library, and Marjorie found an afterschool job typing the Church bulletin, while trying to decide whether or not she was missionary material. Ultimately, the lack of plumbing in 3rd world countries convinced her that she was better suited for an office position. She would meet the love of her life at a church square dance while wearing a blue poodle skirt, her long taffy hair bouncing off the crisply starched shoulders of her prim white blouse as she dosi-doed. She would give birth to four children, two of whom she named after "Little Women" Alcott characters and all of whom she'd spend eighteen years raising before finding her niche as Risk Manager for the government. What better job for the firstborn in a family of limited means with a history of alcoholism.

Betsy, the middle child with the deep green eyes and wafer thin, five feet two figure, kept her dark brown hair short, probably in homage to Brynn, and collected dress patterns which she made into stunning outfits – and still does. Friendly and vivacious, she met tons of cute sailors at the USO dances she attended with her best friend. But while they were gaga over her, she seldom gave them the time of day. Then, when nobody was looking, she lost her heart to one of Marjorie's beaus, whom she would later marry. He moved her to the land of split level houses and Ford Thunderbirds in the suburbs of Dulaney Valley, where she had a daughter with short dark hair and a blue eyed, blond baby boy she named after our beloved Danny. She would spend the latter part of her life volunteering as secretary of everything, from the Daughters of the American Revolution to the French Huguenot Society.

Our baby brother Garland achieved childhood notoriety by standing in front of a telephone pole while his best friends threw Bernie's thrown-away butcher knives around the edges of his body, sending the blood spurting a foot in the air from the severed artery in his left arm. He would later distinguish himself in the Marine Corps before going on to a lucrative career as a businessman. He married a lovely German girl and produced two fine sons before retiring to raise horses amid the rolling hills of Maryland, near the Mason Dixon line.

And I would lose and find my way through several marriages, producing two beautiful daughters before going back to school and launching a career as a family therapist, working with special needs children and alcoholics. Despite the early influence of Patricia Ann, I finally gave up smoking.

But no matter where we live or what direction our lives take, my sisters and brother and I will always think of 24th Street as a warm, mostly safe haven, surrounded by a world at war. We watched people lose loved ones with brave, broken hearts, as well as immense courage and optimism about the future. I will forever think of those as the tender years, sitting around the dining room table with Mama, Hazel, Lila and Brynn, even the little Japanese woman who turned out to be Chinese and, of course, Lucille, Mick and Bernie. But most of all, I miss our darling Danny who could have brought so much joy and sanity to our sometimes uncertain lives. We had very little materially but everything we needed in matters of the heart. I would go back and do it all again tomorrow, if I could.

Marjorie

Betsy

Daddy, supervising from the window.

The End

CPSIA information can be obtained
at www.ICGtesting.com
Printed in the USA
LVHW081945050219
606480LV00014B/159/P